❧ About the Author ❧

E. C. Hibbs is an award-winning author and artist, often found lost in the woods or in her own imagination. Her writing has been featured in the British Fantasy Society Journal, and she has provided artworks in various mediums for clients across the world. She is also a calligrapher and live storyteller, with a penchant for fairytales and legends. She adores nature, fantasy, history, and anything to do with winter. She lives with her family in Cheshire, England.

Learn more and join the Batty Brigade at

www.echibbs.weebly.com

🌹 Also by E. C. Hibbs 🌹

RUN LIKE CLOCKWORK
Vol I: The Ruby Rings
Vol II: The Eternal Heart

THE FOXFIRES TRILOGY
The Winter Spirits
The Mist Children
The Night River

THE TRAGIC SILENCE SERIES
Sepia and Silver
The Libelle Papers
Tragic Silence
Darkest Dreams

Blindsighted Wanderer
The Sailorman's Daughters
Night Journeys: Anthology
The Hollow Hills Tarot Deck

Blood and Scales (anthology co-author)
Dare to Shine (anthology co-author)
Fae Thee Well (anthology co-author)

AS CHARLOTTE E. BURGESS
Into the Woods and Far Away: A Collection of Faery Meditations
Gentle Steps: Meditations for Anxiety and Depression

For Paula,
Welcome to the Lake!
Happy reading!

Blindsighted Wanderer

10TH ANNIVERSARY EDITION

E. C. HIBBS

First published 2012
Second edition published 2016
10th Anniversary Edition published 2022

Cover design, cover artwork, book production and layout by E. C. Hibbs

Cover images from Pixabay

Interior images from Pixabay & created by E. C. Hibbs © 2022

www.echibbs.weebly.com

Dedicated to the memory of my grandparents

Edna Baker and Eric Hibbs.

Thank you for making life wonderful.

Prologue
The Peasant and His Princess

WHEN ON THEE I GAZE NEVER SO LITTLE,
BEREFT AM I OF ALL POWER OF UTTERANCE,
MY TONGUE IS USELESS.
THERE RUSHES AT ONCE THROUGH MY FLESH TINGLING FIRE,
MY EYES ARE DEPRIVED OF ALL POWER OF VISION,
MY EARS HEAR NOTHING BY SOUNDS OF WINDS ROARING,
AND ALL IS BLACKNESS...
A DREAD TREMBLING O'ERWHELMS ME...
AND IN MY MADNESS
DEAD I SEEM ALMOST.

Sappho of Lesbos
translated by E. M. Cox

Septymbre, 1113

The night sky was open and endless, spangled with stars, and half-moon light shone down onto the Lake. Adrian saw the shimmers of the waves even before he emerged from the forest. He guided his white mare onto the bank, then dismounted near a small group of boats, tethered in the reed bed. With mastered silence, he threw a bundle into the furthest one, took up the oar, and pushed off.

He had come here so often, and done this for so long. As always, his face was calm and collected. But tonight, his palms sweated, and his breath trembled, no matter how hard he tried to hide it. Nerves tied his stomach in a knot. He knew this was dangerous, that it was terrible… but that didn't matter. He had waited long enough, done all he could. He just prayed it wouldn't show, when the time came.

The night was cool still, but Adrian knew that all around, countless creatures were going about their business. He heard owls and nyhtegales in the trees, and the soft splashes of fish following the boat. A pair of swans glided across the Lake, side by side. Their magnificent wings folded perfectly against their backs. Together for life.

Adrian reached a tussock, half a mile from the bank, and began to sing under his breath.

"Sweet loved-one, I pray thee,
Thou love me awhile long;
I shall bemoan my song
Upon thee to whom it is sung."

Movement stirred in the depths. It was faint at first, but then grew, and a face peered up at him through the water. Her skin was a lustrous blue-green, with dark emerald hair, studded with a pearlescent headdress. A long white gown waved about her slender frame. She looked sixteen – just a few years younger than Adrian himself – but he knew that wasn't so. She had lived for much longer than him.

She pushed her hands upwards, straining with the effort, then hauled her entire body out of the water. She knelt upon it, and it took her weight like the strongest stone.

"Merrin," Adrian smiled. He laid down the oar, and wiped his palms on his tunic.

"I worried thou wasn't coming," Merrin said.

"Of course I would have come."

Adrian reached inside the boat and drew out a white rose, plucked from the bush outside his house. He passed it to her.

"A gift for my love," he said. "The most beautiful flower in the Valley."

Merrin chuckled. "Not my amarants?"

"Nay. Those are too plain for the likes of thee."

Merrin cupped his face in her hands. Her fingers were long, delicately webbed with a translucent membrane.

Adrian leaned in and kissed her. Her lips were wet, and tasted of the damp Lakebed far below.

"I have missed thee," Merrin sighed. "Why didst thou not return sooner? I wish to introduce you to my father."

Adrian blinked. "What?"

"You should meet. He is anxious for it."

"But… what will he think of me? I am a mere human."

"I don't care," said Merrin. "I love you. You know this. He knows it, too. And for that, he already thinks fondly of thee."

"Merrin, listen," Adrian said. "I… God, help me. I want you so much. But I *am* human. The summer is all but passed now. And my life will be like a single summer in comparison to thine.

You will outlive me. And then—"

"Hush," Merrin whispered. "I will speak with my mother. She may know a solution. She is the Mistress of Magic, after all."

"Magic? What good will that do? And don't your parents already think our meetings are a fancy which will pass? I am but a farmer. You are a princess."

Merrin shook her head. "That doesn't matter. How will we know, unless we ask? She is the most powerful of us."

"Even more than you?" asked Adrian.

Merrin kissed the tip of his nose.

"Even more than me," she smiled mischievously. "Unless thou displeaseth me!"

Adrian chuckled. The love had come as swiftly as a dawn chorus: a thing of frenzy and sweetness: dew upon fresh leaves. Merrin was much older than him, but she was still young for her kind, and acted as such. So trusting and enamoured with him: the handsome one who had ridden through the western forest, and sought to speak with her. The one who had heard of her people's beauty, and wandered closer than many would dare.

But as strong as a bond could be, to draw together one of Land and Lake, that final knowledge was always there. Death waited for no-one, whether they had ten years to live, or ten centuries.

Merrin caressed Adrian's hair. It stood out against her skin: red upon green. Adrian placed his hands on her waist and drew her closer. They grasped each other over the rim of the boat. Adrian ran his fingers down the long fin protruding from her spine. It shivered at his touch, and as she kissed him again, he reached behind him, to the bundle. The moment was nigh.

"Thou cometh here freely," he whispered. "You love me?"

"You know I do," said Merrin.

Adrian kissed her again. "*Sweet loved-one, I pray thee for one loving speech.* Would you truly accept me? Where one goes, the other follows?"

She gazed at him with eyes like amethysts.

"What's wrong? You are tense."

Adrian's mind raced. It was now or never.

"Nothing at all," he said smoothly. "Merrin, my darling. Merrin, wilt thou be mine?"

She smiled. "Always."

Adrian gritted his teeth. "Good."

He whipped open the bundle, revealing a tightly-woven net, and threw it over her.

The two swans flapped away in fright. Merrin fell backwards with a shriek, but before she could dive, Adrian snatched her and hauled her into the boat. He tied the bottom of the net shut, then grabbed the oar.

Merrin screamed and thrashed, and tried to leap over the side, but Adrian pinned her with his leg. She stared up at him in horror.

"What are you doing?" she cried. "Let me go! Adrian!"

He ignored her.

"Let me go! *Now!*"

Merrin drove her knees into his back. Adrian doubled over, and dropped the oar into the water. He tried to grab it, but it drifted out of reach.

"Damn it!" he shouted. He looked around for something else he could row with, but there was nothing. Not even a floating branch.

Merrin kicked out again. Adrian caught her and forced her down. Oar or no oar, he would figure out a way to get back to the bank. But he couldn't let *her* get away. This moment was the entire reason he had courted her in the first place. She was the princess of a place uncharted by man. A thing unhuman, of magic and beauty and darkness. She would bring him and his wife riches and fame beyond imagining – treasures for his descendants to inherit forever.

And all it had taken was smiles and caresses and words.

Merrin's shock melted into fury. She fixed him with a venomous stare. Her fin flickered, like a rattlesnake tail.

"What are you doing?" she snarled.

"You're coming with me," Adrian replied.

"It will kill me!"

"Not if I'm careful."

"Let me go! I mustn't leave!" Merrin demanded. "How could you? I trusted you! Traitor!"

"Traitor?" Adrian scoffed. "To whom? You are not my princess. You do not command me."

Merrin bared her teeth. "Then I shall do worse."

She thrust her hand through the net and seized his. White light seared Adrian's vision. Something burned – so hot, he thought the flesh might slough off his bones like wax. He screamed; tried to throw her away, but Merrin held on too tightly. She didn't look away.

"Thou sought to lead me like a blind child?" she shouted. "Thy *sweet loved-one?* Where one goes, the other follows? Then it will be so, traitor!"

She flung herself against Adrian. The boat flipped; the water roared in his ears. Through a haze of silver bubbles, he saw Merrin tear free of the net. She swam at him and snatched him by the neck, holding his nose just above the surface.

"You would have killed me," she hissed. "Now you will think on me every day. You will see no other. A curse upon thee,

Adrian Atégo! Thou shalt rue this night for all time!"

She yanked his hair back. Adrian choked on the water – for a terrifying moment, he thought she might drown him. But then she let go, and vanished into the depths.

Adrian didn't waste a moment. He swam for the bank, clumsy with pain and fright. The Lake splashed over his head and the trees loomed above him like claws. The entire place was alive. It knew what he had done.

He reached the bank and clambered onto his mare's back. She took off at a gallop, eyes rolling with fright. It took all of Adrian's strength to hold her mane. The sting in his hand was unbearable, like he had thrust it into a bed of embers. He had always known Merrin was powerful, but to burn him like that…

By the time he returned home, the sun was rising. And when it broke the horizon, Adrian let out such a scream, the whole village came running. The sound wormed its way into every house: a single note which sang of desolation, terror, and the endless torment to come.

Chapter I
Fayreground Days

THE LAKES ARE SOMETHING WHICH YOU ARE UNPREPARED FOR;
THEY LIE UP SO HIGH, EXPOSED TO THE LIGHT,
AND THE FOREST IS DIMINISHED
TO A FINE FRINGE ON THEIR EDGES,
WITH HERE AND THERE A BLUE MOUNTAIN,
LIKE AMETHYST JEWELS
SET AROUND SOME JEWEL OF THE FIRST WATER, -
SO ANTERIOR, SO SUPERIOR,
TO ALL THE CHANGES
THAT ARE TO TAKE PLACE ON THEIR SHORES,
EVEN NOW CIVIL AND REFINED,
AND FAIR AS THEY CAN EVER BE.

Henry David Thoreau

Jyune, 1219

Summer in the Elitland was never anything short of beautiful. The Valley was a pocket: a lush island in a bleak and unforgiving stone sea, crested for miles with the summits of high mountains. Over the lip of the Eastern Ridge, the rising sun bathed the land in a symphony of pastel light. The air was warm and fresh, and a chorus of starling song rolled with the wind.

Cartwheels rattled on the road as the two eldest Atégo brothers made their way to the fayre. Eighteen-year-old Raphael perched in the driver's seat, while fifteen-year-old Silas walked alongside the donkey, one hand on the bridle. The younger children had wanted to come too, but there was far too much work to be done back at the farm.

And then there was their father…

Silas's boot hit a stone. He stumbled, almost dragging the donkey down with him.

Raphael chuckled. "Watch where you're going, thy clumsy fool!"

Silas glanced over his shoulder. "Oh, aye?"

"You can take a turn sitting up here. You've been walking for miles."

"Nay. I prefer this."

Raphael sighed. "There's nothing we can do about Pap all the way out here, Si."

"I know," Silas said morosely.

If only it had been possible to forego the fayre. Then they could have stayed at home. But this was the only trading opportunity of the year; the only time the mountain pass was clear enough to allow entry for outsiders. It was held for a few days before Midsummer, and was the highlight of everyone's calendar.

And the Atégos lived in the very village which hosted it: Fanchlow; the closest one to the entrance to the Valley. They would be stupid to miss it.

Music drifted from over the hill: shawms, lutes, fiddles, a pipe and tabor. Drunken laughter followed. And then the fayre itself came into view. Everywhere was a cacophony of activity and excitement. A large boar roasted on a spit beside a great keg of ale, and the mouth-watering smell of meat was pungent in the heat haze. A juggling duo performed tricks with leather balls filled with sand. Two men dressed as a king and a queen sat opposite one another, engrossed in a game of chess – and watched by onlookers who seemed just as interested. Silas supposed that there was some kind of bet between them, in favour of the 'king' or the 'queen' winning.

And there were stalls. Lines upon lines, with people thronging between them like ants. Many had travelled from the outlying villages to barter crops and crafts. Some groups sold fabrics, meats and tools, while others offered more expensive items, such as new cartwheels.

But those weren't what the brothers had come for.

At the edge of the square, a troupe of Cart-folk had taken up space. They came every few years, bringing all manner of exotic bounty. And although there might be some takers for their leather goods and embroidery, most of the Valley-folk were focused on the foreign spices. Stocking up with sacks of it would be essential in pickling the meat for winter. But even as goods passed between hands, everyone threw the Cart-folk nervous glances. Silas did the same. These people were outsiders, and everything about them was different. Their skin was darker, their clothes more colourful, their words almost like another language.

Did they have a word for *themselves* in that strange tongue, he wondered? *Cart-folk* was only the Valley term, from the tilted wagons which always carried them. But Silas supposed it was better than the other one he had heard. *Raptors*: 'thieves.'

They didn't know the ways of the Elitland. They didn't know how it was to be bound to a place, to be born and to die in the footsteps of one's forefathers. Their existence was a rootless one, belonging nowhere. The very thought of it made Silas shiver.

Raphael slid off the driver's seat and elbowed his way to the front of the crowd.

"Three sacks of salt and one of spice, if you please."

A Cart-girl turned to him. "What 'ave ye got for 'em, me redhead sir?"

Silas brandished some trout and a hoe. The girl looked at them for a long moment. Her eyes shone like polished stones.

"Alrigh'," she said. "Toss 'em over."

Silas handed them to Raphael. He watched the girl as she fetched the sacks, hauling them around as easily as if they were full of feathers. She was about his age, and so tanned, he wondered if she had ever spent a day indoors in her life. Thick black hair cascaded around her face, laced with beads.

She glanced up, straight at him. Silas suddenly realised he had been staring at her. Blood rushed to his cheeks, but before he could turn away, the girl shot him a sharp-toothed grin and winked. Then she shoved the sacks into Raphael's arms.

"Mind how ye go," she said.

"Likewise," Raphael replied. He tossed the sacks atop the cart, and Silas quickly manoeuvred it away from the crowd.

"Hold on," said Raphael. He approached the brewer's stall and took two leather tankards of ale.

The man spat at his feet. "Hell-kissed wretch. Get thee gone."

"Merry Midsummer to thee, as well," Raphael said with a pointed smile. He offered one of the tankards to Silas. "We can't come here without toasting. To health and life!"

They tapped together and drank. But Silas swallowed his slower than normal. It felt wrong to be doing this. Last year, he and Raphael would have stayed at the fayre for longer. They would have made merry, and watched as the balefire was lit – albeit from a distance, where none of the neighbours could glower at them.

But not now. Not while their father lay in bed, wracked with illness.

Silas tried to think positive. That was what Raphael always insisted on. Julian Atégo was a strong man. He had thrice fought off influenza in Silas's lifetime alone. Surely, he wouldn't be beaten now.

But Silas wasn't an optimist. He was a realist. And the reality was, nothing was ever for sure.

Silas had been on his feet all day, but he still insisted on walking home, rather than riding on the cart. With every step, he held himself straight and sturdy, like an oak. He was short for his age, but substituted it well enough with physical strength. Everyone could work for hours on end in the fields, but Silas took it in his stride as easily as though each blow of the scythe was the first.

He kept his eyes on the road. Swallows darted in front of him; pollen floated on the breeze. The faint rumble of lowing cattle drifted down from the summer pastures above. Every detail, no matter how tiny, was welcome. It meant he didn't have to think.

Then the Cart-girl appeared in his mind. He blushed again.

How could hair shine like that? What were those beads made from? Knowing her kind, she had probably stolen them.

He shook his head in frustration. It didn't matter. In a couple of weeks, she and her people would be gone. Everything would go back to normal. Or so he hoped.

Normal. That was what the Valley was. Unchanging and faithful, simple and secure. Only one way in and one way out, and no reason to ever leave. Aside from the creature comforts which the Cart-folk brought, everything the people needed was on their doorstep. There were pastures for grazing, and a river for water, sparkling in the sun as it turned a mill wheel at the side of the road. The edges of the Valley were too steep to climb, but hardy trees had taken root upon them, in an emerald montage of oaks, rowans, birches and willows. This place was a green gem, cradled in the heart of a mountainous labyrinth.

But even so, there was danger here.

Silas turned his eyes to the west. There, stretching the entire length of the Valley like a huge snake, was the Wall. It had been built one hundred years ago: miles upon miles of drystone, ten feet high. Nobody ever crossed it. That was the greatest rule of all. The other side was far too dark and evil to risk.

Silas swallowed nervously. Everyone lived in the shadow of the Wall, but it seemed to be doing its job well. There were no demons coming in the night to terrorise people. It was a fragile truce, but an effective one.

"You alright, Si?" Raphael asked.

Silas jumped.

"Oh, my Silent Si," laughed Raphael. "What are we to do with thee?"

Silas tugged on the donkey's bridle.

"We should make haste. We've been out too long

already."

"We're going as fast as we can. You'll make the old girl keel over at this rate."

Silas kept quiet. Realising he wasn't going to get any more conversation out of his brother, Raphael began singing.

"Sweet loved-one, I pray thee,
For one loving speech;
While I live in this wide world
None other will I seek.
With thy love, my sweet beloved,
My bliss though mightest increase;
A sweet kiss of thy mouth
Might be my cure."

Silas pursed his lips. Why had Raphael decided on *that* song? What kind of kiss could be a cure for anything, let alone for what awaited them back home?

When their father had first fallen in the field, and the fever came down on him, they had thought it was the sweating sickness, which would have been bad enough. But then the hot and cold spells turned to a permanent chill. He gasped for breath like a drowning man, yet coughed up nothing, not even phlegm. Their mother Araena had worried it might be an evil spirit, so the priest had come and prayed over him, but it didn't work. Nothing did. Nobody knew what was happening.

Never had Silas felt so powerless. And despite his brother's mirth, he knew Raphael felt it even harder. He was the eldest son: the heir to the farm. One day, he would be the man of the house. And now, that one day felt closer than ever before.

The sun hung low in the sky and turned the mountaintops gold. Women appeared with candles and rushlights for the village lanterns. While Raphael greeted them warmly, Silas kept his head down. The neighbours rarely acknowledged them anyway.

They headed around the hills and past the barns, following the river, until they came to the scattering of houses on the outskirts of Fanchlow. Silas wasn't sure if he felt better or worse when he saw the furthest one. It was always good to be home, but he dreaded what awaited inside.

The house was small, but well-built, from huge cruck timbers which towered high above them. The thatched roof sloped almost to the ground, thin in places, from where the wind had torn through. Silas heard mice rustling in it as he passed. He guided the donkey through the herb garden, into the cart shelter, then unhitched the poles and bridle.

"Good girl," Raphael said to the donkey. He leapt down from the seat and eyed the rose bush. It was filled with huge white flowerheads, the stems bending under their weight.

"We should cut it back this autumn," Silas said.

"I say we leave it. The fragrance is pleasant."

"The thorns are not."

Silas hoisted the spice sacks into his arms. Raphael caught his eye with a half-smile, then called towards the house.

"Ma! Mekina! We're back!"

The door swung open, harsher than normal. Their fourteen-year-old sister Mekina appeared, a frantic expression on her freckled face.

"Thank God!" she cried. "Both of you, make haste!"

A stone dropped in Silas's stomach. He bolted inside, Raphael on his heels.

He heard his father before he saw him: a horrid death rattle, like fluid bubbling in his lungs. The cot was practically hidden by people: Silas's younger siblings, his mother, and even the village priest, Father Fortésa.

The sight of him struck Silas in the heart. When the exorcism hadn't worked, the priest had stayed away, like everyone else in the village. If he was back now, it was for only one thing. To deliver last rites.

Silas and Raphael ran to the cot. Silas almost forgot to breathe. Julian looked like a corpse, mouth wide open, lips blue, eyes bloodshot. His hands were in fists around the blanket. Nothing held tighter than a dying man clinging to life.

"Pap?" said Raphael, all frivolity gone from his voice. "Pap, dost hear me?"

Julian coughed. "My sons…"

"We're here now. Silas and I are both here."

"My sons…"

Silas stroked his father's wrist. Julian gazed up at him.

"Take care of them…" he wheezed. "Swear to me!"

Silas nodded. "We will."

"We both will," said Raphael.

Julian whimpered, gasping for breath like a fish. Silas had never heard a man make a sound like that. It was like he was drowning in the air.

The moment stretched itself out over an eternity. The house became dark – only Mekina broke away, to soak dried rushes in the grease pot and set them alight. They only gave a soft glow, but it was enough for Father Fortésa to see his Bible. He placed a wafer on Julian's tongue, and helped him sip from a cup of wine. Julian almost choked on it, but to Silas's relief, he kept it down.

Night fell across the Elitland. Silas held onto his father with one hand, and Raphael with the other. And there they stayed, until the inevitable crashed upon them like a wave.

Over the next two days, the music of the fayre faded, replaced with the hammering of a chisel, carving a new wooden crucifix for the graveyard. The Cart-folk packed up their wares and took shelter in a corrie above Fanchlow, far enough from the Valley-folk to keep both parties happy.

Silas heard them laughing in the evenings, and saw the glows of their fires, but tried to not pay attention. In its way, the sound of his family's weeping was more comforting than the mirth of strangers. As always, it was them against the world, keeping each other together, even as their foundations crumbled.

He had suspected that not many people would come to the funeral, but he was dismayed to be proven correct. Behind the six remaining Atégos, the pews were all but empty. Only their closest neighbours had bothered attending. A few others lingered at the back, as far away as they could.

Silas refused to look at them. They weren't there out of respect. It was out of fear of offending God by allowing a death to pass unmarked. In such a small community, there was no excuse to shun somebody. Unless they were different.

As a child, Silas had thought it was their hair. Hardly anybody in the Valley had red hair. Once, he had dived into the river and smeared it with mud, hoping that would change things. But it only made people stare even more. After that, he gave up and surrendered to his sullen nature. If they refused to speak to his family, then he would refuse to speak to them.

Father Fortésa led the requiem mass quickly, as though the words burned his tongue when he spoke them. Silas forced himself to not look irritated. Even the priest wanted to be done with the Atégos as fast as possible.

When it was done, Silas and Raphael joined the others who had volunteered to carry the coffin. They walked out to the churchyard, where a grave lay open and waiting. Silas bit the inside of his cheek when he saw it. Everything – the size of the hole, the weight of the body – it all seemed too little. Too unreal. He felt as though he were hanging suspended in a bottomless lake, unable to move. Perhaps *unwilling* to move.

Nonetheless, he kept his eyes fixed on the earth as the coffin was lowered into it on strips of leather. Not many people had remained to watch this, but he could sense them, throwing wary glances and muttering among themselves. If his mother and siblings were aware, they paid no mind. Araena, a black mourning wimple over her hair, was too busy comforting the twins, Uriel and Selena. Raphael, meanwhile, stood as still as a statue, trying to keep his tears at bay.

Father Fortésa recited the final prayers, then sprinkled holy water onto the coffin lid. As it landed, drizzly rain began to fall through the humid air: a silent harbinger to a coming storm.

That was the cue for the mourners to leave. They hurried back towards the village like ants, drawing up hoods to cover themselves. Silas shook his head as he watched them. It was hardly acid. It couldn't hurt.

"We should go, too," Raphael said quietly. "I don't want anyone else getting sick."

"I'll join you anon," said Silas.

Raphael looked at him. "Are you… alright?"

"I just need a moment."

Raphael squeezed Silas's shoulder, then led his mother and siblings down the path to the churchyard gate. Araena practically fell against him, as though the faintest breath of wind might shatter her. Raphael was only young, but he took her weight as though he had been born to do it. Overnight, he had become the man of the house.

A crashing roll of thunder filled the sky. Silas didn't move. Behind him, Father Fortésa hobbled closer, squinting with aged eyes. He was older than most; his spine had bent over and his feet dragged along the ground. But even though his sight was fading, his voice was still as sharp as a needle.

"No words?" he said. "Thou hast not shed a single tear. Brave boy. Or foolish."

Silas didn't reply.

"Did you even pray for him?"

"Of course I did."

Father Fortésa sniffed. "I don't understand thee. Always so brooding. You have been lucky enough to survive childhood, yet you walk as though touched by some dark thing. What dost thou carry upon thy shoulders?"

Silas refused to look at him. "Nothing."

"Thou lies."

"Nay. Speak not to me of falseness. It is they who show it to us, and for what?"

"Slander thy neighbours no more. Thy family be cursed enough."

At that, Silas did turn around.

"*Cursed?*" he said. "How can you say this when we stand here, beside the grave? My family has nothing but good people. We have never wronged anyone."

The priest glared at him. "And yet the sins of the fathers taint thy name."

Silas's blood boiled. "My father was an honest man."

"Aye," said Father Fortésa, "but it's not to him I refer. This isn't the first time this has happened, boy. Your grandfather died the same way. I remember it. And my own mother told me it was so even before that. Father before father, all falling like this. But always the men. It never claims the women."

Silas couldn't believe what he was hearing.

"Ye don't know it's a curse," he insisted.

"Then what wouldst thou call it?" Father Fortésa snapped. "What mere illness claims only those who carry the name?"

"Every illness has a cure."

"If there was any kind of Earthly cure, it would be known by now."

Silas stared at him. Then he looked over the old man's head, into the west, at the long dark shadow of the Wall. It seemed black beneath the heavy clouds, like an ink stain. Or a chasm, waiting to swallow him.

The land of the demons.

"Have *they* done it?" he asked quietly.

Father Fortésa drew down the cross. "I am certain of it."

"Why?"

"I thought *you* might know. Acting as you do."

Silas blinked. "I don't."

The priest grumbled. "Well, then, thou canst do nothing. Away with thee. May God have mercy."

He hobbled towards the church. Silas had a mind to follow him and demand more information, but he knew it would be for naught. So he just stood there, shock turning his body to stone, eyes fleeting between the coffin at his feet and the Wall in the distance.

A huge crack of thunder split the sky, and the rain came down, so heavily, it seemed the angels were weeping.

Chapter II
The Tomb Garden

THE ASRAI WANDER'D, CHOOSING FOR THEIR HOMES
ALL GENTLE PLACES - VALLEYS MOSSY DEEP,
STAR-HAUNTED WATERS, YELLOW STRIPS OF SAND
KISSING THE SAD EDGE OF THE SHIMMERING SEA.

Robert Williams Buchanan

Ripples spread across the Lake as the rain fell. The entire surface danced with them. Lightning tore through the sky, but Merrin was too far down to really see it. She never swam high enough anymore.

She coasted alongside a shoal of silvery minnow. Their wide eyes watched her as she swirled and dived with them, always keeping pace. Moving like this, it could be so easy to forget. And she needed that now: simple distraction. The moment she stopped, the moment she would remember how the world was changed forever.

She stayed out for as long as she could, following the flashes of fish, around mountains of rocks and forests of weeds. In many places, they were sculpted and cut into patterns: the result of decades of work by her people. Hardly any light penetrated the Lake, but that didn't matter. The Asræ were a nocturnal race. And all were able to spin magic, so for centuries, they had laid out lines of it like thoroughfares, to allow everyone to see.

Some things never changed. That was what she needed to hold onto now. The Lake would always be their vast Mother, and the Asræ would always be Her children, watching over all of the fishes, the reeds, the frogs, the diving birds. Unlike them, She would last forever.

When Merrin could delay no longer, she sank down, to the very bottom. She made sure to move slowly, in a spiral, so she could grow used to the weight of the water. Then, when the sun was nothing more than a flicker overhead, she swam towards the city.

Everywhere she looked, she saw houses, built into the rocks themselves. All were spaced modestly apart from their neighbours, so everybody had room. People moved between them; children played hide and seek in the long reeds; songs drifted, phantom-like, through the water. And in the square, a small crowd had gathered, spinning around each other as they rehearsed a dance. No creature could dance like an Asræ. Even on the surface, where they were no longer weightless in the water, it was a sight Merrin never tired of.

She had a mind to linger and watch them, to further delay herself, but she knew she had been gone for long enough already. So she turned away and swam into the palace. It was a colossal green and grey building, sprawling across the Lakebed in a maze of turrets and gables. It was all made from stone, low to the ground so it wouldn't crumble, fringed with long mosses which waved when she moved past them. Fish fleeted in and out of the open windows like the birds of the air, and other Asræ followed them: men and women just like Merrin, with long green hair, shimmering teal skin, and purple eyes like cut gems.

They bowed their heads when they saw her. Merrin tried not to grimace. They had always been respectful, but now, it was different; deeper. Now, it would always be this way. That was no longer a bow to a princess.

One of them kicked his legs and came towards her.

"Penro," Merrin said. "I didst not expect to see thee out and about."

"There's much to be done, Your Majesty," he replied.

Merrin flinched. "Must you call me that? It's… too soon."

Penro cast his eyes down. The fin down his back waved softly from side to side. He was a little older than Merrin, and she had known him all her life; first as a child, then as her father's advisor.

"I know. But I must," said Penro. "And I must tell you that your mother is looking for you."

Merrin sighed through her gills. "Where?"

"The King's Room."

"It couldn't have been anywhere else?"

"She insisted," Penro said apologetically. "Forgive me. Now I have seen you, I must go."

He went to swim away, but before he could, Merrin grasped his hand.

"Penro, wilt thou come to me after moonrise?" she asked. "I… need to talk about something other than all this."

Penro offered a small smile. "I'm afraid I shan't be able until tomorrow. It will be a busy night."

"Fine," said Merrin. "I just wish for your company. Please."

"You'll have it," Penro promised, then he bowed to her, and disappeared into the gloom.

Merrin hung still in the water, using her fin to keep herself steady. Penro had always looked out for her. Even after that horrific night over a hundred years ago, when so many had turned away. She knew she could trust him. He was one of the few to whom she awarded that respect.

She slipped into the palace through one of the open doors, and made her way through the corridors to the King's Room. It was a modest place, despite its name: spacious enough to move in, but with little in the way of furniture: only a throne at the far end.

"Take a seat."

Merrin's mother, Dylana, appeared from behind a pillar. Her skin was wrinkled, her green hair streaked with white, and her fingers were puckered, like those of a human's who had lain in the water for too long. She was old, and it showed. But she had her wits about her, as sharp as a reed-leaf; and her eyes sparkled as though she carried the moon itself behind them.

"I cannot," Merrin said.

"You can," said Dylana. "Come hither."

She took her daughter by the hand, guided her closer, and gently pushed her upon the seat.

Merrin squirmed. She had always known this time would come. But she had hoped it would still be centuries away.

She looked down. Woven around her wrists were two thick sleeves, made from reeds and ancient leather, preserved by magic. She still hadn't grown used to them. In a place ruled by water, where even the finest crown could be lost unless it was braided into the hair, these were the true mark of the monarch. The Royal Bands had originally encircled her father's arms. And now they were hers.

"I know this is difficult for thee," said Dylana. "It is for me, as well."

"You are not the one who must sit here," Merrin scowled.

Dylana didn't rise to her daughter's anger. She just swam closer and floated before Merrin's face.

"Tell me what's troubling you."

"Thou knoweth already."

"But it will help you to voice it."

Merrin closed her eyes. The words formed in her mind, pressed upon her shoulders like rocks. This was too difficult, too close…

"I have no desire to be Queen. Not yet," she whispered.

Dylana stayed quiet. She knew there was more, even before Merrin did.

"I wish to use it to atone for my frivolity. But for my whole life, it's been Father's position. I'm not ready."

A smile of understanding flowed across Dylana's thin lips. The depth of it brought more relief than Merrin could have hoped for. Her mother was grieving too, for the man she had loved all her life. And she was the most powerful Asræ in the Lake. She had been practising magic for longer than any other; had the power to commune with the memories of those who had passed. She had given that same gift to Merrin, but no matter how many times she visited the Tomb Garden outside the palace, it brought no comfort. It still meant that the King of the Lake was dead, and Merrin now had no choice but to take up his mantle.

"Listen to me," Dylana said, with the quiet voice of one who had allowed everything to leave its mark on her. "Thou art young, still. Less than two thousand years old. Frivolity is permitted."

"Frivolity almost killed me," Merrin said acidly.

"Think of the minnow," her mother continued. "They are born, know no mother nor father, and must swim alone through a strange new world. Just like we Asræ did, once. Do you think they ever pause to berate themselves, or lament their loneliness? Of course not. They take life and live it, and they survive."

"Not all of them," Merrin pointed out. "That's why so many are born. Because fewer still will survive."

"Ah, but you have something they don't," Dylana said. "Years. Centuries. The ability to learn and grow. No-one feels ready to take up a weight when it comes down upon them. It matters not whether it is expected, or is a gift or a burden. You make of it what you will. You are as ready as you allow yourself to be."

Dylana grasped Merrin's chin gently in her fingers.

"You will be wonderful, my dear. I understand your burden, to follow in his finstrokes, but you must believe in yourself."

Merrin trembled. "He has always been our King. Even since before we came to this place. Who am *I?* I'm nothing."

"You are *everything*," Dylana insisted, and pressed her lips to Merrin's forehead. "But you must release your past grudge if you are to become the most magnificent Queen you can be."

A cold weight grew in Merrin's chest. *Release it?* No, that was impossible. If she did that, from where could she possibly draw her strength?

"You can do it," Dylana insisted. "I would undo it, but thee is the one who cast it. It must be thee who counters it. I can lend thee my power…"

"Nay."

"Merrin, I beg thee."

Merrin shook her head. She still remembered the tight net around her legs; the hand holding her down; the face she had loved turning to betrayal…

"I want you to hold the coronation here," she said. "I won't go up there."

Dylana caressed her cheek. "Merrin, I know you are afraid…"

"I am not afraid!"

"You are. And I don't blame you. But you must come to the surface with us. Coronation or not, it's the only way you can age."

Merrin gripped the arms of the throne.

"I shall go close enough for the moonlight to touch me, but I will never step into the air again. Dost hear?"

"You must see past that," said Dylana softly. "It has been so long. Nothing will happen to you now. Not unless you choose to inflict it upon yourself."

"I inflict nothing but self-preservation," Merrin snapped. "Is this the only reason you asked for me? To chide me? I will be worthy of my people, but in *personal* matters, I know what is best for myself."

Dylana shook her head. "It dismays me to see you like this. You should try. There is a week yet before the Rise. Go high. Take your time with it. Grow your confidence enough to put your hand through."

Merrin glared at her. "*Nay.*"

She pushed her legs down, shot above the throne, and swam from the King's Room as fast as she could.

The familiar hallways warped around Merrin as she swam towards her father's bedchamber. Tears formed in her eyes, and were immediately lost to the water. She was glad of it. Nobody saw her weep. Ever. Not for anything.

She lingered in the doorway, but it wasn't long until the old King noticed her. He beckoned with a frail hand.

"Merrin, come here," he called. His voice, strained and quiet, was like grit in her chest.

She braced herself, and approached. He was lying on his bed, a thin sheet covering him from the waist down. Veins stood out in his neck like ropes. His eyes found Merrin's, and she laid her head onto his chest. She wanted to embrace him, but didn't dare, in case it hurt him.

"Don't leave me," she whimpered. "Please!"

He stroked her hair. Merrin focused on it: the shaky movement of his fingers on her scalp. It was such a small movement, but soon, it would be gone.

"Worry not for me," he said quietly. "I have… led a long and full life. My time is nearing, but I am not afraid. Merrin, look at me."

She did, trying to commit every feature of his face to memory.

"Thou shalt do fine," he said. "You are strong."

"I'm not!" Merrin cried. "I need you!"

"I will always be with you," her father whispered.

He held her as tightly as he was able, then called over the top of her head.

"Penro!"

Merrin kept still. She knew what was coming, and she had

dreaded it. This would make it all too real.

Penro appeared and bowed his head.

"Your Majesty?"

"Come," said the King, "and remove the Royal Bands from my wrists."

Merrin kept her eyes closed throughout the whole thing. She couldn't bear to watch those symbols of authority leave her father and pass to her. But it wasn't enough. Even without looking, she felt them: tight, woven, fibre upon fibre. Just like a net…

Merrin, wilt thou be mine?

She opened her eyes, and jolted so hard, she rose off the bed and floated above it. She looked around frantically. But there was nothing; she was alone in her chambers, the water cool and still on her skin. It had only been a dream.

She glanced at the Bands. They still seemed wrong. Nobody was permitted to wear anything around their wrists unless they were the monarch.

She swam to the mirror and stared at herself. It didn't matter that nobody was here. She needed to get herself under control.

Would sleep ever come easily again? First, the loss of her father. Now, succeeding him as ruler. And to go to the *surface…*

In the past, it had never bothered her. She went willingly, night after night, climbing atop the water and dancing until she could barely stand. But the memory of the last time still burned inside her like a brand. The memory tied her stomach into a knot, and in the mirror, her face became as hard as stone.

It was her mask; her wall. She drew it around herself whenever she was afraid. If that moment could not destroy her, then neither could anything else.

She blinked, and her reflection copied the movement without hesitation. A gown of flowing white gossamer flowed about her body, inlaid with minnow scales. But behind all the glamour, and the same high, delicate features of her people, the girl in the mirror looked so small. A frightened child. Not a Queen.

She turned to the window. The water was lighter – the sun was shining far above, but she could tell from the colour that it would soon set. Then there would be nothing but a waxing moon above. Something which could not hurt.

She snarled under her breath. There was no use in lingering here, alone with her thoughts. The least she could do was be productive.

She pulled on a dress and swam through the window, into the depths. She kept close to the wall, and followed it down. Long weeds stroked her legs as she passed. A shoal of minnow flickered overhead, the lamplight flashing off their scales. Everything was so green; so beautiful.

One of the guards called up from below.

"Who goes there?"

Merrin held out her arms so the Bands were clearly visible.

"Only me, Lachlan."

The guard bowed his head. "Oh, I beg your pardon, Your Majesty."

"Please don't call me that yet," Merrin said. "And there is no need to apologise."

Lachlan swam closer to her. He was the chief of them, and like all the guards, he carried no weapons, because there was never any combat among the Asræ. Their role was one of ceremony and privacy, to ensure the palace was not disturbed.

"If I may," he said, "I advise thee to return to thy quarters. The sun shall rise soon."

Merrin glanced upwards. "I have no intention of going high enough to be harmed. I… am going to the Tomb Garden."

Sympathy filled Lachlan's eyes.

"Would you allow me to accompany you?"

Merrin hesitated. If it had been Penro in front of her, she would have accepted the offer in a heartbeat. But instead, she shook her head.

"I wish to be alone," she said.

"Very well," said Lachlan. "I shall be here, should you need me."

He bowed again, then the two of them glided away from each other.

Merrin descended to the Lakebed, swimming slowly. She twisted onto her back and stared at the surface. Dawn had not arrived yet, but everyone had already retired to their homes. No Asræ ran the risk of being too exposed in the summer, when the nights were so short. Merrin's people had always been born of darkness, and every child was warned against being touched by sunlight. If they were, their skin would blister and burn, and no kiss from the Lake would ever be enough to cool it. And if they did not find shelter, then they would die.

Merrin shuddered. So many things up there spelt doom. Her parents had told her that. Still, she hadn't listened.

A ghostly light, paler than the ones around the buildings, bloomed out of the water like a flower. Merrin kicked towards it, and arrived at the Tomb Garden. It stood on a steep east hillside, so it could easily face the moon. It was the site of remembrance for all who had died. Asræ were so long-lived, there were only a few stones, but each was well-tended and kept free of moss. And her father's was at the very top, perched upon the summit like a beacon.

Merrin eyed the surface warily. It wasn't too close, but the moonlight still managed to shine down and touch her. This was as high as she would venture, even during the Rise.

A faint orb hovered above the grave like a star. As soon as Merrin looked at it, she felt her father there.

I miss you, she said in her mind.

The orb flickered. *I am with you.*

Merrin knelt on the ground. His bones lay beneath her, casting his memory into the light. All Asræ could draw comfort from them, but only she and her mother could see them. It was a power even older than Dylana – the one which, according to legend, had made them Asræ in the first place.

Far from where anyone might see her, Merrin bent over the grave and wept.

Chapter III
Silas's Decision

IN SPRING OF YOUTH IT WAS MY LOT
TO HAUNT OF THE WIDE WORLD A SPOT
THE WHICH I COULD NOT LOVE THE LESS-
SO LOVELY WAS THE LONELINESS
OF A WILD LAKE, WITH BLACK ROCK BOUND,
AND THE TALL PINES THAT TOWERED AROUND.
BUT WHEN THE NIGHT HAD THROWN HER PALL
UPON THAT SPOT, AS UPON ALL,
AND THE MYSTIC WIND WENT BY
MURMURING IN MELODY-
THEN- AH THEN I WOULD AWAKE
TO THE TERROR OF THE LONE LAKE.

Edgar Allan Poe

Silas lay on his cot, fully clothed save for his boots, and stared at the ceiling. A thin shaft of moonlight broke through it, thick with dust motes. In the gloom, he watched a fat spider spinning a web between the wall and the fishing net hanging from the beam.

Silas kept his eyes on it. The sound, purposeful movements helped his mind to wander.

The house stank of damp – the rain had saturated the thatch on the roof, and seeped through in places, turning the floor to mud. Raphael had thrown down some straw to soak up the worst of it, but that had only brought the smell inside. It was dark, too. The children had blown out the rushlights as soon as the evening meal was over, and they felt their way around using only the glow of the embers. Dinner had been taken in subdued silence, broken only by Araena's sobbing. It was plain food: lamb and rye bread, but Silas was glad of that. He couldn't have stomached anything heavier.

Now, everyone was abed: scattered around the room on low cots. Raphael snored softly in the corner, flanked by Selena and Mekina. Uriel lay separate from them, because he often kicked in his sleep. Near the fireplace, their mother was curled into a ball like a frightened mouse.

Silas looked at her. She was a healthy woman, but she seemed so small now, as though her skeleton had shrunk inside her body. She would never grow used to the empty space beside her.

Father Fortésa's words clung to Silas's mind like a cold mist. Could it be true? Could the family really be *cursed?*

He thought of the Wall; of the forbidden demonic land beyond it. The priest had claimed that at least two more generations of Atégos had drowned in the air, the same way as Julian. That would make it close to one hundred years. Close to the time when the Wall was built.

A chill ran up Silas's spine. It had to be a coincidence. But could *anything* be a coincidence, when an entire realm of evil lay just a few miles away?

"*Weargh!*"

Silas jumped. Uriel was sitting bolt upright. His legs flailed so violently, his blanket fell to the floor. His eyes were blank and unfocused.

None of the others stirred, too used to his restlessness. But Silas crept over, placing his feet carefully so he wouldn't step in the mud, and eased his brother back down.

"There's a leech in my pillow," Uriel mumbled. "I don't want it to eat me. It wants to get me..."

Silas tucked the blanket around his chin. Uriel kicked out again, whimpering.

"Nay, don't tie up my fishing line... there's a leech that'll get over there..."

Silas stroked his forehead to soothe him. After several fitful moments, Uriel finally settled.

Silas returned to his own cot with a sigh. He knew he should try to get another few hours' sleep. It was still the middle of the night, but this close to Midsummer, the sun rose early, and the Valley-folk with it.

However, the more he tossed and turned, the more awake he felt. How was he supposed to relax, to go about work as normal, with gravedirt still clinging to his boots? How could he ever look at the Wall again? Or his brothers?

That thought made him feel sick. If it was a curse, and only came for the men of the family...

Silas looked at Raphael. He was the eldest. It would take him next. And then Silas himself. Sooner or later, it would kill them all.

Unless there was a cure. Or, failing that, a way to appease.

"Don't you wreck my fishing line..." Uriel mumbled again,

Silas's eyes snapped back onto the ceiling, to the net. An idea leapt, fully formed, into his mind. Those things were valuable – Raphael had traded for it at the last fayre, and it cost almost all the strawberries they had managed to pick. To sacrifice it would be no simple matter.

But neither was the curse. Not now.

Before he could convince himself it was a bad idea, Silas pulled on his boots, tied a knife to his belt, and lifted the net down. He glanced back at his mother's empty bed. It might be too late for his father, but perhaps, if Silas did everything right, he might yet save his brothers.

You've lost your mind, he thought. Then he slipped out of the door.

He ran from the house, the net over his shoulder. The river shimmered like silver; the fields and mountains shone blue under a fat waxing moon. Another week, and it would be full.

The village lanterns fell behind him as he emerged into the flat bottom of the Valley. He jumped hedgerows and brooks, crept past the mill with its huge creaking wheel. His legs burned, but he didn't slow down. If he did, he knew he might not muster the courage to begin again.

Eventually, he reached the river. The Wall itself was still half a mile away, but the fields ended here. No-one dared risk farming so close on the other bank. So now, all that lay between it and Silas was a meadow: cornflowers, pansies and wild roses. It might as well have been virgin snow, daring him to mark it with his footprints. Once made, they would never be erased.

And the Wall itself... Even looking upon it made Silas tremble. He had never been this close. He doubted anybody had, in over a hundred years. He felt like an ant in its shadow, about to be crushed.

Land of the demons. The unknown, forbidden place. The constant reminder that some things could not be controlled, and were much better shut away than thought about.

Nerves gripped Silas's belly like an iron fist, but he fought through it, and waded across the river. When he reached the meadow, stems and grasses snagged his ankles, as though trying to hold him back. He fought on as the Wall loomed higher. It was even taller than he had imagined: almost twice his height, made of dark, jagged stone. Pale lichen stuck out from the cracks, and an ivy curtain fell from the top. White morning glories pierced the gloom like massive eyes.

Silas tried not to look at them. He took a deep breath, then wedged his toes between the stones, and began to climb. The rough surface chafed his hands; he slipped on moss and almost fell. But he hung on. He had come this far. He couldn't turn back now…

He reached the top, swung his leg over, and sat straddled to catch his breath. The lights of Fanchlow sparkled behind him, trying to call him back. Above them, the sky had begun to shift into the faint blue of dawn. It cast a soft dewy glow over the Valley; blackbirds and goldfinches filled their air with their song. The sun would rise soon.

That made Silas feel a little better. Demons were beings of darkness. Nothing could hurt him in the light.

He tightened the net around his shoulder, gripped the ivy, and shimmied down the far side of the Wall.

When his feet met the ground, he stood still, preparing himself. The place already felt colder than normal, as though it had never known the touch of summer. The air he breathed was heavy and thick. Damp.

He turned around.

A dense forest greeted him: hazels, willows, silver birch. It was a labyrinth of wood and bramble, shrouded in white mist. The leaves whispered in the breeze: a million voices tumbling over each other.

Silas trembled. All these things, he had seen and heard before. But *this* was different. The thorns on the shrubs looked more vicious. The trees bent against the sky like fingers. The entire place seemed *alive*.

Muttering a prayer, he stepped forward. He walked with care, wanting to disturb the surroundings as little as possible. Every single time he moved, he expected something terrible to spring out of the undergrowth and strike him down.

But nothing came. And that worried him even more. He hadn't seen any demons, but they must have realised he was there.

The dawn light grew stronger, but it made little difference. The canopy of the trees was too thick. Silas kept his eyes down, so the height of the branches wouldn't terrify him.

What was he doing? This was so foolish! He had broken the truce… What was to stop the monsters from bringing more death upon the family for this?

At last, the trees thinned. A strange rhythmic sound reached Silas's ears, like water in the wind. He saw something shining. He walked towards it, stumbled down a hillock. The spongy earth became wetter, pierced by fat bullrushes and thick red blossoms. Amarants.

And before him, stretching from north to south like a giant black hole, was a lake. It stretched so far, it simply melted into the mist. The surface glittered like diamonds, broken here and there by waves lapping softly along the banks.

For a moment, Silas forgot his fear. He stared in wonder. Never had he seen such a massive body of water. Nothing like this existed on the eastern side of the Valley. This seemed too huge to even be a lake. It was too dark. Too menacing. Did it even have a bottom? Or did it just stretch on forever, straight through the Earth?

Did it lead to Hell?

The waves swept towards his boots. Each one seemed to hiss at him. *Thou art not welcome here!*

Silas gritted his teeth so hard, his jaw ached. Then he spotted something he hadn't been expecting. Drawn up in the shadow of a huge hazel were some boats. They looked ancient – he wasn't sure they would even still be watertight.

But the demons were down there, in the lake. He knew it. What else might be responsible for a curse which drowned men in air, than those who dwelled in the depths? The boats might be the only way to reach them; to meet them on their own ground.

He checked the boats. There were three of them, with oars inside. All sturdy. All made using the same techniques Silas still knew. They must have been from before the Wall was built, when this place was open to the Valley. How often had people come here? Did that mean it was safe, once? That the demons could be reasoned with?

He glanced at the water. A cold wind blew through him as though he wasn't there. Every knot in the trees, every ripple and stubby brown reed-head – all were like eyes, watching him with an intent that was anything but human.

"Lord, give me strength," Silas whispered.

He gave the nearest boat a shove. The reeds strained against the keel, but he pushed through them, and leapt inside. Then he grabbed an oar and paddled away from the bank.

The lake's mist closed around him. Frogs croaked. The shadow of a goosander flew across Silas's face. He drew the boat to a halt, and leaned carefully over the side. His reflection stared back at him. But down there, far below, he could see something moving. It was faint, but it was there.

"I… I come to make an offering," he said, barely above a whisper. "My name is Silas Atégo. I beg thee, lift thy curse upon my family."

He took the net, hefted it up, and threw it. It spread out like a huge wing, then slapped down onto the black surface, and sank. The line snagged on the end of the boat, but Silas didn't notice. He just kept his attention fixed on the depths, and waited.

A sudden tremor rattled over the surface. Merrin's eyes snapped open, but she didn't move. It was just a dead tree, finally giving way and tumbling into the water. That happened sometimes.

But it didn't *sound* like a tree. It didn't even sound like a sapling. And was that a *voice* she heard? It was distorted, but there were words.

Chills stabbed at Merrin like pike teeth. The noise echoed off the slopes and rocks. It was something not of the Lake. Something far too raucous and clumsy to belong anywhere down here.

Then a shadow fell over her. She looked up.

A *boat*. And drifting down from it, an open blanket of ropes and knots…

Merrin tried to swim away, but it was too late. The net covered her face; wrapped around her neck. Her gills slammed shut. She tore at the thick twine, but it was woven too strongly.

Terror stabbed through her chest. A familiar face pushed

into her mind, with that red hair and those lying lips…

"*Nay!*" she shrieked. "Penro! Lachlan! Help me!"

The net began to rise. Someone was pulling it up. Towards the surface.

Merrin fought with all her might. She kicked and struggled, trying to dive, but whoever was in the boat had tied it fast. Her fin broke free of the water. She drew a breath to call for help again, but it was pure air. And then she tumbled onto hard wooden panels.

This couldn't be happening again… She had to escape…

She opened her mouth and screamed.

Silas clamped his hands over his ears and stared at the creature in the bottom of the boat. He hadn't expected to catch anything, but when it tried to swim away, it had almost capsized him. He should have just cut the rope and let the net sink…

Now, he was trapped in the middle of the lake, with a *demon* at his feet.

He propelled himself backwards until his shoulders hit the prow. The boat rocked from side to side as the creature thrashed. It looked like something out of a nightmare: green all over, with a spiny fin down its spine, and thick webs between its fingers and toes. It reared and scratched like a wild dog, shrieking with every breath. And that terrified Silas more than anything else. It sounded so *human*.

"Pray, calm thee!" he cried. "Don't summon any others! 'Twas an accident! Please!"

The demon looked straight at him. Silas gasped in fright. The pale dawn sky shone in its eyes. They were bright purple, burning with anger.

"You!" it snarled.

Silas held up his hands.

"Don't be vexed! I am of the family Atégo–"

"*You!*" the demon roared.

It sprang at him. The impact knocked the breath from Silas's lungs. Then the entire boat swayed, and he crashed into the water.

The demon knelt above him, as though the surface was a solid sheet of ice. While it continued struggling with the net, Silas began kicking his way towards the bank. His strokes were clumsy – he had never swam out of his depth before. He couldn't even see the bottom of the lake. What if some awful monster loomed from the darkness and dragged him down? There could be *anything* in this place…

He came up for air. But the demon was waiting for him. Free at last, it smacked his head so hard, he saw stars.

"How dare it be *you!*" it shouted. "How dare you come here!"

"Please!" Silas cried. "Oh, God! I didn't mean to–"

"*Liar!*"

The demon seized a handful of Silas's hair and pushed him under. Panic pierced his body. It was going to drown him.

He felt something swim close to him. He screamed, but the water tore his voice away in a flurry of bubbles.

"Merrin, let him alone!" a voice snapped.

"I will not!"

"Stop! Leave him and come hither!"

Suddenly, the demon released Silas. He rose with a frantic gasp. The demon went to plunge back into the depths, but the water refused to yield. It tried a second time, but still, nothing happened.

"What's wrong?" asked the other creature.

"I cannot descend!" the first demon cried. It looked at Silas again. "*You* did this!"

The other one grabbed its wrist before it could advance on him.

"There's no time! You must take cover!"

The demon's fury snapped into fear. It looked up at the sky, growing lighter by the moment. The sun was almost risen.

"Get to the cave on the east bank!" said the second demon. "I shall return to thee at dusk! Leave him! Just go, now!"

Without another word, it dived, and was lost to sight. Silas turned around, kicking water in all directions. The bank was just twenty feet away…

The demon snatched his hair again. He took a breath, terrified it would push him underwater. But instead, it ran; sprinting over the surface and dragging Silas behind it. Then it flung him down in the shallows and knelt on his shoulders, pinning him.

"Thou think'st it safe to chance me?" the demon hissed. "Ye shall never know peace! I bring upon you the same as I did him!"

It grabbed Silas's hand.

Agony tore through him. It was like the hottest flame, searing into his flesh, down to his bones, shooting up his arm, to his skull and his eyes…

The demon let go and bolted into the trees. Silas lay still, trembling with pain. Why had it released him? It had meant to murder him; he was certain of that…

But it didn't come back. He couldn't even hear anything, save for the calls of frightened starlings.

He leapt onto his feet and ran as fast as he could. His heartbeat slammed in his ears like a drum. He could hardly breathe; he had never known pain like this...

The sun finally broke over the mountains, and struck him.

Silas fell onto his knees. His vision turned black, shrinking by the moment. He opened his eyes wide, but that didn't do anything. Within moments, his sight was completely gone.

He screamed in horror. He spun in all directions, trying to get his bearings. What had happened? How was this possible?

What had the demon done to him?

He found the hillock. Frantic, he raced up it, hands out to feel his way. He slammed into trees and tripped over roots. Mist wormed down his throat. Sharp thorns tore his arm like knives.

He didn't stop. He just needed to get back, out of here, and home... Raphael would help him...

He touched rough stone; ivy. The Wall. He scaled it as quickly as he could, hissing with pain as the edges cut his palms. Then he flung himself over the top, fell through empty air, and landed flat on his face in the meadow.

Silas spat soil out of his mouth and carried on, listening for the river. He felt as though he had spun in a hundred circles. Nothing was where he thought it was. Where did that hill come from? Why couldn't he hear the mill wheel creaking?

Time blurred. He still couldn't hear anything. Surely, there would be people in the fields by now?

"Raph!" he tried to shout, but it came out as a strangled squeak. The pain was too much. He was going to faint...

Then he heard voices. They sounded strange – definitely not his family – but they were people. Humans. They had to help him...

His knees buckled. His cheek hit the ground. Even his own

breathing felt far away.

Footsteps approached. Hands appeared under him. Then slumber beckoned, and he dived to embrace it.

Chapter IV
The Missing Atégo

I AM: YET WHAT I AM NONE CARES OR KNOWS.
MY FRIENDS FORSAKE ME LIKE A MEMORY LOST;
I AM THE SELF-CONSUMER OF MY WOES,
THEY RISE AND VANISH IN OBLIVIOUS HOST,
LIKE SHADES IN LOVE AND DEATH'S OBLIVION LOST.

John Clare

The cockerel's crow sliced through Raphael's slumber. He sat up, finger-combed his hair, and changed into a fresh tunic and pair of hose. He rubbed his knuckles into his eyes with a groan, then began going from cot to cot.

"Time to rise," he said to Mekina, before tickling Uriel's foot. His brother yelped himself awake.

"I thought thou was a spider!" Uriel cried.

Raphael flashed a smile and curled his fingers into a claw.

"Get up. There's work to be done."

Mekina awoke Selena and began dressing her. Their mother, however, didn't move. She just lay there, with her back to them.

"Ma?" Uriel said anxiously.

"Leave her be," Raphael whispered.

He tried to keep his expression soft, for the sake of his siblings, but in truth, he wanted nothing more than to do exactly what Araena was doing. The idea of going about the daily chores opened a huge hole in his chest. Yesterday, at the funeral, there had been an excuse to stop. But now, life would return to normal. Even though it could never be normal again.

Raphael's eyes lingered on the empty cot. He breathed deeply, so he wouldn't cry.

"Raph?" Uriel said. "Where's Si?"

Raphael turned around. Silas's bed was empty.

"Thou knoweth him to rise early," Mekina said. "Look, his boots aren't there. He's probably outside already."

Raphael nodded in agreement. Silas's cot was closest to the door – he was the lightest sleeper out of all of them; often the last to retire and the first to awaken. It wasn't uncommon for him to have begun work before the others had even eaten. He would slip about like a shadow, deliberately taking the quietest chores: weaving fresh wattle into a wall or tying bundles of wheat together.

Mekina laced up her stays, edged past their mother's bed, and threw a handful of bark into the fireplace. The embers had burned low, but quickly reignited, and she fed the newborn flame with twigs until it was burning healthily. Then she hung a cauldron on a hook and began heating some leftover pottage. It would be a quick breakfast, but one which could sustain them for the entire day.

While it heated, Raphael stepped outside. There was no sign of Silas. He walked to the cart shelter, checked the donkey in her paddock, but his brother was nowhere to be found.

"Si?" Raphael called.

His voice echoed back. Nobody answered.

Selena poked her head around the door. "Isn't he here?"

"Nay."

"The river? He may have gone for water?"

Raphael paused. That was a good point. The pails had been in need of refilling, and the river was far enough to warrant rising early.

"Well he'd best make haste to be back," Mekina said from inside. "The food is ready. Raph, come hither."

"Be sure to leave some aside for him," Raphael said. He returned to the house and accepted a portion of the pottage, spread on a plate of flat unleavened bread. Then he took a second helping and brought it to Araena.

She looked up at him with eyes bloodshot from tears.

"Ma, thou must eat," he said gently.

Araena let out a breath which moved her whole body.

"I cannot."

"Try. Just a few mouthfuls will do thee better than nowt."

Raphael broke off a little of the bread for her. Araena chewed on it, but there was no strength in her jaw. She stared into nowhere, barely even blinking. She was only in her early thirties, but her age seemed to have doubled overnight. Never had Raphael seen his mother look so frail. It was as though everything inside her had been sucked out.

He put an arm around her shoulders, and helped her to eat. By the time she was done, his own breakfast was cold, but he didn't care. He just swallowed it as quickly as he could, then washed it down with a cup of ale.

"Well done," he said to Araena.

His mother managed a tiny grin. Even when Raphael wasn't smiling himself, he could always bring it out in others. No matter the situation. No matter how much he was also hurting.

"Now, to work," Mekina said. "I'll wash and tidy in here. The stable and coop must be cleaned – Selena, you do that, and empty the chamber pots. Uriel, Raph, could you go to the hay field and start cutting it?"

"Is it not a little early for that?"

"Nay, I checked it the day thou travelled to the fayre. The south patch is ready. The summer has been kind."

Raphael eyed the holes in the roof. "I'll fix those first, lest we have more rain. The hay can wait. Or Uriel can start without me. I'll join him anon."

"Si can help me when he gets back," Uriel added.

Raphael glanced at the door again.

"I'll keep watch from up high," he said. "Come. We don't want to fall behindhand."

With that, he headed outside with Uriel and Selena. While they headed in opposite directions, Raphael fetched a bundle thrashed straw from last year's harvest, tied it to his back, and clambered up a ladder until he sat atop the roof. Piece by piece, he began laying the new thatch, pushing it as far back as possible, so no water could seep through. It was hard, monotonous work, but that was exactly what Raphael needed.

The sun crept higher. The sky turned as bright as polished glass. A soft breeze blew sweet with the notes of wildflowers, and bees buzzed around Raphael's head. He didn't bother waving them away. They were the fat, furry kind, which didn't sting. Once they realised he wasn't a blossom, they would leave him alone.

Someone shouted. Then a yelp tore across the hay field.

Raphael spun around. A group of neighbouring children

were standing at the edge of the farm, throwing stones and sods of earth. Uriel tried to hit them away, but one struck his face and knocked him down.

Raphael scrambled down the wall and ran over.

"Enough!" he cried, leaping in front of Uriel. "What's the meaning of this?"

The children took a few steps back, but didn't break eye contact. Vitriol painted their faces.

"Cursed ones!" the tallest boy snapped.

"Aye, 'tis true!" said another. "Father Fortésa told of it!"

"What say you?" Raphael demanded. "This is nonsense. Leave us alone in our grief."

The tall boy spat at him.

"You don't scare us. You should build another Wall here! Keep away from us!"

Raphael shook his head. "Thou art pitiful. Get home."

The children sneered, but nonetheless took their leave. Raphael stood still until they were gone from sight, then turned to Uriel. His brother was whimpering, but Raphael sensed it was more from fright than pain.

"Are you hurt?" he asked.

"Nay," Uriel muttered tearfully. "I didn't do anything wrong!"

"I know," Raphael said. "Pay them no mind."

"Why would they say that?"

"They're fools."

Raphael pulled Uriel into a hug; felt his little body trembling. He supposed it was a good thing that he had faced the boys. If Silas had seen them, he would have stared them down until they fled, and if that didn't work, he would have boxed their ears.

Raphael peered towards the river. It had been almost an hour. And still Silas hadn't come home.

A heavy smell of incense saturated the air. It spun around in Silas's head and dragged him out of slumber. But he kept his eyes closed. He could still remember what had happened... It would be so much worse to open them and see nothing.

Then he realised he *couldn't* open them, even if he'd wanted to. A cloth had been wrapped around his head, covering them. There was a very soft pillow under him, stuffed with fine down, which must have taken several large birds to fill. Another bandage was wrapped around his arm. His wounds had been cleaned; the ones on his hands lay open to the air so they could heal quicker. He carefully touched his left palm, and recoiled with a hiss. That was the one the demon had grabbed. It still felt like the fiercest burn.

There was a sudden rustle of clothing, and a tinkling sound, like beads knocking together.

"Uncle!" a girl shouted. "Uncle, he be a'wakin'!"

Silas went to sit up, but smacked his forehead on what felt like a thin beam. The whole room shuddered, and he yelped in shock.

"Ai, now," the girl said, her voice softer. "Be careful! Lie back down an' be still."

Silas frowned. She didn't sound like anyone he knew. The room – was it a room? – felt very small, and the wind howled around the outside, unnervingly close. He reached out, touched the wall, and frowned. It wasn't a wall at all, but a thick sheet of canvas. He was in a tent.

Who lived in a *tent?* Was he even still in the Elitland?

Before the girl could answer, someone else entered. Someone big.

"How's he doin'?" a deep male voice asked, and Silas felt a hand close around his wrist. Instinctively, he pulled away and tried to run.

The man pushed him down.

"Ai, ai! Yer'll not do any good!"

Suddenly, Silas noticed his clothes were gone. Beneath the blanket, he was dressed only in a linen chemise. He was defenceless.

"Where are my things?" he demanded.

"They be a'dryin'. They were soaked through."

"Where am I? Let me go!"

Silas tried to kick the man off, but it was no use. He would have had more luck moving a boulder.

"Calm thee!" the man snapped. "We mean ye no harm."

Silas stilled. There was a warmth in that voice – a stern kind of warmth, like hardening honey. But his nerves didn't dissipate. In a single day, he had buried his father, crossed the Wall, almost been killed by a demon. Rendered *blind*.

Blind. A life of sightlessness. It was as much a burden as being crippled. If the creature had made him deaf or mute, then at least he would have still been able to work. But how was he supposed to do anything now? He couldn't harvest the crops, or set traps, or chop wood.

He would never see his family again. He would never see the shattering of freckles across Mekina's face, or Raphael's warm smile...

He refused to cry. That would hardly help. See them or not, he needed to get back to them.

A wooden rim pressed against his lips.

"Drink this," the girl said.

"What is it?" Silas asked warily.

"Ale."

Silas hesitated, but then opened his mouth, and realised how thirsty he was. He gulped it until the cup was drained.

"I'll fetch more in a bit. Keep an eye on him," the man said to the girl. Then Silas heard him leave. There was a hollow tap as the cup was put down on a hard surface.

"So, what be yer name?" the girl asked.

Again, Silas listened to her voice. He was sure he had heard it before, but she definitely wasn't from the Valley.

"Thou art Cart-folk?" he asked again.

"Oh, aye," the girl replied, and Silas had the idea that she was smiling as she said it. "But we 'ere don't go by that. We're Peregrini."

"Peregrini?"

"Meanin' 'Wanderers'," she explained. "Now, what be thy name, lad?"

Silas pressed his lips together. He wasn't sure whether giving his name would be a good idea.

"Hmm?" the girl pressed.

"Silas," he replied. His first name was harmless and common enough among Valley-folk.

"Alrigh'," she said. "Mine's Irima. An' ye be in our humble camp, on the mountainside. We found thee collapsed down yonder. An awful sight, yer were. What happened?"

Silas shook his head. He couldn't bring himself to say it. How could he know she was trustworthy? She wasn't of his world. Even those in the Valley would turn on him if they learned the truth. What if Father Fortésa found out? Another curse to add to

61

the first one…

"Yer for sure a quiet one," Irima said. "Are yer hungry? If thou won't speak, eat instead."

Before Silas could protest, she pushed something into his hand. He felt it carefully; smelled it. It was meat: cooked and then left to go cold, heavily pickled with spices. He took a tiny bite; recognised the texture of mutton.

"Thou slept awhile," Irima carried on. "'Twas at dawn, we came across yer."

"And what is it now?" Silas asked.

"Evenin'. The sun will be settin' shortly."

"I… must return to my family."

"Yer can't right now. It be too dangerous to walk down there alone. Stay another night, recover thy strength. We can help yer to Fanchlow upon the morrow, if yer want."

Silas gave a single nod. It was taking all his concentration to decipher her speech. There was a strange lilt to it which he hadn't noticed at the fayre, like a high wind playing with clouds until they formed a million shapes.

He listened to her move about the tent to stretch her legs. A tawny owl hooted outside, very close.

"So," Irima said suddenly, "how did yer lose yer sight? Was yer born blind? Or was it some kind o' accident?"

Silas hesitated. He remembered the demon pinning him down, snarling in his ear…

"An accident."

"Not long ago, I'm guessin'?" Irima said. "Ye wouldn't 'ave been stumblin' about, otherwise. Thou poor thing."

Silas bristled. She sounded genuinely sympathetic. But he hated being so helpless, so pitiful. He didn't even tolerate his family fussing over him when he was hurt or ill. Raphael might be the eldest, but Silas was firm where his brother was gentle. No matter what happened, he remained strong. Never weak. Ever.

"What 'ave yer got in yer head?" asked Irima.

Silas frowned. "What?"

She tapped his temple gently, and the sudden touch made him flinch away.

"What be the matter?" Her words were soft and strangely comforting. "Yer face held all the sorrow o' the world just then."

"It's nothing," said Silas quietly.

She sat beside him. The tinkling noise came again as she moved. Silas was amazed at just how much he was hearing, now that sight couldn't distract him. Things he had thought to be quiet were now unbelievably loud. And there were new sounds: so obvious, he wondered how he'd ever missed them. He heard the distant hum of conversations in other tents; bleats of sheep and goats; the snorting of the horses and the pawing of their hooves against the earth. The wind whistled through the trees nearby, and he shivered. That sound reminded him of the waves on the lake.

There came a tapping sound: two pieces of flint being struck together.

"Just lightin' the lamp," Irima muttered. "The sun's set. It's gettin' too dark to see what I'm doin' in 'ere."

At last, she put the flint down. There was a faint skitter as one of the pieces rolled across the floor.

Silas froze. The cloth was still over his eyes, but through his lids, there was light.

He slowly lifted it.

"Ai, don't! Thou has a cut there!" Irima protested. She went to stop Silas, but he smacked her hand away, and opened his eyes wide.

The light exploded in front of him. He recoiled with a yelp, then tried again. A wash of colour assaulted him. Lines and shadows found their proper places. The lamp which Irima had lit glowed like a miniature sun.

He struggled to breathe. How was this possible? The demon had stolen his sight…

Irima whimpered in fright. Silas looked up at her, and his mouth fell open. He recognised her. Tanned skin, black hair hanging with ornaments… She was the girl who he and Raphael had traded with at the fayre.

She leapt to her feet and ran outside, screaming for her uncle.

Panic hit Silas like a sudden hail. What would these people think, when they saw his sight had returned? That he was a demon? Silas himself might have believed that, if he was in their position. What would they do to him now?

He jumped up, staggering like a drunkard, and snatched hold of the tent beam before he could fall. Then he flung back the flap.

A twilight sky opened around him. The campsite was small, encircled by tethered horses and tilted carts, but Silas saw past them, and realised just where he was. They were in the Fanchlow corrie, high up on one of the mountainsides behind the village. It all looked tiny on the slopes: a few faraway dots of light and dark smudges in the shapes of houses.

No matter about his boots or clothes. He needed to get down there.

Stones dug into his heels as he ran. His head swam with fright. He headed towards a gap in the carts, but instead of passing through, he slammed into something big and rounded. He blinked hard, and leapt back in alarm.

Almost invisible in the darkness was a black stallion. It

tossed its head and snorted, flashing the whites of its eyes. Then it raised a leg and kicked Silas in the stomach.

He flew onto his back. All the breath snapped out of his lungs. He tried to stand, but it was impossible. Were his ribs broken?

A huge man strode over to him. Silas looked up into a face the colour of leather. A sooty beard covered his chin, and his hair hung with pale beads, just like Irima's. A dark purple kerchief was tied around his neck, embroidered with intricate patterns.

"Yer mad imbecile!" the man snapped. Silas flinched when he heard his voice. This was the man who had been in the tent with him and Irima.

Silas looked around. More people were beginning to approach. Men, women and children: all swathed in colourful scarves and sashes. They muttered among themselves; some drew the cross over their chests. Irima stood separate from them, carrying a burning torch. She stared at Silas as though he were a ghost.

The man drew a blade. Silas shrank back in terror. Irima's uncle looked like he could have snapped him in two like a twig. And he bore another strength: a cool deep kind, of warranting respect. Silas recognised it – he himself often called upon it when he was taking charge of his siblings. This man was in charge, and he knew it.

"Who are yer?" he demanded. "*What* are yer?"

Silas held up his bandaged hands and tried to speak, but he was too winded.

"Irima saith his blindness is gone!" a woman called. "There's magic o' some sort about him!"

"Magic?" Irima's uncle repeated. His hand crept to an iron crucifix around his neck.

Silas bit back the pain and forced his words out.

"I'm but a man!" he wheezed.

"Then explain yerself! How be it that thee can see, after bein' found helpless?"

"I knoweth not! Please believe me, sir! Please! Have mercy!"

A horrible silence fell. At any other time, Silas might have withdrawn into it, as naturally as breathing. But now, it grated against his bones like a millstone. He didn't dare take his eyes off the knife. It was long, sharp: the kind used for carving meat.

What would happen now? These people weren't of the Valley. And they had to be called Raptors for a reason... Would they steal *him* away? They had already taken his clothes. What was left to do? Strip his bones clean and cook him for dinner?

Irima's uncle bent closer.

"My niece saith she saw yer a few days past. Red hair like this be rare."

"Take it," Silas cried. "Cut it off and sell it. But don't hurt me!"

"I'll do no such thing."

"Then what dost thou want?"

"There was another with yer," said Irima. "At the fayre. A bit older. Yeh've a brother?"

Silas's heart leapt. "Holy God, please don't go to my family! We have naught!"

Irima came closer. "We're not savages. We just be afraid. What's happenin' with yer?"

"Be careful!" said a tall man. "He might be some kind o' demon!"

"Nay!" Silas insisted.

"Then how is it possible?" the man barked. "What yer

done ain't natural! If not a demon, he be cursed!"

Silas stomach flipped over.

"I doubt that," Irima's uncle said. "What happened to yer? At the fayre, yer were fine, correct? An' now ye be covered in cuts and bruises. An' *that*."

He flicked the knife at Silas's left hand. Silas looked down at it, and forgot to breathe. Beneath the wounds from scaling the Wall, his flesh was bright red and shiny, as though he had pressed it onto a heated pan.

"A burn," he said quickly. "And the cuts are from pruning a rosebush."

"An' why were yer so far from home?"

"I sleepwalk."

Irima's uncle cocked an eyebrow. "An' bein' soaked head to toe wasn't enough to wake thee?"

Silas bit the inside of his cheek. "I... It did. But then I lost my way. I couldn't see the village lantern."

Irima's uncle twisted his beard between two fingers. Silas didn't dare look away. Had they believed him? He hated to lie, but how else was he supposed to get away from this alive?

"No word about yer eyes?" Irima's uncle pressed.

"I swear to thee, I don't know how it happens."

"Yer tell the truth?"

"Aye."

"Alrigh'. Listen 'ere. We've no intentions o' harmin' anyone, an' it seems neither do ye. Yer seem like nowt but a scared lad. Still injured, though. It would weigh heavy on me conscience to send yer away now."

Silas gasped. "Thou intends to keep me here?"

"A little while," Irima's uncle said. "Until yer are better, and then go on yer way. Thou be in no danger from us."

Silas didn't relax, but he nodded, to show his thanks. He just needed to recover, and hide the truth from the Cart-folk. That was all, and it would be easily done. His quiet, sullen nature had always lent itself to keeping people at bay.

Irima's uncle got to his feet.

"Yer are to stay in the sick-un's tent," he said firmly. "I want to know where yer are always."

Silas's eyes widened.

"Thou claimed I would be in no danger," he cried.

"And yer shan't," Irima's uncle replied. "But nor will I risk it. Not for thee, or for my people." He glanced up at the crowd. "Everyone go back to yer business! Ai, Andreas! Take the lad back over there. Wash yerself after handlin' him. Sleep apart from yer wife tonight, until yer be clean. An' Irima, you keep watch over him. Make him well."

A burly man stepped forward, gathered Silas in his arms like a baby, and carried him away.

Chapter V
Merrin and Her Wall

DARK AND BURNING EYES, DARK AS MIDNIGHT SKIES,
FULL OF PASSION FLAME, FULL OF LOVELY GAME.
I'M IN LOVE WITH YOU, I'M AFRAID OF YOU.
SAYS WHEN I MET YOU MADE ME SAD AND BLUE.
OH, NOT FOR NOTHING ARE YOU DARKER THAN THE DEEP!
I SEE MOURNING FOR MY SOUL IN YOU,
I SEE A TRIUMPHANT FLAME IN YOU:
A POOR HEART IMMOLATED IN IT.
BUT I AM NOT SAD, I AM NOT SORROWFUL,
MY FATE IS SOOTHING TO ME:
ALL THAT IS BEST IN LIFE THAT GOD GAVE US,
IN SACRIFICE I RETURNED TO THE FIERY EYES!

Yevhen Hrebinka

The afternoon sunlight crept close. Merrin drew her legs up and covered her toes with her dress. Just as Lachlan ordered, she had hidden in the cave. Luckily, it faced north, so the very back had been in shadow all day. But that did little to comfort her. She

69

had been trapped for hours, fury and fright still holding her in an iron grip.

For an awful moment, as she fled, she thought she had forgotten where the cave was. She hadn't been here in so long. One night, she had even come here with *him*. They had sat together, then they had waded into the shallows of the lake, and kissed...

Merrin shook her head. No. She refused to allow that memory to torment her. He was dead. She had seen to that. And he had never loved her. He had only loved the idea of her.

But still, she pictured him. And what happened... It was exactly the same. Crashing through the surface, the air tearing her lungs, the bright sky searing her eyes. She couldn't believe she had been so foolish. Why didn't she swim away faster? Why hadn't she fought harder?

She stared at her hand; imagined it gripping that boy's head of hair. Red. Of course it was red. Even a century hadn't been enough to breed that out of them.

She thought of the boy, of *his* hand: seared and scarred forever. A mark of shame which would mark him for the rest of his life, however short it might be. It was a punishment which only she and her mother were powerful enough to inflict – and one which Merrin herself had dealt only once before.

She shivered. It was so cold up in the air. She couldn't even remember the last time she had been completely dry. And everything was so *heavy*. Here, with no water to support it, her body felt as though it were made of stone. Her skin pressed into the hard rock. The roots of an ash tree had broken through, and groped at her like twisted fingers. The musty smells of earth and last autumn's leaves wormed their way into her nose.

If only the sun wasn't so dangerous, she would have

sprinted to the Lake in a heartbeat. But then what would she do? She hadn't been able to pass through the surface.

And that terrified her. Was she to be confined up here forever? She couldn't live in this cave. What about her people?

"Stop it," she muttered to herself. "Just wait for the night. Thou shalt be able to descend by moonlight."

Merrin hoped the sound of her own voice would convince her, but it only made her feel more alone.

She laid her head on her arms. She wanted to weep, but she was too exhausted. So she closed her eyes, and slipped into slumber.

A swan and his mate glided over the Lake. The reeds whispered to each other. The trees bent their branches and danced with the wind. On the bank, a white mare lowered her head to drink.

Hands slipped around her waist from behind. Soft. Gentle. Unyielding.

Wilt thou be mine?

Merrin woke with a horrified yelp. She brushed her body down; kicked out at the earth as though it might burn her.

She was still here. Still trapped. Still alone.

Frustration overwhelmed her. She drove her fist into the rotting leaf-mould, and screamed until her chest burned. Birds took flight from the trees. She hated them; hated the branches, the soil, the air. This forest was a part of her home – its very name, Delamere, meant Forest of the Lake – but it wasn't under the water. It was too hard and harsh. Everything up here was *wrong*.

She closed her eyes. Perhaps it would be easier if she couldn't look out there.

The air became crisp. The shadows lengthened. Then, at last, the sun disappeared behind the Western Ridge. The pink sky cooled to blue, and stars appeared, shimmering like fireflies. A bird began to whistle. Merrin focused on it. She could hardly remember when she'd last heard such a sound.

"Nyhtegale," she muttered. Yes, that was what they were called.

A new wave of nausea swept over her. *He* had once sang her a song about those birds.

"Your Majesty!"

Merrin leapt to her feet. "Hello?"

"It's safe! Come hither!"

Merrin stumbled out of the cave, brushing soil and leaves off her legs, and hurried around to the Lake. Two green heads were above the surface, waiting for her. Lachlan and Penro.

She almost melted with relief, and ran over the water towards them. When they saw her, they stepped through, and stood level with her.

A shoal of minnow flashed under their feet. Merrin sighed. The feeling of the Lake on her flesh felt glorious after cowering in the cave.

Penro's violet eyes shone. He looked as though he would burst into tears.

"Thank the stars!" he exclaimed. "Art thou hurt?"

Merrin shook her head. "I'm fine. Thank you so much for coming."

"I'm sorry we were forced to leave thee," said Lachlan. "Where is the boy?"

Merrin gritted her teeth. "Gone."

Penro watched her carefully.

"And unharmed?"

"He still has his life," Merrin snarled. "He should count himself lucky. Now, please, enough about him. I want to go home."

Lachlan bowed his head, then stood aside, so she could descend first. Merrin closed her eyes, pointed her toes, and pushed. But the water didn't swallow her leg like it was supposed to. It continued to hold her weight, as though it had frozen over.

She pulled back, tried again. And still, it didn't work. She moved a few feet away and slammed her heels down. Nothing happened.

Shock and fear clogged her throat like weeds around a stone.

"What's wrong?" Lachlan asked.

"I still can't pass through!" Merrin cried.

Lachlan pushed with his own foot, and it slid underwater, as easily as a knife through butter. He looked at Merrin in alarm.

"I shall fetch thy mother," he said, and dived so quickly, he was lost from sight in moments.

Merrin paced back and forth, trying to keep her breathing steady. She wanted so badly to throw open her gills and feel the water passing through them.

"Worry not," Penro said gently. "She'll know what to do."

Merrin didn't reply. She couldn't even bear to look at him.

After several long minutes, she spotted movement in the depths. Lachlan rose out of the darkness, Dylana at his side.

Dylana pulled Merrin into her arms. Merrin held onto her, but refused to relax. She hated Penro and Lachlan seeing her so weak.

"Are you alright?" Dylana asked. "Penro told me what happened."

"I'm fine," Merrin said frantically. "Mother, please! I just want to go home! I cannot bear staying here a moment longer!"

"Calm thyself."

"How can I be calm? I am trapped here!"

"How is that possible?" Penro asked. "Lady Dylana, thou is the Mistress of Magic. You must be able to do something. She must return!"

Dylana drew away from Merrin, but didn't let go of her arms. A sad shine came into her eyes.

"Aye, she must. But there is a reason why she cannot."

Merrin froze. "What is it?"

"You were taken from the Lake by force."

"And... the first time wasn't by force? I returned then!"

"Your *capture* was by force," said Dylana, "but you went to him willingly the first time, Merrin. You passed through the surface under your own power. You weren't dragged through, as you have been now."

Merrin's cheeks burned. Just thinking about this made her feel ill.

"So... I must have passed through willingly?" she asked.

Dylana nodded. "But thou shalt be able to come back."

The relief almost brought Merrin to her knees.

"How?" she demanded. "Please... I can't stay here. I must... I need to do my duty. Father would be so ashamed..."

"Take that thought from thy head," Dylana said firmly.

"I was in the Tomb Garden... I only wished to see him!" Merrin cried. "Dost thou see why I insisted upon never coming here again! It brings only strife! *Nothing will happen*, thou said, and look! I hate this place! Mother, please, do something!"

Dylana took Merrin's face in her hands.

"I can't," she said. "And neither can thee. We may be powerful, but you must wait until the night when we will all be at our strongest. Then we can all help you, and you will be able to pass through."

A stone dropped through Merrin's stomach.

"The Rise?" she said in a tiny voice.

"That's five nights from now!" Penro protested. "What about the sun?"

"It's the only way," said Dylana.

Merrin could feel her hands shaking. She glanced at the water shimmering underfoot: a solid barrier between her and her beloved home. She wanted to fall apart; to open her eyes and find this all to be a nightmare.

Dylana's hands appeared on her shoulders.

"You must be careful," she said. "Continue to shelter in the cave. I shall return every night to see you, and bring food."

"I'll come, too, Your Majesty," Penro volunteered.

Merrin nodded. "Does this mean I must be crowned up here, after all?"

"It does," said Dylana. She pointed to an island in the middle of the Lake, the banks red with amarant blossoms. A single willow tree trailed its branches into the water. "We shall do it there. The moonlight always shines strongly upon it."

Merrin eyed it contemptuously.

"And as soon as it's done, and the Rise is concluded, I can go home?" she asked.

"Aye," said Dylana. "You can do this, my darling."

"I *will* do this," Merrin said firmly. "For my people."

A cool breeze sent a rustle through the shivering reeds. Merrin listened to the sound, for the first time in one hundred years, and heard their hidden words, encouraging her to remain strong.

"And thou should be kind to thyself," Dylana said. "The human who did this… He was an Atégo?"

Merrin's fin snapped from side to side.

"Don't say that name!"

"An Atégo," Dylana repeated, answering her own question. "I thought as much."

"I will hear no more about them!" Merrin barked.

"What didst thou do to him?" Dylana asked. "Did you brand him? Make him blind?"

"What does it matter?"

"Did you?"

Merrin bared her teeth. Her eyes burned like live coals.

"A century has gone by," said Dylana. "You hold the past and present as one in your head. He is innocent."

"That family will never be innocent."

"You know their lifetimes are shorter than ours. The one who hurt you is long gone."

"I care not! That boy still came here! The humans were the ones who decided to build their Wall! They set their own boundary! If any cross it, they must face the consequences!"

"Then you would have sought out *any* human who came here, regardless of reason?" Dylana argued. "Would you truly spend the rest of your life as such? Would you kill *all* of them?"

Merrin faltered. "Of course not. But–"

"Hark!" Dylana said. "These circumstances are awful, I know. And how terrible that it was such a repeat of the first time. But will you have this be your choice, Merrin?"

Merrin pushed her mother's arms away.

"Aye!" she cried. "He did this to me! He knew what he was doing! And so did I! He *deserved* it!"

"Blindness for the rest of his days?"

"You speak of *choice*, Mother? He chose to be blind! He ignored the warnings and dared come to me! Is that not blind enough? Is my reaction not punishment enough? To only see in darkness, as I do?"

"And what was he to you?" Dylana pressed. "Nobody. Did you even know his first name?"

"Enough!" Merrin shouted. "It's done! He must live with it, and so must thee! The humans will do well to keep their Wall! Let this be a warning for that! I will not be weak! And I will not put my people in danger! If one human grows comfortable here, what is to stop all of them coming, with their nets and their lies? Wouldst thou want to see every Asræ ripped away like I was?"

A sharp silence fell. Even the trees and waves seemed to still. Merrin stood shaking, struggling to breathe. She felt as though her skin was the only thing keeping her from flying everywhere at once. She hadn't known anger like this in so long...

Dylana shook her head slowly, then turned and slipped back under the surface without another word.

Merrin's heart sank as she watched her mother disappear. She wanted to call out to her; beg her to stay... But what would she say then? She couldn't apologise for something she wasn't sorry for.

Penro took a step forward. Merrin's eyes snapped onto him. She had forgotten he was there.

"Please don't be vexed," he said carefully. "Thy mother speaks wisely."

"So thou taketh her side?" Merrin asked miserably. "Thee, who witnessed what happened?"

"I also witnessed a terrified boy begging you for mercy," said Penro. "Merrin... I have known thee long. You were never like this."

"That was before," Merrin said, hating how her voice trembled.

"Hardening thy heart is not the answer," he insisted. "That

is not the trait of a monarch. Your father was compassionate. I know you are, too. You are strong, yet kind. Please don't forget that."

A cold mist descended upon Merrin's shoulders. She looked at her hands, then at the Royal Bands around her arms.

"I haven't forgotten it," she said. "I have simply learned that only a few are deserving of it. And mark me: if any more Atégos come here while I am trapped, I will do more than brand them. I will kill them."

Chapter VI
The Lightless Dawn

ANYONE CAN CARRY HIS BURDEN, HOWEVER HARD,
UNTIL NIGHTFALL.
ANYONE CAN DO HIS WORK, HOWEVER HARD,
FOR ONE DAY.
ANYONE CAN LIVE SWEETLY, PATIENTLY, LOVINGLY, PURELY,
TILL THE SUN GOES DOWN.
AND THIS IS ALL LIFE REALLY MEANS.

Robert Louis Stephenson

Raphael and Uriel had spent all day in the field, mowing the long grass with scythes, then collecting it on the donkey cart, to be tied into hay bundles. They would be stored in the fodder house, ready for when the livestock came down from the summer pastures on the mountainsides. It was hard, heavy work, under a blazing sun, and Raphael's tunic was soaked through with sweat. He had worn a straw hat to protect his face, but he could feel the back of his neck beginning to peel. He splashed some cool water on it, then took both scythes under one arm.

"Come," he said to Uriel. "Let's make for home. We've done enough for one day."

He cast his eyes towards the setting sun. It was late, but still, there had been no sign of Silas.

A knot twisted under his ribs. This wasn't like his brother. Not at all.

He led Uriel by the hand, up the hill, towards the house. They passed one of the village lanterns, moths clustered around the flickering flame inside it. Raphael gently blew on them, and they fluttered into the air.

"Aren't moths just butterflies?" Uriel asked.

"Night butterflies," Raphael said. "They're not as colourful, though I think them pretty, in their way."

"Like nyhtegales?"

Raphael smiled. "Aye. They're hardly swans, but what a song they have."

Uriel tugged on his wrist. "Wilt thou sing it? The nyhtegale song?"

Raphael rolled his eyes melodramatically.

"When the nygtegale sings,
The trees grow green,
Leaf and grass and blossom springs,
In Averyl, I believe;
And love has to my heart gone
With a spear so keen,
Night and day my blood doth drain
And my heart, to death it aches."

"I don't remember it being so sad," Uriel said. "Why would anyone ache for death? Pap didn't. Did he?"

Raphael paused and knelt down, so he was his brother's height. Uriel was so young – between his lips, Raphael could see the gap where he had lost both his front milk teeth. And in his wide, innocent eyes, Raphael recognised his own grief, as though he were looking into the deepest pool.

"Nay, he didn't," Raphael said. "He wanted to stay with us. But we all must pass, sooner or later."

Uriel's lip quivered. "*I* don't want to. Those boys... Before thou arrived, they said we are cursed. That all the men in our family will die the same way Pap did..."

Raphael shook his head. "I told thee, they're foolish. I am fit and healthy. So are all of us."

"But... what about Si?" Uriel asked. "Didst he not want to stay with us?"

"Of course he does."

"Then where is he?"

Raphael sighed. "I don't know. Perhaps he's home already. We'll probably find him waiting for us. Here, jump on."

He patted his back. Uriel climbed up it; Raphael moved the scythe blades away from his brother's feet, then held onto him and carried him to the top the hill.

Raphael was glad to not have Uriel looking at him anymore. Now his face was out of sight, he let a scowl steel across it. He knew he should be angry with Silas for disappearing, but it wasn't in his nature to hold grudges. More than anything, he was worried, and that walked hand-in-hand with his grief. He had to stay strong for the sake of the others, so he kept smiling. But that only held the same effect as swatting at a cloud of midges. It granted a few moments of relief, but then it would return, as thick as ever.

Twilight had fallen by the time the two of them stepped through the door. The smell of warmed pork made Raphael's mouth water.

"Making use of the spices from the fayre?" he asked.

"Aye," Mekina said. She flipped the meat in the spider pan, then nestled its three iron legs deeper into the coals so it wouldn't fall.

Raphael set Uriel beside Selena, then perched on his mother's bed. Araena still hadn't moved from how they had left her that morning.

"Good eve, Ma," Raphael said softly. "Hast thou drank today?"

"A little," she muttered, her voice strangled from sobs.

"Take some more."

Raphael fetched a cup of ale and passed it to her. She sipped a few mouthfuls, then laid back down on the cot.

Raphael caught Mekina's eye. "Si isn't here?"

"Nay," she said. "And he's obviously not with thee."

"The fayre has concluded, hasn't it? He wouldn't be in the village?"

"If he was, he would have returned by now. It's hardly a whole day's errand."

"Mm," Mekina sighed. "And I doubt anyone would make us particularly welcome in Fanchlow, these days."

She stuck a knife into the meat to check it was cooked, then divided it into wooden bowls. She filled only five of them. Raphael glanced at the two vacant ones at the back: one for Silas, one for their father.

Araena whimpered. She didn't speak – she didn't need to. Tears streamed down her face like a waterfall. The sight was a dagger in Raphael's heart. His poor mother had lost her husband; the love of her life. And now Silas was gone. Silas, who kept everything in order and watched over everybody with his firm, silent eyes. One by one, her family was slipping away.

Raphael took a deep breath. He knew that what he was about to say would hurt her even more. But there was no choice.

"I shall find him," he announced.

Everyone turned to look at him. Even Araena rolled over.

"What if you don't come back, either?" Selena asked nervously.

"They'll throw stones!" Uriel cried.

Raphael raised a smile. "They won't. And it will take more than a few stones to hinder me."

"Raph, I don't think this is wise."

"Neither is leaving Silas alone. The Elitland isn't a large place. He must be here somewhere."

Mekina caught Raphael's eye.

"Where will you go?" she asked.

"I'll search Fanchlow tonight," Raphael said. "Failing that, I'll take the road south. First to Cederham, then on to Ullswick, if needs be."

"That's the other end of the Valley!" Araena protested. "Holy God, Raph, please don't leave us! Will Uriel be the man of the house without thee?"

"A few days, at most," Raphael promised. "That's all I need. And I will go on foot."

"Take the donkey," Selena said.

"Nay, she must haul in the hay bales," replied Raphael. "Worry not for me. I will find him. And we'll come home together. I swear."

A flat shine came into Araena's eyes. Raphael knew why. He hadn't intended it to be heard that way, but she was imagining him returning with his brother's body. Coming home together could mean one of two things, especially when the entire village seemed to be turning against them. And if the children had taken to throwing stones, what were the adults capable of?

"I *will* find him," Raphael repeated. He looked at Mekina, and she nodded once. With both the eldest brothers gone, she would protect the others as best she was able. It was all they could do.

Silas drew back the tent flap and peered outside. The fire in the middle of the campsite had burned out – there wasn't even a hint of smoke left. Overhead, the sky had turned pastel blue, the stars beginning to fade. Dawn would come soon.

All around, he saw the tents: a circle of mounds, tapering at the top like bells, all made from willow staves and canvas tarpaulins caked in tar. They looked spacious enough to sleep perhaps five people, and yet were small enough to easily transport. The wooden carts surrounded them in a wall. Now Silas looked closely, he realised the wheels were more thickly-built than any Valley wagon, to withstand longer journeys, over rougher terrain. In places, the carts were painted the same bright colours as the clothes he had seen, forming flowers and butterflies with beautiful symmetry.

As for the site itself, Silas had been correct when he first recognised it. The corrie was a hollow, high up on the mountainside, that had been worn away by ice centuries ago. The only remaining trace of that ice was the small circular lake nestled in the ground. Silas had seen this spot sometimes, when he went up to the pastures to check the sheep.

It was so close to home, it hurt. His family were only a few miles away, probably worried sick about him…

"What are yer doin'?"

Silas spun around. Irima was lying on the mattress across from his own, her eyes open and fixed on him.

"Don't be a'tryin' to go," she said. "Me uncle told yer."

"I'm not," Silas said gruffly. "I just wanted fresh air. It stinks in here."

Irima chuckled. "The incense be good for yer. Bad smells will only make thee sicker."

"I'm not sick."

"Nay, but ye be injured an' unclean."

Silas frowned. "What? Of course I'm clean. Didst thou not see to that, when thee stole my clothes?"

Irima sat up. She sighed sharply through her nose, then reached behind her and revealed a bundle of fabric. Even in the gloom, Silas recognised his tunic and hose.

"I told thee, they were a'dryin'," she said curtly. "An' now they're dry, I've taken 'em to be stitched, since ye have all but torn 'em to shreds."

Silas pursed his lips.

"I know what thy folk call us," Irima continued. "*Raptors.* Aye, I've heard men speak that word. But what have we ever stolen? Naught but a single sheep to feed ourselves. An' that were long ago. I don't even remember it. But *ye* do."

"Because it was still stealing," Silas snapped. "Valley-folk don't let things go easily."

"So I see," Irima snorted. "Now, come, sit down. I know yer didn't sleep. I didn't much, either. But yer should still rest. The sooner yer heal, the sooner yer leave."

"Wilst thou really let me go?" Silas asked.

"Why, afraid we'll steal *thee* away? Nonsense. Of course yer can go, as me uncle told so."

"Thy uncle, who held a knife to my throat?"

85

"Oh, hardly! Lord above! But can yer blame him for being scared? Thou was scared, too. An' would ye have treated any o' us any different, if yer found us helpless at yer door?"

Silas kept silent. But that was a good enough answer for both of them. Irima cocked an eyebrow at him, then struck the flint until the lamp was alight. It was a long, thin dish, made of hardened clay and filled with oil, the wick hanging out of it like a snake tail.

"Sit down," Irima said again. "Since yer be so mistrustin' o' me, yer can tell me if the stitchin' is up to scratch."

Silas scowled at her as he returned to his mattress. It was a thin thing, padded with straw, and lying atop a few layers of woven mats which formed the floor. He could feel the hardness of the earth underneath it. At least in his cot at home, he was off the ground.

Irima produced a needle and set to sewing his tunic. She worked quickly – within only a few minutes, she had closed up the holes, and even repaired older ones which Mekina had missed.

Silas watched her. Now the lamp was lit, and he was no longer panicking, he noticed for the first time how intricate her clothes were. Every inch was covered with embroidery, right down to her belt and shirt cuffs, and the linen had been dyed in a dazzling array of red and yellow. It must have all taken weeks to complete. Nobody in the Valley had time for any of that. Compared to everyone Silas knew, this girl and her people looked like they had leapt through a rainbow.

"Why is everything so decorated?" he asked.

"Well, on the road, we have only what we need," said Irima. "There be no place for fancy tapestries an' such. So everythin' is useful. But that don't mean it can't be beautiful, too."

Silas could see that. Aside from nature itself, all he knew

had always been plain. The spices were the most exotic thing he might know. And that, in itself, was enough. It was safe, secure, unchanging.

But he looked down at his hand, and a shudder passed through him. Unchanging? That seemed like a joke now. Everything was changing, before his very eyes.

"Done," Irima said. She tossed the tunic at him. "Happy?"

Silas nodded. "No flowers?"

Irima looked straight at him. "I thought yer didn't want to stick around long enough to want 'em."

"And thou doesn't mind caring for me thus? If I am unclean?"

"Why else do yer think I'm the only one 'ere? Keep it to as few people as possible. So, me an' Andreas, who found yer. That way, it don't spread."

"There's nothing to spread," Silas argued. "I told you. I'm not sick."

"And I tell thee, we can't know that," Irima snapped back. "Better safe than sorry. An' don't take such a tone with me. I'm not a little sister who yer can boss about."

Silas growled under his breath. "Thou art rude."

"To ye, maybe," Irima said. "Look, yer must understand. Goin' from place to place as we do… we're used to others findin' us strange. Anyone who's not one o' us, we need to treat with caution, in case they harm us. So many innocent troupes, just like us, have got wiped out, just 'cause outsiders decided to hate 'em. Me parents died that way. A mob came, set their tents afire. Me uncle won't let that happen again. Not to anyone."

Silas picked at the hem of his tunic. He couldn't deny that the Cart-folk had been kind to him. Kinder, perhaps, than even his neighbours in Fanchlow. Surely, if they did intend to hurt him, they would have done it by now. There had, after all, been ample time while he was blind and defenceless.

And Irima… She spoke so nonchalantly about her parents, it must have been a long time ago. But it plucked at his own grief like a mournful tune on a lyre. To lose them like that… Silas tried to imagine it: the tarpaulin and poles in flames; and the tar coating would only make it burn hotter…

"I'm sorry for your loss," he said, and he meant it.

Irima gave him a small smile. Then she set her thread aside, and as she moved, her hair beads sparkled in the light.

"What are they?" Silas asked.

"These?" Irima ran her fingers over a line of beads. "Pearls. Yer get 'em out o' oysters."

"Oysters?"

"Thou's never seen an oyster? Yer eat 'em. Quite slippery, mind. But sometimes, when yer open up the shell, they have these things inside."

Silas's head swam. "So… they are like snails?"

Irima shook her head. "Bigger. About the size o' yer hand."

"I've never seen the like," said Silas.

"Yer wouldn't," Irima replied. "Yer can only get 'em at the sea. An' ye folk never leave this place. Too afraid o' what's outside."

Silas ground his teeth together, but decided against challenging her. He was too curious. He had heard tales of the sea: lakes filled with salt, and so huge, it was impossible to see the other side. So how could someone even tell the difference between the water and the sky?

"And thou is never afraid?" he asked instead.

Irima smiled to herself. Her entire face seemed to light up

with it, as though she was hearing a song not for Silas's ears.

"There are many things to fear," she said, "but why should the world be one o' 'em?"

"But… ye are rootless. No home."

"Of course we have a home. We just take it with us."

Silas glanced at the tent above him. The canvas was growing lighter now, as the sun crept closer.

"That's not the same," he said.

"Oh?" Irima smirked. "If yer sturdy house were to crumble to dust right now, would it not be more important to have those yer love? To us, our *kin* are our home. An' so long as we're together, we'll be alrigh'."

Silas stared at her, a million words tangling in his throat. But instead of speaking them, he turned his face away and pulled on his tunic.

"Thank you," he muttered.

"Yer welcome," Irima said warmly. "Now, let's have a look at yer wounds."

She crawled closer to him. Silas sat perfectly still as she inspected his palms, running her fingers over them with a feather-light touch. The cuts had turned to scabs, but the burn mark was as fierce as ever. Just looking at it made Silas's heart beat faster.

"Can that be covered?" he asked. "Please. I hate the sight."

Irima glanced around the tent, then leaned behind a mound of blankets and rummaged in a wooden chest. Eventually, she withdrew a single leather glove; slipped it over Silas's hand. It fit perfectly.

"That's thine now," she said. "Me uncle was goin' to throw it, anyway. He lost the other one."

"What's your uncle's name?"

"Garrett. I've already told him yer name."

Irima pushed up Silas's sleeve, then unwound the bandage, and held her hand close to his skin to feel for heat.

"Ai, that be well on the mend," she muttered. "Yer a quick healer. Lucky."

Silas scoffed. He *wasn't* lucky. Not at all.

"Oh, find some mirth in ye," Irima said, softer now. "Yer not dyin'."

"Don't," Silas snapped.

Irima frowned, and a deep shine came into her eyes.

"What's wrong?"

"*Don't*," Silas said, and turned away from her. But she didn't retreat.

"I meant no offence," she said. "Alrigh'. Brace yerself. I need to clean yer arm."

She took a bottle of ale, pulled the cork out with her teeth, and poured the liquid over Silas's wound. He yelped in pain, screwing his eyes shut.

"Sorry 'bout that," Irima said. "I'll bind it afresh now."

Silas sucked in air between his teeth. At least she knew what she was doing.

Irima tied a new bandage around his arm. Then Silas opened his eyes.

He recoiled. He fell back onto the mattress, and felt the whole tent shake as he hit one of the poles.

"What is't?" Irima asked.

Silas held his hands out in front of him frantically. The left one stung, as strongly as it had the day before.

"I can't see!"

Irima gasped in horror. "What?"

Silas snatched out for her, found her wrists. He strained his eyes, but there was nothing. Only blackness.

"Oh, God! Don't leave me! Please!" he cried.

"What's happenin' to yer?"

"I don't know! Please stay with me! I... I..."

His words trailed off. He lowered his head wretchedly, trying not to cry. This was all too much... What had that demon done to him? What would his father think of all this? He had broken the oldest rule, disgraced them all, brought a second curse down upon himself...

Irima's hand appeared on his face.

"I'll not leave," she said, trying to keep the tremble out of her voice. "Lord... Yer eyes. They be like milk."

Silas whimpered. Unable to hold his strength anymore, he turned away and wept harder than he ever had before.

Chapter VII
A Revelation in Ullswick

HOPE IS THE THING WITH FEATHERS –
THAT PERCHES IN THE SOUL –
AND SINGS THE TUNE WITHOUT THE WORDS –
AND NEVER STOPS AT ALL –

Emily Dickinson

Raphael's sleep came broken and short. He knew he should try to gain as much energy as he could, but the anxiety held him too tightly, like the talons of a monstrous bird of prey. He had walked every path in Fanchlow; knocked at every door, only to be met with unwelcome sneers. He had called Silas's name until his throat became hoarse. He had even taken a rushlight and checked the church. All to no avail. It was as though his brother had disappeared into thin air.

Raphael sat up and stared at the cot near the door. It looked so wrong, like a hole punched through the fabric of reality. It was difficult enough to see the empty space beside Araena, without *this*.

A horrid vision invaded his mind. Silas, lying next to their father, faces as pale as the moon…

"Stop it," Raphael said to himself. "You're doing the right thing. You'll find him…"

"Si!" Uriel cried in his sleep. "There's a leech! In my pillow…"

Raphael sprang across the room and tucked the blanket tighter around him.

"Ssh, ssh," he whispered. "Calm thee."

"Si…" Uriel mumbled. "Don't go near my fishing line…"

"It's alright," Raphael said, and softly began to hum under his breath. He stroked Uriel's forehead in time to the tune, and eventually, his brother became still.

Raphael, however, knew that more sleep would be impossible. So he dressed himself, pulled on his boots, and stepped outside. The roses on the bush glistened with morning dew. Raphael touched one of them, and a few of the petals came away in his hand. They were so pearlescent, as though they were made of moonlight.

He let them fall, and listened to birds striking up the dawn chorus. He heard a nyhtegale among them, putting all the blackbirds and robins to shame. No other bird sang like that: so intricate and ethereal, like light made music.

He stayed there, in silence, as the sun rose behind him. The Valley came alive with crowing cockerels and lowing cattle. Swallows burst out of the roof thatching and darted between the houses like arrows.

He heard movement within the house, and slipped back through the door. Everyone was awake, with Mekina bent over the cauldron, cooking another breakfast of pottage. Selena walked from cot to cot, tidying the blankets. Araena was sitting up in the corner and running a comb through her long hair.

Raphael raised a small smile. At least she was out of bed today. That was an improvement.

"Still no sign of him?" Mekina asked.

Raphael shook his head.

"Then thee shall go?"

"Aye."

"Alright. I'll make you a knapsack after breakfast."

Mekina shared out the pottage on the unleavened bread. There was less of it than the day before. Everyone ate slowly, to make it last, so they would feel less hungry later.

"I'll go to the forest," Selena volunteered. "The strawberries are ripe. I'll pick them before the birds find them first."

"And I'll dig for pignuts," Mekina said. "It won't be much, but it will do, for now."

She finished off her food, then gathered a small loaf and two apples into a square of fabric, added some flint pieces to make fire, then tied it at the top.

"I'm sorry it's not more," she said.

"It's enough," Raphael smiled. "I shall forage along the way. And... hopefully the people in the other villages will be hospitable."

"More than *here*, thou means?" Araena muttered. "Speak not your name, Raphael. How are we to know that's not what doomed Si?"

"Si is fine, Ma," Raphael insisted. "He's smart, and tough. Thou knows it will take more than fools to harm him."

"Unless the fools are many," his mother said darkly. "Thy hair is a mark enough. Please, God, be careful!"

Raphael swallowed the last of his pottage, walked across

the room and hugged her.

"I will," he promised. "Don't be afraid. I will return. Both of us will."

He kissed the top of her head, then went to each of his siblings in turn. Selena and Uriel looked up at him with huge, frightened eyes. Raphael flicked their noses playfully.

"Behave yourselves," he said. "I don't want to hear of any grief when I come home. And nor will Si."

"Thee won't," Selena said in a tiny voice. "Raph, I don't want you to go."

"And nor do I," Raphael replied. "But I must. So do what Mekina and Ma tell you."

He turned to Uriel. But his brother looked away, and squinted at the opposite wall.

"Raph," he said, "do we not have enough fish?"

Raphael glanced over his shoulder, at where the net hung. But it was missing.

He gasped. How had he not noticed that before?

"We do have enough," Mekina said, a frown in her voice. "Dost thou think that's what he's done? Gone to fish?"

Raphael's brow furrowed in thought. "But I went to the river. He wasn't there."

"Would he have gone to the corrie up yonder?"

"With the Cart-folk having made it their camp? Nay, don't be foolish. He knows better."

"Then where?" Araena asked. She suddenly held a hand to her mouth. "Oh… Surely he wouldn't have gone across…"

"He'd never do that," Raphael said. "Ullswick. That has a lake around it."

"But why would he go that far?" Araena cried. "It makes no sense!"

"Sense or no, it matters not," Raphael replied. "I shall leave now. Ullswick is a long walk."

He raised the best smile he could muster, then took the knapsack from Mekina and walked outside. She followed him, caught his hand, and shoved a cloak into it.

"Keep thyself warm," she said.

Raphael looked at her. She held her spine as straight as a pole, but he could still see the nervousness shining in her eyes. She was only fourteen, and already forced to grow up so quickly. When he opened his arms, she all but fell into them. She felt so small, as fragile as a bird.

"Thou art so good to us all, Mekina," Raphael said. "Stay strong, and don't be afraid. I will return."

He steeled himself, turned around, and walked away.

Every step felt a mile further than the one before it, and every breath tore at his chest as though he had swallowed thorns. He was leaving his family. Something he had never thought he would ever do…

"Thou can do this," he muttered. Hopefully, if he said it enough, he would start to believe it.

He walked down the hill, into the village; past the square and the chicken coop. The church loomed in the distance, and he threw a glance at it, drawing the cross over his chest. Then he turned onto the road. It opened before him like a book, rolling over the fields and around little drystone walls. Raphael hesitated for a moment, but hurried on before any of the neighbours could spot him, and soon, Fanchlow disappeared behind him.

He felt sick. He hadn't been this far from home since childhood. And the last time was with Julian.

"Father, be with me," he said to the sky. "Help me. Take me to Si."

A warm breeze blew at his back, and the branches swayed, throwing honeyed sunlight through their leaves. Long grass waved in the fields. With every breath, Raphael smelled pollen and wildflowers. The Valley's colours wrapped around him like a blanket: a patchwork of green and blue, melting into towering grey mountains on their sides. Perfect. Unchanging. Secure.

But a shadow still shaded Raphael's heart, like a cloud across the sun. If it was so perfect, he wouldn't be walking the entire length of it, weighted by grief, driven by worry. And there would be no need to conceal his identity.

That gave him a sudden pause. At the funeral, Silas had remained; Raphael had seen him speaking with Father Fortésa. And those children who taunted Uriel had mentioned the priest's name. Surely, he wasn't the one spreading malicious rumours about them? But if he was, and Silas had taken heed of them…

Raphael quickened his pace. As soon as he got to Ullswick and found his brother, they would return home, and he would have words with the old man. He would find out the truth behind the hatred, once and for all.

Raphael walked all day. He paused at a brook to drink, then filled his canteen and splashed water on his face. It was cool and crisp, having flowed straight down from the mountaintops. He ate mid-stride: a crust of the loaf and one apple, right down to the core. He had hardly anything to trade, save for a couple of iron rings around his belt. The Elitland knew no currency – everyone dealt in goods and equal worth. He just hoped it would be enough for lodgings, otherwise, he would have to tie himself into the branches of a tree.

The road itself was empty. Every now and then, he spotted people working in the fields, but they were too far, and too busy, to notice him. Lonely houses and water mills dotted the landscape, and he heard the ringing of a hammer from a blacksmith's forge.

Raphael kept his head down as he passed. Silas wouldn't have stopped at any of these places, and he would have been easy enough to spot.

Eventually, when the sun reached its noon point, Raphael arrived at the next village. Cederham was twice the size of Fanchlow, perched atop a terrace of land that jutted out above the Valley floor. The river flowed over the lip in a small waterfall, and its spray showered him as he approached.

The streets, however, were as abandoned as the road which led to them. Everyone was at work, mowing hay and digging up vegetables. But Raphael wasted no time. He knocked on the door of the first house, and was met by a ruddy-faced woman. She blinked in surprise when she saw him, looking him up and down as though he were a stray dog.

"I beg your pardon," Raphael said, "but hast thou seen a youth of fifteen years, red-haired, carrying a fishing net?"

The woman's brows lowered. "Nay. Not here."

She shut the door so swiftly, it almost smacked Raphael in the nose.

He went to the next house, and then the next. Each time, the occupants said the same thing, and it quickly dawned on him that Silas was nowhere in Cederham. His hunch had been correct. Ullswick was the only place his brother could be now.

He rejoined the road and walked on. A couple of people watched him warily from their windows. Raphael felt their eyes on his back like daggers, but he refused to turn around. It was rare, though not unknown, for a stranger to be wandering through. It was just his hair which had caught their attention. That was all.

The sun began to set, and blisters rose on his heels. Raphael leaned against a tree with a groan. There was no chance of reaching the last village before dark, and neither was there time to turn back to Cederham. He would have to bed down for the night.

He spotted an old goat shelter, practically disembowelled from harsh winters, but it was better than nothing. He crawled under the broken planks, curled into a ball in the corner, and covered himself with the cloak. He fell asleep quickly, but tossed and turned on the hard earth, and the stink of mould permeated his dreams.

The wind howled around him, distorted by the shelter into an eerie moan. It blew from the west, cold, straight off the mountains. Raphael thought he smelled dampness on it. And was that crying? It sounded far away, but so desolate, as though the sobs had been held in silence for an entire lifetime…

His eyes flew open. It wasn't dawn yet, but he could tell from the position of the stars that it wouldn't be long. So he ate another few mouthfuls of bread, then set on his way.

The sky turned pink, laced with violet clouds. Raphael drank from the river and washed himself as best he could. But even as he tried to focus, he noticed his hands were shaking. How could everything have gone so wrong?

He wanted to pray, but he didn't dare stop to do so. He needed to carry on. There was no choice.

The wind blew again. Raphael turned his head, and his eyes found the Wall. All the way, it had followed alongside him like a grey snake. Here, the Valley floor was wider, so the Wall had been built further back, but that didn't lessen his nerves. No matter how far he walked, he would not escape the demons. They were always there.

The mountains were larger this far south, holding in the Elitland like impenetrable walls. At the very end, marking due south, stood the most gigantic of them all. Raphael had seen it from the pastures above Fanchlow, but from there, it was only a blurred silhouette in the distance. Here, it reached so high, it hurt his neck to behold it. The summit was hidden under a blanket of snow which never melted, and from halfway up its giant flank, a waterfall roared over the rocks. The sun hit it at just the right angle, turning the torrent into a moving rainbow.

Raphael climbed up a steep hill, and relief consumed him. Finally, there was Ullswick: the largest of the three villages, nestled inside a lake which curled around it like a horseshoe. That sight alone lifted a weight from Raphael's shoulders. Of course Silas would be here. The lake was deep, full of trout and bass. He would probably appear as if from nowhere, and chastise his big brother for worrying so much.

Raphael's legs were aching from his journey, and his blisters had only grown larger. But he gritted his teeth, fought through the pain, and headed towards the village. Men looked up from working in the fields and shielded their eyes with their hands.

One approached, his cheeks burned bright red from the sun.

"Why have you come, stranger?" he asked.

Raphael offered a smile. "I seek my brother. Hast thou seen him? Fifteen, with a look of me, but shorter? He likely carries a fishing net."

The man shook his head. "I've not seen any such man."

Raphael's heart sank. "Not at all?"

"Nay. But this is a large enough place that I may have

missed him. Where do ye come from? Cederham?"

"Fanchlow."

The man's eyes widened, then he glanced at Raphael's hair. Nobody else was near, but he leant closer and spoke in a whisper.

"Thou be an Atégo?"

Raphael tried not to react.

"Don't deny it," the man hissed. "I know what your kind look like."

"My *kind?*" Raphael repeated incredulously. "I'm no different to thee."

"Wrong."

"How do you know of us?"

"Oh, because a hundred years ago, this was where thy line began," the man said coldly. "Some of them are still here. Cursed folk! So either take thyself away, or to thy kin. But get thee gone from my land. I'll have no demon-touched feet walking hither."

Raphael's mouth fell open. "I am not cursed!"

"Get thee gone!" the man snapped again, and shoved him backwards. Raphael snatched a low-hanging branch before he could fall. Then the man wrinkled his nose, as though smelling something rotten, and hurried back into the field.

Raphael stared after him. How could everyone in the Elitland be so inhospitable, simply over a *name?* Had the horrible rumours spread this far south *already?*

But he pushed that worry aside. He had kin here? There were other Atégos, hidden away at the very bottom of the Valley? All his life, he had believed his family to be the only ones. And if they were as ostracised as Raphael, surely they would help him.

He crossed the little bridge of land which led into Ullswick. Everywhere, he saw people fishing in the lake, but Silas wasn't among them. They all watched Raphael with suspicious eyes, whispering to each other and pointing at his hair. He heard his surname, the syllables overlapping each other like waves. Never had he felt so sickened by it.

The warren of streets made his head swim. The houses were stacked tightly together, each leaning upon their neighbour like a game of dominoes. Clothes lines hung between the windows, all full, to take advantage of the hot summer day. Doors had been swung open so the rooms within could be aired, and Raphael knocked on each one he came across, but he received the same cold response as he had in Cederham.

And with each one, his hope dimmed. The places where he might find Silas were shrinking by the minute. How could he have come here, and not be seen by anybody?

Blood began to seep through Raphael's shoes. Still, he staggered to another house, set further back from the others. An old corn dolly, made from last year's husks, hung above the lintel as a good luck charm.

"Hello?" he called, his voice dry and cracked. "Please… Might I trouble thee?"

The door opened a crack. A woman peered out, her eyes shining in the darkness like embers.

"Who are you?" she demanded.

"My name is Raphael," he replied. "I've come seeking my brother. And… a drink, if thou would be so kind. I have travelled far."

The woman stared at him, as though he were a strange insect. Then she swung the door wide, and the light fell upon her. She was a few years older than Raphael, in her early twenties, but permanent lines were etched into her forehead and bags hung heavy under her eyes. A linen cap covered her head, similar to

102

what Mekina wore when she was in the fields. But beneath it, Raphael noticed a few strands of hair, just as red as his own.

Realisation settled over the two of them at the same time. The woman tossed her head, beckoning Raphael inside, and he hurried over the threshold.

The house was similar in layout to what he knew, but there were only two cots, on either side of the fireplace. A third stood propped against the wall, being used as a makeshift hanger for clothes. Dried herbs hung from the rafters, filling the air with their fragrance.

An older man sat near the hearth, whittling a piece of wood. He coughed, and his lungs rattled as though they were filled with water. Raphael froze. Julian had sounded like that, when the illness had him. This man didn't look as sickly, but how much longer would his health last?

"What's this?" he asked in alarm.

"Tell him who you are," the woman said to Raphael. "Tell us both. And I have guessed, but thy surname as well."

"Raphael Atégo."

The man's mouth fell open. He stood up slowly, as though he were beholding a spooked horse, and approached with his hands raised. As he came closer, Raphael noticed his hair: it was receding, but it too was red.

"I never thought thy like would return here," he said, voice trembling. "My boy... Oh, God, yes I see it!"

"I heard the villagers mention another branch of the Atégo family," Raphael said. "That is thine?"

"Aye," the man beamed. "I am Abraham Atégo; this is my daughter, Nalina. Oh, come hither and sit! You look exhausted. Wouldst thou care for meodu?"

Raphael nodded as Abraham pushed him down into the

chair. Nalina sprang to a keg and held a leather tankard beneath it. When she passed it to Raphael, he drank deeply, not even bothering to taste the sweet honey within. He was too thirsty, too exhausted.

"I'm seeking my brother," he gasped. "He disappeared a few days past. Did he come here?"

Nalina studied Raphael's features. "Nay, I've seen him not. And we would have known."

"He's a quiet one. Not the kind to make a fuss," Raphael insisted. "He took a net with him, so I believe he went to fish."

"And not at yonder river?" Abraham suggested. "Would that not be closer to thee?"

"For certain. But I've searched there already. This place is my last hope," said Raphael. He drained the last mouthful of meodu and leaned forward in the chair. "I can't believe I'm before thee! Why didst thee not come to us? Or to the fayre? Surely, we would have seen each other; known each other before now!"

Abraham heaved a sigh, which ended in a feeble cough.

"As ye can surely hear, I am ill," he said. "And Nalina is all I have. She cares for me. Travel is impossible."

"Did you know we were in Fanchlow?" asked Raphael.

"Of course," Nalina said as she refilled his tankard. "But going there has never been easy. We have so little; nay, not even a donkey. None of our neighbours will help us. They think us unlucky."

Raphael grimaced. "They saith the same of us."

"It's been that way for so long, I can't imagine it otherwise," Abraham muttered sadly. "Our name is cursed."

Raphael shook his head. "I refuse to believe that. We are unlucky. That's all."

Abraham scoffed. "*Unlucky* is an understatement. Doth

thou truly think they hate us simply for our hair? Nay. Tell me this, my boy: hath any of thy family suffered as I do, with this infernal cough, drowning in the air? Any *men?*"

Raphael nodded. "Aye. My father. Not long ago."

"I thought as much," Abraham sighed. Nalina laid a hand on his shoulder and he clutched it like a lifeline.

"None of our men are safe," she said. "Not even as far away as thee, it seems. It's been so for generations. *That's* why they hate us so much, you see. They know."

"Know what?" Raphael asked. "Pray, tell me."

Nalina and Abraham exchanged a dark glance.

"He's as innocent as a lamb," Nalina whispered. "Perhaps it would do him better to–"

"Nay," said Abraham. "Better he learns from friendly lips."

Raphael watched them carefully. Nalina drew up a second chair and helped her father sit. Then she perched on the rim of the fireplace, her back to the flames, and clasped her hands together to stop them shaking. A shadow fell upon the room, like a dark stain where a carcass once lay.

"Our family has endured the same thing for so long," Abraham said. "And all because of one man. Adrian Atégo. He lived about a hundred years ago, with his wife and their son. He was the one who began the building of the Wall. Because he had dealings with the creatures on the other side."

Raphael almost dropped his tankard. Nothing could have prepared him for that.

"What… kind of dealings?" he asked in a tiny voice.

"He never spoke of it," replied Abraham. "But it was enough for him to know how dangerous the demons are. And they cursed him for it. They marked his palm with a terrible burn that never healed. With every sunrise, he would become blind and wretched, only to have it restored under the night. It drove him insane. But before he could end his own life, he was struck down with an illness. *This* illness. And it killed his son, and every son there has ever been since."

Abraham reached out and grasped Raphael's hands.

"Do you understand?" he wheezed. "*They* murdered him. They will murder all of us, until we are nothing but a memory to this land. I told thee, my boy. We are cursed. Dost thou believe it now?"

Chapter VIII
Unlikely Saviours

I SHALL BE TELLING THIS WITH A SIGH
SOMEWHERE AGES AND AGES HENCE:
TWO ROADS DIVERGED IN A WOOD, AND I,
I TOOK THE ONE LESS TRAVELLED BY,
AND THAT HAS MADE ALL THE DIFFERENCE.

Robert Frost

Silas barely moved for the whole day. He sat, stiff as a board, against one of the tent's thin vertical beams, with his eyes wide open. True to her word, Irima stayed with him, working on her embroidery, but close enough for Silas to hear her.

The two of them hardly spoke, but each could feel the other's wariness and fear like waves of sickly heat. Silas knew she had guessed why he was trying not to even blink if he could help it. His sight had returned once. If it did again, he refused to miss the moment.

The day was one of the longest he'd ever lived. He hated the feeling of there being no difference whether his eyes were open or not. The world was a black hole into which he fell and swam and wallowed. Its choking embrace surrounded him; limitless boundaries stretched on forever. He had never felt so helpless, and he knew he looked it.

He heard liquid being poured into a cup, and Irima pressed it against his palm. He sipped it slowly, to make it last.

"It's nearly sunset," Irima said quietly.

Silas nodded. He could feel it. The temperature was dropping.

"Are yer hungry?" she asked. She tried to hide the tremble in her voice, but Silas still noticed it. Without his sight, he was hearing so much more.

"Nay," he muttered. "Please don't be afraid of me."

"I'm not. Not o' *thee*," she replied. "But *this*…"

"I know. I don't understand it, either."

Irima swallowed. "Do yer… think it will always be so? Every day?"

Silas couldn't bear to reply. Was this truly better than being constantly blind? It would be a constant reminder of his transgression: the sin burned upon his soul. To chance a demon; to rip it out of the water and lay eyes upon it… Did he deserve it, after all?

He listened to the sounds outside the tent: chopping wood, scattered conversation, crackling fires. The horses pawed the ground and children ran about. Somewhere, a group began playing music. He heard a fiddle, drum, shawm…

"They be a'practisin'," Irima said lightly. "We like a party every now an' then. No better time for it than Midsummer."

"Thou celebrates it?" Silas asked in surprise.

"Doesn't everyone?"

"In the Valley, yes."

"Well, this 'ere Valley ain't the whole world," Irima said pointedly.

Silas went to retort, but he let it go. He didn't have the drive to be defensive anymore.

"Your people are... not what I expected," he admitted.

Irima gave a small chuckle. "Is that a good thing?"

"I think so."

"So yer no longer think we'll do ye harm?"

Silas turned his head towards her. "Nay."

"Well, that's an improvement," said Irima. "Now, drink the rest o' that ale. Yer'll pass out, otherwise. An' I've got enough to do without throwin' water over ye."

She tried to sound jovial, but Silas knew she was still fretting. He could hear it in the way she moved: more fitful than before. When she inhaled, it wasn't enough to fill her lungs. She was watching him, waiting, like a hare ready to spring.

A pinprick of light suddenly appeared. Silas gasped and sat bolt upright.

"Is it a'comin' back again?" Irima asked quietly.

Silas didn't dare tempt fate by answering. He just focused on the dot of light. Slowly, it grew, bleaching away the blackness into an overwhelming white. Then it settled, into beiges, browns, greens. He saw tarpaulin and wooden beams; the patterned blanket over his legs. And at his side, there was Irima, with the pearls shining in her hair.

She stared, but to his relief, she didn't run. Instead, she raised her hand.

"How many fingers am I holdin' up?"

"Three," Silas replied without hesitation.

Her mouth fell open. "Lord above... 'Tis a miracle!"

"I wouldn't say that," Silas muttered. He stared at the mats on the floor, saw how tightly and beautifully they had been woven. He never would have paid notice to that a few days ago.

Under the glove, his left palm tingled, as though he had slapped it.

Irima touched his shoulder. "Yer scared. Aren't ye?"

"Scared?" Silas repeated. "I'm terrified."

"What did this to thee?"

"I cannot say."

"Do yer think it will frighten me more than what I've seen since yer came?"

"Aye. Thou wouldst turn from me and never look back. It's what everyone would do, if they could."

Irima frowned. "Do yer mean yer neighbours?"

Silas nodded. "They despise us. I always thought it was because of our hair. This colour... it's not normal in the Valley. Hell-kissed, I've heard it called. But now... I know it to be more than that."

Irima shuffled closer to him.

"Is it somethin' to do with the Wall?"

Silas bit his tongue so he wouldn't react.

"Look," Irima said, "I know yer hidin' somethin'. Yer can trust me."

Silas shook his head. "Like thee, I trust none but my family."

Irima kept hold of him. "I know yer people think there are demons in this place. An' I've never known any blind man regain his sight, before I met ye. Only *here*." She leant closer. "Did yer cross the Wall?"

"Nay," Silas hissed. "Nobody crosses the Wall."

"Except ye?" Irima said, more a statement than a question. "Look, I'm not from around 'ere. Yer knows, as well as I do, that yer Valley ways ain't my ways. Will I truly judge ye worse than them?"

"I don't know, and I won't risk it," Silas said. "For that very reason, you wouldn't understand."

"I, who have been judged me whole life long?" Irima pointed out. "Ai, forget it. 'Tis like tryin' to get blood from a stone."

Silas shot her a ferocious glare. It had the effect he wanted: she backed off at once.

"This is my burden," he snapped. "It is mine alone to bear. And I will bear it even when I am gone from here. So leave it be, and it can never taint thee."

Irima fell silent. Silas worried he had hurt her, but then he pushed it aside. He had spoken harsher to Selena, and she was five years younger than Irima. If a child could take it, then a woman was more than capable.

But he sensed Irima wasn't cowed, like his sister. It would take more than his austerity to shake her. Even if a monster were to rear its head, she might be afraid, but all the same, Silas imagined she could still take up a knife and fight. It wasn't the way of a Valley-girl, but he still respected it.

Footsteps sounded outside, and the tent flap opened. Irima quickly lit the lamp, and in the soft light, Silas recognised the imposing silhouette of her uncle.

"I thought I'd come an' check on things," he said, staring straight at Silas. "Yer still have yer sight?"

"Aye," Irima said, before Silas could speak. "He's recoverin' well. I actually think he be clean enough to wander about the camp now. If it please ye, Uncle."

Garrett grunted. His face was as unreadable as a stone. His eyes fleeted over Silas, and paused when he saw the glove.

"Helped yerself to that, have ye?"

"I made a gift o' it. The burn needs protectin'," Irima explained.

"An' I see thou hast stitched up his clothes."

"I had to keep busy somehow."

Garrett nodded slowly to himself. "There's been no more happenin's? Nothin' I should be concerned about?"

"Not at all," Irima said.

Silas glanced at her. She was covering for him?

"In that case, yer can feel free to wander, lad," said Garrett. "I dare say folks will do well to see yer mean no harm. But I still advise ye against leavin' just yet. Yer still be recoverin'. Let Irima care for yer a little while longer, an' then I'll take yer back to Fanchlow meself. Alrigh'?"

Despite himself, Silas managed a small smile. "Thank you, sir."

"'Tis fine," said Garrett. "Now, that tunic be dry an' stitched well enough, but it still needs a good washin'. Get out o' it. I'll fetch thee a spare one for now."

He left without another word. As soon as he was out of earshot, Silas turned to Irima.

"Why did you do that?" he asked. "Thou lied to him. About my sight."

"Ai, I but omitted a truth," Irima said flippantly. "It's nowt we should worry over, until it proves itself so. And am I not to prove ye can trust me? How else than givin' yer free reign enough to get comfortable?"

Silas pursed his lips. "Thank you."

"Yer welcome," Irima replied, a shine in her eyes. "When me uncle returns, get changed, then I'll take yer hither. Yer can meet some o' the others. They'll see that ye be no demon. An' ye shall see that nor are we."

The night brought coolness to the air and a faint breeze whistling down the Valley, but Raphael was too hot to sleep. Nalina had spread out the spare cot for him, and if he closed his eyes, he could almost have imagined himself back at home, with his siblings slumbering around him like kittens. But then he would look around, and see a strange roof at strange angles; feel a blanket which smelled like someone else. And that would bring the sobering reality that he was not home, and Silas was still missing.

His mind raced. Even the whistling nyhtegales and hooting owls weren't enough to calm it. He thought of Father Fortésa, standing in the graveyard, speaking with Silas whilst Raphael had led everyone else away. Should he have stayed? What might he have overheard which could have pointed him in the right direction?

Never had he felt so despondent. He had searched every place he could think of. There was nowhere else his brother could possibly be.

And what of Adrian Atégo? Raphael tried to picture him: perhaps his age or a little older, slowly losing his mind and his sight, year by year. Yet despite that, he had built the Wall. How long must it have taken? The regular drystone ones were a feat in themselves, and they weren't even half the height. And as for the length, mile upon mile…

He must have been terrified. What man would dedicate his entire life to cutting off half the Valley, if there wasn't true evil on the other side? Something evil enough to curse all the men descended from him? Something he knew well enough to have *dealings* with?

Raphael shuddered. He could hear Abraham's breath rattling even as he slept. It was so similar to what the Atégos had heard before Julian's death. And now Raphael himself was the eldest man. Would he be next? Abraham and Julian were in their forties… Did that mean *he* might have another twenty years of life? Or would it be a life lived in fear? Could anyone risk changing their fate, when it had been laid down by creatures of darkness?

Suddenly, a horrid chill descended over Raphael. Silas was too smart and sensible to just disappear. But what if he had also figured all this out? What if he had tried to take matters into his own hands? What if he had brought the net not to catch fish, but for something else?

Raphael looked out of the window. The shutters were closed, but he could see between the planks, and there, in the distance, was the black line of the Wall.

"Oh, nay," he muttered. "You wouldn't. You fool; you *wouldn't* have…"

But the words sounded thin and hollow. Deep down, he knew it. Silas was nowhere to be found, because he had done the unthinkable.

Terror paralysed Raphael to his bones. He had journeyed this far – to the other end of the Valley – but did he dare go further? What if he vanished, too?

Determination cut through his fear. There was no choice. Silas had to come home.

As quietly as he could, Raphael pulled on his boots. Then he slipped the iron rings off his belt and left them by the hearth, where Nalina could easily find them. Those should be enough to show his appreciation and pay for his lodgings.

He gazed at his slumbering kin. Would he ever see them again? He hoped so. If he managed to find Silas, and together they discovered the cause of the illness, perhaps Abraham might even survive.

That thought was the final steel his heart needed. Raphael fetched his cloak, pulled the hood over his hair, and sneaked outside. He stole through the empty streets like a shadow, past the lake and the village lanterns, over the road and the river. The Wall stood before him: a huge smear against the night sky. Just looking at it made him feel sick.

He spoke the Lord's Prayer under his breath, held Silas in his mind, and began to climb.

Merrin walked across the Lake. With each step, she dragged her toes, pushing them as deep as she could manage. But it was as impenetrable as ever; the water didn't even cover her by an inch. Fish swirled underneath her, coming close, curiosity getting the better of them. She knelt down and swept her hand over the surface, and they scattered like snowflakes.

She couldn't bear to go back to the cave. There was another, a little larger, further south. That would suit her better than the cramped one, which still held the echo of that horrible memory. So she wandered for miles, following the Lake, listening to its whispering waves and the rattle of reeds in the shallows. A pair of swans flew by. Merrin watched them in silence, then turned her head away.

She laid down on the water. The back of her dress soaked through. She closed her eyes, relishing it, pretending that she was once again where it was weightless and soft. Nothing could hurt.

Nothing could ensnare. There was just her, and her home, and her people.

What must they be saying about her? They were so close and yet so far. As promised, Dylana had come during the hours of darkness, with supplies of trout and watercress, and spoken to her. But Merrin remained quiet. She knew what her mother was trying to do: guilt her into admitting she had done wrong.

What was wrong with protecting oneself? Or dealing justice? The punishment must fit the crime, and time after time, that family had almost destroyed her. What would have happened if they succeeded? The end of the Royal Line; the end of everything the Asræ knew.

She refused to let that happen.

She stared up at the moon. It had dropped low in the sky; there wouldn't be long until dawn. And then, in another few days, it would be full. The full moon closest to Midsummer. Then she could finally go home, and be Queen.

She still didn't feel ready – the very thought sent a cold dart of anxiety through her chest. But her father hadn't felt ready, either. He took up the mantle when he was about her age, and he had been alone until Dylana stood at his side.

Merrin sighed. She had her mother, too; and Penro. But they were all she needed.

The water waved beside her. She turned her head, and spotted Penro swimming closer. His soaking hair clung to his cheeks. Merrin couldn't help staring. For over a century, she had only ever seen her people under the surface, where hair and clothes floated like living things. But up here, it looked limp and dead. Just like everything.

"Your Majesty," Penro said.

"Call me by my name," Merrin sighed. "I'm too tired for

titles right now."

Penro nodded sympathetically, then gestured to the surroundings.

"I couldn't find thee yonder. So I followed. Are you alright?"

"I'm fine," Merrin said flatly. "I just needed to get away from that place."

"Be sure to take shelter soon," Penro warned, shooting a glance at the sky. "There is another cave, over there, on the east bank."

"I know. I remember where it is. 'Tis why I stopped, so I can reach it swiftly. But I want to stay out here for as long as I can. I… *need* to stay here."

Merrin hated the wretchedness in her voice. She sounded like the frightened little girl she had pushed down inside.

Penro moved his hand through the surface and laid it over hers. Merrin drew a deep breath, trying to keep tears at bay.

"Thou shalt come home," he assured gently. "You are so strong. I've always admired that about you."

Merrin didn't look at him. "You don't admire me for everything, though. Do you?"

"We all make mistakes."

"It *wasn't* a mistake. And I don't want to talk about it. I've heard enough of it from my mother. Where is she?"

"Making preparations for the coronation," said Penro. "I've brought thy food for tonight. I'm only sorry I didn't come sooner. I did not realise you had moved."

He passed her a woven bag. Merrin quickly slipped its strap over her shoulder so it wouldn't sink, and it hung below her, submerged in the water.

"I've upset her," Merrin said softly.

"She'll not hold that against thee," Penro insisted. "Do not begrudge your circumstances. You are here. You are grieving."

"So is she," Merrin pointed out. "She hath lost her husband, as much as I lost my father. *Everyone* down below grieves for him. That's no excuse for me to be…"

Weak. She couldn't bring herself to say it.

"Aye. That's no excuse," Penro said, firmer now. "But I see it not as an excuse. I see it as honesty. And you must be honest with yourself, as much as any other."

Merrin pursed her lips. "I have been so. No good ever cometh of it."

"Am *I* not honest with thee?" Penro asked. "Has that not always been my purpose? To advise? Let me do that now, Merrin. We are all working as hard as we can, to ensure all is made easy for your return. And I know thou feels alone up here, but it is not so. *I* am here. So is thy mother. We would be with you all the night long, if only there was not so much to be done."

"I understand that," Merrin said. "I just want to be down there with you. I hate it here. Penro, I hate it so much!"

She sat up, teeth bared, and slammed her fist into the water. It held like stone. But even though she knew that would happen, it snapped something within her. She pulled her knees to her chest and began to weep.

Penro pushed himself through the surface, knelt at her side, and put an arm around her shoulders. Merrin's fin flickered. She wanted to curl into him like a child, but refused to let herself. That was *too* close.

Penro felt her stiffness. He sighed, then tapped her wrist.

"Thou had best find shelter. Dawn is near," he said. "I'll accompany you."

"Nay, I can manage," Merrin muttered. "I… don't want

thee to see me like this."

"Oh, Merrin, thy tears don't frighten me."

"All the same, I don't wish for them. And nor do I wish you to take the risk of leaving the Lake. But come to me again tonight. Please."

Penro smiled. "I shall."

He laid his hand on her head, bowed, and slipped back under the surface. Merrin watched him through the rippling water. He floated underneath her for a moment, looking up, then dived until he was lost from sight.

Merrin dragged herself to her feet. She felt as though her legs had turned to iron. And yet it still wasn't heavy enough to break through and take her home.

The sky and the Lake both transformed periwinkle blue. She hurried to the bank, earth clinging to her feet with every step. She grimaced at the sensation. She felt filthy up here.

The undergrowth was thick and wild; undisturbed for decades, brambles and thistles rose to hip-height. Merrin held her skirt tightly to keep it from catching on the thorns. Spiderwebs streaked across her face and she raised her arms to swat them away.

One of the Royal Bands snagged on a branch. Merrin tried to pull free, but it pierced straight through the weave. Desperate, she leapt up, in a bid to unhook it. She tugged as hard as she could, hoping the Band might even snap. But the angle of the branch was all wrong; pointing upwards, holding her in place.

Panic tightened around her throat like a noose. The tree canopy overhead wouldn't be enough to shield her. And the forest was growing lighter by the moment. If the sun reached her, she would die. It would melt her into a pool of water; there wouldn't even be anything left to place in the Tomb Garden…

"Penro!" Merrin shouted. "Penro! Help me! *Please!*"

She screamed so loud, her throat burned. But she knew nobody would come. They wouldn't be able to hear her, deep under the Lake. And even if they did, to surface now would also spell death for them...

Then, incredibly, she heard footsteps; the rustle of movement through leaves. It was behind her. She tried to twist her head, but the tree blocked her view.

"Who is't?" she cried. "Help me! There's a cave yonder where we can shelter!"

The leaves rustled again.

"Wh–what are you?"

Merrin froze. That was no voice she recognised. And the way it spoke... *Another* human? Two, in the space of three days?

She gritted her teeth. "Thou is not welcome here!"

"Are you a demon?" the voice asked shakily.

"I shall be, if you come closer!" Merrin hissed.

"But... you were calling for help."

"Not *your* help!"

The human came closer, and finally Merrin saw him: a little taller than her, muscular, wearing an old brown cloak and hood.

She struggled like a fish on a hook. She whirled about, going to raise a leg and kick him. But he was quicker than her, and warm fingers closed around her wrist. Then, he lifted her, as easily as if she were a bird, and unhooked the Band.

Merrin whirled away, her face ablaze, and drove her foot into his stomach as hard as she could. He stumbled to his knees, wheezing.

"Get away!" she barked. "How dare you come here!"

The human held up his hands. Merrin shook with anger.

She should reach out, snatch them, teach him a lesson he would never forget…

"I mean thee no harm!" he cried, staring at her. "I… What are you?"

"Well, take heed that I mean *thee* harm!" Merrin shouted. "Get out, or on your head be it! *Now!*"

A ray of sunlight pierced the leaves, and struck Merrin's arm. She gasped with pain, and spun away, but the damage was already done. It felt like the touch of a thousand nettle stings.

"Nay!" she cried. She spun around, but all she saw were walls of trees.

"It harms thee?" the human realised. "You must get to the cave I passed?"

"Where is it?" Merrin demanded.

The human locked eyes with her. "Revoke thy threat and I will take you."

Merrin bared her teeth. "Insolent boy!"

"I have saved thee once already," he retorted. "What say you?"

Merrin threw a glance skyward. There was no time. No choice.

"Agreed," she snapped. "Just make haste!"

The human stood with a groan, one hand nursing his stomach, then beckoned for her to follow him. He took huge strides, flattening the thorns with his boots to clear a path. Even that way of moving stoked Merrin's ire. So clumsy; so full of weight. Not of the Lake. Nothing like her. And everything like him.

Eventually, she spotted the mouth of the cave. It was more worn than she remembered, but that didn't matter. It was in darkness, deeper and larger than the one on the north bank. It would protect her.

She shoved the human to the ground and leapt past him. She retreated as far back as she could, until the sunlight could no longer reach her, and checked her arm. The skin seared with pain, and when she touched it, she felt blood.

"You're hurt," the human said.

Merrin didn't look at him. "I spared thy life. So, flee with it."

"Nay. I have questions."

"You impertinent…"

Merrin raised her head, and her snarl died on her tongue. He was still lying where she had flung him, and his hood had fallen back, revealing thick red hair. And now the sunlight fell upon him, she almost crashed to her knees in horror. Brown eyes, strong features; eighteen or thereabouts. He looked so similar to…

"What's wrong?" he asked.

Merrin gritted her teeth. "Get out."

"Please, mercy!" the boy cried. "I did not come here with evil intentions, I swear to God! I come in search of my brother. All I wish is to find him, and then I'll never turn in the direction of this place again!"

"You know to never come here," Merrin growled. "*Thee* should know it best of all, Atégo. And so should thy brother."

His eyes widened. "You know who I am?"

"Everyone here would recognise the likes of you."

"And my brother? Thou hast seen him?"

"Oh, I have seen him," Merrin snapped bitterly.

The human stepped closer. Merrin remained exactly where she was, staring him down like a hunter. This was too horrible… A hundred years had changed some things, but this boy's face was so similar to the one which she had caressed and kissed…

"Where is he?"

"Why should I tell you anything?" Merrin snarled. "You are the trespasser here."

The boy's brows lowered. "What have you done to him, demon?"

Merrin scoffed. "*Demon*. Of course that's what your kin have taken to calling mine. Apt, if not incorrect."

"Then what are you?"

"We are Asræ. The People of the Lake."

"There are more of you?" the boy asked.

"More than you can count," Merrin said proudly.

He glanced over his shoulder, towards the Lake. "But none who can come out in the sunlight? None who can help you?"

Merrin's eyes narrowed. He was smart. And that unnerved her even more. Smart ones were dangerous. They knew how to get what they wanted.

"Where is my brother?" the boy asked again, firmer now.

"Do you think you frighten me?" Merrin replied. "I am not some little girl you can command. I could kill you right now. I *should*."

"If thou could step into the sun to reach me," the boy pointed out.

Merrin stormed to the mouth of the cave, as close as she dared. He leapt back in alarm. The reaction – finally one of fear – satisfied her enough.

"Why are you here, if it harms you so?" he asked, a little softer. "Should you not be under the water?"

"Aye," Merrin snapped, venom in her voice. "Now, hark: your brother is not here. No other humans are. So just take your leave, stay on the other side of your Wall, and trouble me no further! Think thyself lucky I cannot reach thee!"

The boy's eyes fleeted over her. Merrin fought the urge to squirm. He would never have seen such a being as her before, with her green hair and violet eyes. Of course she must look like a monster, straight out of the tales from his forefather. She hoped they were all filled with terror. *Fear her. Never cross her. She will destroy you…*

"One question, I ask of thee," the boy said. "Is my brother alive?"

Merrin nodded. "Very much so."

"You saw him? You speak truth?"

"I detest lies. I speak nothing but the truth."

He nodded. "Then your reassurance is enough. I know he's strong. If he could survive here, he could survive anything."

Merrin cocked an eyebrow. *Survive?* Twice, the sun had foiled her with this family. If his brother had dragged her through the surface just a little earlier, she would have had ample time to drown him. And she would have relished it.

"You're still here," she noted coldly. "I answered your one question. Now, go away."

But to her horror, the boy shook his head.

"Nay. If he's crossed back into the east, I believe thee. But while I'm here, there are some things I must know. And while I remain, I'll not let ye come to harm."

He pulled off his cloak and tossed it towards Merrin. She recoiled in disgust.

"The sun may still reach thee. Use it to shield thyself," he said. "Do I have your permission to forage on your land?"

Merrin refused to satisfy him with an answer. She turned her back and retreated into the shadows of the cave, her fin quivering with rage. As soon as night fell, or he came within arm's reach, she would take that filthy cloak and strangle him with it.

Chapter IX
Conflict Within

IT IS THE HOUR WHEN FROM THE BOUGHS
THE NIGHTINGALE'S HIGH NOTE IS HEARD:
IT IS THE HOUR - WHEN LOVER'S VOWS
SEEM SWEET IN EVERY WHISPER'D WORD;
AND GENTLE WINDS AND WATERS NEAR,
MAKE MUSIC TO THE LONELY EAR.
EACH FLOWER THE DEWS HAVE LIGHTLY WET,
AND IN THE SKY THE STARS ARE MET,
AND ON THE WAVE IS DEEPER BLUE,
AND ON THE LEAD A BROWNER HUE,
AND IN THE HEAVEN THAT CLEAR OBSCURE
SO SOFTLY DARK, AND DARKLY PURE,
THAT FOLLOWS THE DECLINE OF DAY
AS TWILIGHT MELTS BENEATH THE MOON AWAY.

Lord Byron

Raphael's heart pounded in his ears as he walked through the forest. Every tree and bush felt like it was watching him. Even the birds had fallen silent. They knew he wasn't supposed to be there. The demon girl had made that clear enough.

No, not a demon. She had called herself an Asræ. Raphael focused on the word, rolling it around his mind. It certainly sounded less terrifying than the one he had always known. But did it make her any less dangerous? She spoke like him; had arms and legs and features just like him. Was she more human than monster? Or had she been, long ago?

He picked some strawberries, the Lake shining next to him like a mirror. It cast a coolness onto the summer air, and Raphael stopped near its edge to fill his canteen. The water was as clear and crisp as a mountain stream, and he pulled off his boots to splash some on his blisters.

He tried to imagine a whole society of people living under the surface. It was certainly huge enough to accommodate them. Even from where he stood, Raphael couldn't see either end, and he could only guess as to how deep it was. All three of the villages could have probably fitted inside the Lake basin, with room to spare.

He headed towards the cave. With every step, he spotted amarants, spreading over the ground like a carpet. He had never seen so many of them. The little red flowers danced in the breeze, as though they were all bowing in the direction of the Asræ girl.

Everything in this place felt alive. Even the shadows looked darker and deeper than what Raphael would have expected for such a bright day. It seemed to him that the entire forest was watching over her, unwilling to let her come to harm.

She was still huddled against the stone wall at the back, her body turned to the side, so no sunlight could touch her. She fixed her steely eyes on him. Raphael fought the urge to flinch. He felt like she could break his bones just by glaring at him for long enough.

"Use the cloak," he insisted. "I've no need for it at the moment."

"Nor do I," she said pointedly.

"Thou shalt burn."

"I don't need *you* to tell me how to care for myself, boy."

Raphael held up his hands to placate her. "I meant no offence."

"Your *presence* offends me," she snapped. "I want thee gone."

"I will go. But not yet," said Raphael.

He sat down in the cave mouth: within sight of her, but a safe distance away. He couldn't stop staring. Now his initial shock was gone, he couldn't deny how beautiful she was. It was a fierce kind of beauty, like rain: soft and gentle at first sight, only to thrash everything in its path and deafen all ears with its thunder. And those eyes… Such ice; such hatred and wrath…

"Quit your gawking!" the Asræ barked.

Raphael swiftly looked away. He split the strawberries into two portions, and rolled half them across the floor to her. She glanced at them as though he had thrown mud. Then she opened the bag over her shoulder, removed a whole trout, and took a bite straight out of its side.

Raphael pressed his lips together so his jaw wouldn't drop. Juices flowed down the Asræ's chin. She watched him as she chewed, waiting for him to recoil. But he didn't. He refused to let her unnerve him any more than she already had.

"You're not what I expected," he said.

She bit the trout again. "I can be everything you would

expect."

"And you don't frighten me."

"Liar. I'm not fool enough to believe empty words like that."

Raphael swallowed. She was right. He was afraid. But he wasn't going to let it stand in the way of finding answers.

"Then do you believe me," he said, "when I tell thee I wish to help you?"

The Asræ scoffed, and busied herself with finishing her meal.

"I only want to ensure you survive this day," Raphael continued. "I would hate to have helped you, get information, and then leave. Tonight, thou can return to thy home, correct?"

Still, she didn't look at him.

"I must abide you until nightfall?" she muttered.

"I know my company is unwelcome," Raphael said carefully, "but I hope it's not impolite."

"Why canst thou not just run after thy brother and leave me be?" the Asræ snapped. But Raphael heard an edge of wretchedness in her voice.

"I *will* go after him. But he's likely made for home already, after coming here. 'Twas no wonder I couldn't find him. Why did he cross the Wall?"

"I know not."

"But thou saw him?"

"He is the reason I am up here!"

The Asræ thrust the half-eaten trout back into her bag, so forcefully, scales flew in all directions.

"What does that mean?" Raphael asked.

"He netted me and pulled me out of the Lake," she snarled.

Raphael's heart leapt. "What? He came hither for *you?*"

"I don't know why!"

"Did he wish to speak with thee? You see... our father died only a few days past. He drowned in the air. And I've been told that he is not the first man to suffer as such. I think Silas knew that. I think that is why he sought thee out."

"To do what?" the Asræ snapped. "That was a long time ago."

"So it's true?" Raphael pressed. "There is a curse?"

"What does thou want me to say? What good would it do? I have told you all I know! Please, just stop talking!"

She shuffled further back, and twisted away from him as much as she was able, tucking up her legs so they wouldn't fall into the sunlight. Raphael noticed the long spiny fin extending down her spine, shivering with anger.

"Perhaps things will be better if I introduce myself," he said.

"I know who you are."

"Nay, you know my family name. As many do, it seems. But my first name is Raphael."

The Asræ didn't move.

"Dost thou have a name?" Raphael asked.

"Of course I have a name," she replied. She paused for a moment, then glanced over her shoulder, snatched the cloak, and wrapped herself in it.

"Fine," she said stiffly. "If I've no choice but to abide you, then the least I can do is make my life easier with co-operation. My name is Merrin. Queen of the Lake."

Silas walked away from the tent. He placed each foot carefully; one hand held before him, and the other clutching a stick to touch the ground. Irima lingered behind him with a watchful eye, but Silas tried to ignore her. He wanted to find his way without her aid. If he managed that, perhaps he could convince himself that he was not helpless.

He stumbled over a mound and crashed to his knees. Irima ran over to help him, but he waved her off.

"Are yer hurt?" she asked.

Silas shook his head. He got back up, brushed dirt off his hose, and carried on. The earth turned hard underfoot; crunched as it gave way to scree. He counted his steps between here and the sick tent. Thirty-two. Then he reached out with his toe and tapped it until he felt water. There was the lake. Finally, he bent down, pulled off his glove, and began to wash.

"Well done," Irima said. "Yer found it faster than I thought yer would."

"I've been up here afore," Silas muttered. "A while ago. My family used it as a pasture when I was a child."

Irima's pearls jingled as she shrugged. "But all the same, not for a while. An' yer did well just now."

Silas smiled, but didn't turn his head so she could see it. He concentrated on the water. He scrubbed it over his face and hands; rolled up his sleeves so he could reach his arms. Garrett had loaned him a shirt, and Silas was stunned by how comfortable it was, as though the stiff linen had been woven with something soft and supple. Like all Peregrini clothes, it was lavishly decorated; even in his blindness, Silas could run his fingers over the embroideries and follow the patterns they made. Flowers, birds, waves...

It had only been a few days since he escaped the demon,

but already, he had begun to learn how to manage. His sight came and went, remaining intact only during the night. But there was no pain in the changes – it was as though somebody simply slipped a blindfold over his eyes at dawn and removed it at dusk. He saw the world without seeing it: the softest crunch of the grass under his boots with every step, the slithering of clouds down the hills as their cool shadows passed over his face. Everything was still there, and to compensate, his ears, fingers, nose and tongue had sharpened. But all the same, when his vision disappeared, Silas kept his eyes shut. It was easier that way, to fool himself that he was sightless by choice. Better that than to look around, with the hot sun beating down upon his face, and find nothing.

The water splashed nearby as Irima washed her own hands. Silas listened, and by sound alone, knew exactly what she was doing. First her hands, then her arms, her feet, and finally, her face. Then someone else appeared on his left, further away, and he heard the soft flap of wet fabric.

"Good morn, Ida," Irima said.

"An' to ye," a woman answered, nerves at the edge of her voice. "How might yer charge be a'doin?"

"He's come along well," Irima replied. "Uncle has given him permission to go about the camp."

The woman drew a shaky breath. "Is he... safe?"

"Aye. Ye can believe me on that."

"But what about... Well, thee knows."

"Worry not," Irima said firmly. "His affliction is nowt that can be dangerous, not to him, nor us."

The woman cleared her throat uncomfortably, then turned back to the water. Silas listened again, and realised she was washing some clothes.

"Why dost thou do that?" he asked. "Clean everything so

thoroughly, all the time?"

"'Tis our way," said Irima. "Everythin' should be spotless. When yer travel as much as we do, it's easy for stuff to get dirty."

"But ye aren't travelling now," Silas pointed out.

"It don't matter. It's still important," the woman said. "An' everythin' has an order. The clothes are never done in a place where a body goes. Hence why I'm at a distance from yer both. It would be better in a river, with a current, but this will suit for now."

"Speakin' of," Irima said, "are yer done, Silas?"

"Aye."

"Then come along. Yer must meet some o' the others."

Silas hesitated. "Will they accept me?"

"Ai, don't worry," Irima insisted. "If yer were goin' to cause any trouble, ye would have done it by now!"

"And likewise, thee to me," Silas admitted. "I had... such fears about what ye might do."

"Well, that's a start," Irima said warmly. "Maybe soon, thou might even realise I can be trusted."

She took his wrist and guided him away from the lake. Silas concentrated on everything around him. There were children running about and laughing; the soft creak of willow being woven into baskets. He heard a gentle tune from the fiddler and shawm-player. The strong smell of cooking and spices hung in the air: a thick vegetable stew, similar to what he had eaten since arriving. Preparation of the food took most of the day, but the meals were large and communal, shared between all the families within the troupe.

Deep down, his heart warmed. These people were so strange, so different. But they were kind and honest – more so than many Valley-folk. They hadn't needed to rescue him. They could have just stripped him of his knife and clothes, and left him to die where he fell. And yet, they had saved his life. They had given him food and shelter, without a single word about paying it back.

How could he have assumed the worst in them? How could anyone? They were no more Raptors than Silas was a demon.

"So," Irima said, "yer've met Ida just now. She's me older cousin. Her parents were from another troupe, same as mine. They've been dead awhile, but Andreas – the one who fetched yer when ye were unconscious – he's her 'usband. She's expectin' a babe soon."

Silas nodded. That would explain why Ida had sounded particularly unsure of him. If she had already known the perils of strangers, that was a difficult barrier to break.

Irima led him from tent to tent, and introduced everyone by name. Several were nervous – he heard it in their voices – but others greeted him with warmth. One man even came close and shook him by the hand.

"Art thou sure this is a good idea?" Silas whispered to Irima when they left the last tent. "I mean… they saw me. When my sight returned."

"Which is exactly why yer should put 'em at ease this way," Irima replied. "I know thee's sound, and so does me uncle. The others will see that too, if yer show 'em, as yer showed us."

"But… what of thee?" Silas asked. "You have been so generous. For what?"

"Because it's the right thing to do," said Irima softly. "An'… I suppose I've grown a tad fond o' yer company."

Silas was taken aback. His *company?* Someone *enjoyed* being with him? The only person who he had ever truly bonded with was Raphael. All others – his kin and neighbours alike – were much too wary to get close to him.

But as he thought of his family, the respect they gave him struck his heart like a stone. He cared for them so much. Yet, ever since he had been old enough to give orders, he had done so. None of his younger siblings dared argue with him. But did that mean that he had forgotten how much he loved them?

The memory of his father swam through his mind: first alive and smiling, then drowning in the air. How could that have happened only last week?

"What 'ave yer got in yer head?" Irima asked, and tapped Silas on the temple.

"Nothing," he muttered.

"Yer a haunted one," she said quietly. "Not used to company. Are yer?"

"Nay."

"Why?"

"It's never been my way."

Irima sighed. "You Valley-folk 'ave some peculiar ways."

"Nay, not them," Silas said. "*Mine*. I just… It's easier that way. To protect people."

"Yer protect no-one by puttin' up walls," Irima said gently. "That only pushes 'em away."

Silas scoffed. "Hence why thou only knows *cloth* walls."

Irima chuckled. "They do their job well enough! Keep out the wind an' weather. Collapse small enough to move. 'Tis all we ever need."

"But do ye not crave security?" Silas asked.

"Yer mean a solid house? A field o' big fat milk cows, what can barely walk for their udders? No. If yer were to wish a Peregrini to stop wanderin', yer would need to cut off our legs at the hip. It's in the blood. Can't ever get rid o' that."

"Not even for safety? If thou were not so… different, then…"

"Then they'd accept us?" Irima finished dryly. "Welcome us and stop callin' us thieves? Come, now. Do yer really think that would be the end o' it? An' why should we change for them? I say this as one who nearly lost everythin' when they killed me parents. I was afraid, for a while. But now I wear pearls in me hair and look every man in the eye. They can't frighten me. An' they can't change me. I'll never let it be so."

Silas nibbled on his bottom lip. Her voice struck him like a hammer. Such passion and pride… and such acceptance. How could something be so hard and yet soft? Or a person be so rootless and yet so free?

"May I ask thee something?" he said.

"O' course," Irima replied.

"What's outside the Elitland?"

Chapter X
The Human and the Asræ

COLD THEY WERE AS THE PALE MOONBEAM,
COLD AND PURE AS A VESTAL'S DREAM.
SERENE THEY DWELT IN A SILVERN WORLD,
WHERE THROBBING WATERS STOLE DUSKY-WHITE,
WASHING THE FEET OF DARK CAPES STAR-PEARL'D,
AND ARCH'D BY RAINBOWS OF RIPPLING LIGHT.

Robert Williams Buchanan

The Atégo boy had sat at the mouth of the cave all day. He had tried to engage Merrin in conversation, but she refused to look at him, much less respond. This was exactly what it had been like at first: polite words and charm. Sweet bait, leading to the trap.

The sun moved around. It came awfully close to her, but she tucked up her legs, and the cloak added another layer of protection. When she thought she could bear it no longer, the light began to dim and the air cooled to a pleasant dampness. Evening was drawing in. The moon appeared in the sky, fat and silver; almost full.

Eventually, the boy's tiredness overwhelmed him, and he fell asleep, leaning against one of the trees. Merrin turned slowly, worried that the tiniest noise would awaken him.

Brazen human! He had believed her to be a demon... Was he now so comfortable in her presence, in her dominion, that he would let his guard down that easily? Even after she had made her hatred so clear? Did he realise how much danger he was in?

Merrin didn't care. The sun was setting. The shadows were long and deep enough for her to move.

She rose to her feet with the fluidity of a dancer, pulled the cloak off her shoulders, and twisted it until it became long and thin. The boy's head lolled back against the trunk. She could strangle him before he even realised what was happening. Or she could brand him with blindness, like she had his brother and forefather. He deserved it. All Atégos deserved it...

She hesitated. They might deserve it, but this one had saved her. Even as he feared her, he had come to her aid and kept watch. Could she really kill him after that?

She sighed, and dropped the cloak.

"What's this?"

Merrin's eyes snapped up. She had been so focused on the human, she hadn't even heard Dylana approaching, a new bag of supplies over her arm.

"Merrin," she said, "what are you doing?"

Merrin's breaths shook.

"He's one of *them*," she hissed. "A brother of the last one. He's been here since dawn... I can reach him now..."

"And what are thy intentions?" Dylana said. She walked closer, dripping water with every step. As she passed the boy, she bent close, peering into his slumbering face.

Merrin didn't move. She pressed her lips together; felt her

heart pounding in her head.

"He's certainly stayed longer than his brother," Dylana noted. "I should congratulate you for not acting rashly."

"Thee shouldn't," Merrin said venomously. "The only reason he's still alive is because the sunlight stood between us."

"Ah," Dylana sighed. "Penro told me of your threat to kill the next Atégo you saw. And yet you didn't need me to stop you just now. Would you really murder a helpless innocent as he sleeps?"

Merrin flashed her teeth. "I say it again: none of them are innocent. And... it's not *murder*."

"Then what dost thou call it?"

"Protection."

"For us, or for you?"

"Both. Do you want to open this wound again, Mother?"

"It's vengeance, Merrin," Dylana said. "Not protection, not even justice, but *vengeance*. And for what? All the men dying because of a curse thou laid down in a fit of rage? Do you feel any better for it? Listen to me. Adrian is gone."

"Don't say his name!" Merrin hissed.

"Adrian is gone," Dylana repeated softly. "I want you to tell me the truth. Why is this one here? Why has he lingered where no others dare to tread?"

"Because he's a fool," Merrin spat. "He... he appeared seeking his brother. I was trapped. He happened across me and proved himself useful."

"He *helped* thee?" Dylana pressed.

Merrin whipped her head away.

"If that's true, you owe him your life," said Dylana.

Merrin recoiled. "I do not owe an Atégo anything!"

"Not even a heart which has turned to stone?" Dylana shot

back, firmer now. "My daughter, you are better than this. Thy father knew it, too. Wouldst thee rather be lying as a pool of water on the ground, forever lost?"

Merrin shuddered at the thought. It was the most terrifying demise of any Asræ; a fear so primal and deep, it lingered always at the edges of nightmares. The sun was death. Even as she stood there, her arm throbbed with pain where the dawn rays had touched her. She tried to angle her body away, to keep it out of view, but Dylana still saw it.

"Come hither," she said.

Merrin did, glaring at the boy with every step. Dylana wrapped her webbed fingers around the wound and pressed. Her hands glowed, and Merrin sucked in a breath through her teeth. She could feel her skin fusing back together; first the topmost layer, and then further down, like a million needles driving into her. Several moments passed, and then finally the sting subsided, and when Dylana removed her hands, Merrin's arm was perfectly healed.

"Thank you," she said.

"You're welcome," replied Dylana. "I expect thee to extend that same courtesy to thy guest."

"He's not my guest," Merrin muttered. "I just want him gone. But he insisted on staying. He wants answers out of me."

"Then give them to him," her mother said. "And give him a chance. Merrin, my dear girl, I am but a mirror for your own thoughts. I don't always tell you what you wish to hear, but you know what you must do."

Merrin bit the inside of her cheek before she could cry. Her fingers curled into fists.

"I can't help this!" she cried.

Dylana shook her head. "You can. If you're strong enough

to hold onto it so firmly, then you can hold onto something else, something healthier, just as well. This is but a mask that you have forced upon your own face, to keep yourself from being hurt again. It is understandable, but a hundred years ago, thou was nothing like this. A hundred years, it has been, since you had your revenge. Please, you *must* let it go."

Merrin caught a sob in her throat and swallowed it back down.

"I…"

Dylana brushed some stray hairs behind Merrin's ear.

"I'm proud of thee," she said softly. "It is beginning already."

"Is it?" Merrin replied, a curt edge in her voice like a blade. "I still hate them."

"And yet that boy still lives. I watched thee walking towards him. If I had thought you might harm him, I would have intervened. But I did not need to. You stopped by yourself. That is more than you would have done before."

Merrin exhaled sharply and turned away. But Dylana didn't relent. She laid her hands on her daughter's shoulders and embraced her.

"This is not a step back," she said. "It leads forward, into a new beginning. Thou hast wallowed in darkness and fury for too long."

"It's a part of me," Merrin insisted.

"The *scar* always will be," Dylana insisted. "But you need not hold the knife in the wound forever."

Merrin stared straight ahead. She couldn't focus. The trees swam together into a collage of branches and shadows. Even the moonlight seemed paler than normal, as though it were waning rather than waxing. And all the while, she heard the boy breathing.

At last, a tear rolled down her cheek. She made no move to wipe it away.

"I don't know how," she whispered.

"Then start at the beginning," Dylana said. "Open thy heart."

"So it can be torn asunder again?"

"I don't mean it that way. He has been kind to thee, protected thee, despite everything. Do the same. Be patient. Listen. Try not to see what he reminds you of, but see what he is, here and now. And do not be blind to the answers. Thou may surprise thyself."

Dylana kissed the back of Merrin's head, left the bag in the crook of a tree, then walked onto the Lake. Merrin watched out of the corner of her eye as her mother slipped below the surface.

More tears stung her. Such a simple act, to go home…

The boy shivered in his sleep. For a moment, Merrin worried he might awaken, but he just pressed himself tighter against the tree, and mumbled something.

"Silas…"

Merrin pursed her lips. She picked up the cloak again. But she didn't twist it. Instead, she opened it out, and with shaking hands, spread it over him like a blanket.

Something was tickling Raphael's nose. He eased his eyes open, and noticed a shock of brown fur: a vole. As soon as he moved, it shot back into the undergrowth.

"I must say, for a human, you sleep deeply enough to rival an Asræ."

Raphael looked up. The shimmering lake creature was sitting nearby, perched on a rock as though it were a throne. The sun had set, and out in the open, under a starry sky, she looked like something out of a dream. Or a nightmare.

Merrin. That was her name.

Nerves coiled in Raphael's belly. Night had fallen. That meant she could reach him.

"Dost thou intend to harm me?" he asked.

Merrin scoffed. "I had a mind to. But it would have been much easier while you slept."

Raphael sat up from where he had rolled onto the ground. His cloak fell off him. He stared at it, then back at Merrin.

"Thou covered me?" he said in surprise.

"Don't think thyself special for it," she snapped. "I marvel at your idea of *helping me*, as you so eloquently described it. Slumbering on whilst the sun was overhead."

Raphael bit his lip. "I'm sorry."

"Save thy pity. I need it not," Merrin said. "In truth, I was grateful for the blessed silence."

"So thou doesn't wish to speak to me?"

"I never did. I wish for you to leave. So do it."

Raphael got to his feet, slowly, wincing as his blisters flared with pain. How had he even managed to walk this far, let alone scale the Wall?

His eyes settled on the lake, shining lilac under the soft blue sky. Even the amarants under his feet looked purple in the gloom.

"It's beautiful," he gasped.

"Didst thee expect it to not be?" Merrin asked scornfully.

"I don't know what I expected," Raphael admitted.

"Were stories not told to your people?"

"Of course. But they were all mere warnings. Stay away. Never go thither."

Merrin scoffed. "*Mere* warnings? And yet you came. As did your brother. Fools."

Raphael looked at her over his shoulder. "I cannot speak for what Silas did to thee, but I helped you."

Merrin's eyes shone dangerously. "You presume much."

"Only the truth. Thou wouldst not have screamed with such terror otherwise," Raphael said. "Why do you hate us so terribly? One of my forefathers had dealings with your kind, and it seems you were hospitable enough to him. Until you weren't."

Merrin leapt to her feet. Raphael was so startled, he stumbled and fell against a tree. Merrin snatched his tunic with a strength which stunned him.

"Give me one reason why I shouldn't show you my *hospitality*," she snarled.

"I saved thy life!" Raphael cried. "Thee hast cared for me!"

"Hardly! You disgust me! You and your brother both!"

"Why? You speak of stories? What lies have been spread about *us?* We are not monsters, any more than thee!"

Merrin bared her teeth. Raphael fought the urge to shrink back. But then, to his relief, she released him.

"Why didst you not harm me before?" he asked, gentler now. "Why not just return to your home? The sun has gone now. You're safe."

Merrin held his eyes. They burned like hot coals, as though she were viewing the source of all evil.

"I cannot," she said. "Not for another two days."

"Why?"

"Because I am above the surface against my will."

Raphael read between her words at once. "Silas. It's because of him, isn't it?"

Merrin gave a curt nod. "When the moon is full, I will be able. But not until then. We don't belong up here. Asræ are of the water; of the darkness."

Raphael's eyes ran over her. He saw the webs between her fingers, the gill slits in her neck, the fin which ran from the base of her skull to the bottom of her spine. Those alone might have been enough to make him run. But here he stood.

"How did Silas even reach thee?" he asked.

"In a boat up yonder," said Merrin, sweeping her arm towards the north.

"A boat? But... if your people are of the water–"

"They were made by *your* people, before the building of the Wall. Humans used to fish in the Lake. There were fewer of them then, so it didn't harm Her. We allowed it. Or, my father did."

"Thy *father?*" Raphael repeated. "Before the Wall? 'Tis impossible!"

"It's not," Merrin said coldly. "Only *your* lifetimes are pitifully short."

"Thou speaks as though thee remembers this time."

"I do."

"How many years old are you?"

"Many more than thee."

Raphael stared at her. She only looked about his age; perhaps a little younger.

"How is it possible?" he gasped.

"For every century which passes, we only age by one year," Merrin answered. "I remember the time when your ancestors first struggled through the mountains and arrived hither.

144

Before that, 'twas only the Asræ in this place. We were the ones who named it the Elitland. The Land of the Elite. Because we chose it above all others to be our home."

Shock painted Raphael's face. "Then thou is... over a thousand years old?"

Merrin looked straight at him. "Aye."

Raphael shook his head in shock. "Extraordinary!"

"What is?" Merrin said, with a hint of bitterness. "Time passes no faster for us than it does for thee. You think we possess so much life? The opposite could be said for you. That is... one of the reasons why relations between our people have been strained."

"But only recently?" Raphael asked. "It wasn't always so, was it?"

"It was inevitable."

Merrin's eyes flashed with anger. She whirled away from him and snatched out at the tree, so tightly, Raphael thought he heard the wood crack.

"What's wrong?" he asked, as gently as he could.

"I am done with thy questions," Merrin growled.

Raphael hesitated. Despite everything his common sense screamed at him to not do, he laid a hand on her shoulder. Her muscles tensed.

"Do not touch me," she snapped.

"I'll not harm thee."

"And you presume I will promise the same? *Do not touch me!*"

Raphael let go of her. There was something else under her words. Pain. Deep, gut-wrenching, heart-tearing pain; of a kind he couldn't name or comprehend.

Before he could speak again, she bolted away from him,

and ran across the surface of the Lake as easily as if it was a solid road. Raphael's jaw dropped. He stared after her until she rounded a little island and was lost from sight.

He drew the cross over his chest. What was this? Demon magic? No, she wasn't a demon; he had to remember that…

She was an Asræ. *Demon* was just a name given by those in the east. A *wrong* name. There might have been terrible things which happened here, but were they all so innocent?

He sighed. It didn't matter. She hadn't hurt him; he was free to leave. But first, he needed to cool his burning feet.

He stumbled down the bank. The lake stretched before him, waving and breathing like a living thing. A clump of reeds nodded their fat brown heads at him. He heard crickets chirping; frogs croaking. A nyhtegale whistled deep in the forest.

A tiny smile stole across Raphael's lips. This place was more than merely beautiful. The lake seemed to possess its own immense power; something which nothing on the other side of the Wall could match. How could anything so stunning be demonic? How could respect turn to fear in such a way?

He pulled off his shoes, wincing as the leather rubbed against his blisters, and eased his feet into the water. As he washed off the blood, he closed his eyes, and began to sing under his breath.

"Sweet loved-one, I pray thee,
For one loving speech;
While I live in this wide world
None other will I seek.
With thy love, my sweet beloved,
My bliss though mightest increase;
A sweet kiss of thy mouth
Might be my cure."

The water rippled. Raphael opened his eyes, and scrambled back in alarm. Another Asræ had appeared in front of him, treading water. It was a male: like Merrin, he was tall and slender, with blue-green skin and emerald hair, and eyes the colour of lavender. He looked to be in his mid-twenties, but such an appearance only told Raphael that he was much older.

The Asræ pushed himself up, through the surface, and stood upon it.

"Greetings," he said. "So you are the one who came to Her Majesty's aid."

Raphael held up his hands. "Please, have mercy!"

"Thou hast nothing to fear from me, young man," said the Asræ. "I am Penro: Advisor to the Queen. Who are you?"

"Raphael," he replied, struggling not to squirm. Beside such fine titles and ethereal beauty, his name sounded so simple.

Penro smiled. "A pleasure."

"Likewise," Raphael said nervously. "So... she wasn't lying? She really is a Queen?"

"She is yet to be crowned, but yes," said Penro. "And she would not lie, not even to thee. There are few things she loathes more than lying."

"Except humans," Raphael noted.

"She has her reasons. Old reasons, but valid to her, nonetheless. Now, I want to ask thee: what was that song?"

"'Tis but a ditty."

"Oh, I'm sure. But I recognise its colours. I have seen them, here, in this place. *A sweet kiss of thy mouth might be my cure.* Who wrote it?"

"I don't know," Raphael admitted. "It's just an old song."

"I thought thou might say that," Penro said, with a shine in his eye. He walked closer, but didn't leave the lake. Raphael watched him nervously.

"So it's also true that you aren't demons?"

"Nothing of the sort."

The stone of unease in Raphael's chest began to wear away. This Asræ seemed much warmer than Merrin. And he was much less decorated: he wore a tunic and robe of the same shimmering white material, but there were no ornaments in his hair, nor green sleeves around his arms.

"Ah," Penro said, motioning to his wrists. "I see thou hast noticed what she wears."

"One of them became stuck on a tree branch. What are they?"

"The Royal Bands. They mark her as the Voice of the Lake; of all within this place. They were originally worn by her father, King Zandor. I wove them off his arms and onto hers as he laid on his deathbed. And so it shall be with Merrin, hopefully many millennia from now."

"I didn't mean to upset her," Raphael insisted. "I just…"

"It takes little to upset her," Penro replied softly. "As thy brother learned. And thee, so it seems."

"But she was… kind to me," said Raphael.

Penro raised his eyebrows. "*Kind?* Well, that is certainly a difference."

"I presume she is not that way inclined?"

"Thou does not understand. She is a gracious one. Proud, and with such a heavy burden. But she's so young, still; and in mourning for her father."

"*Young?*" Raphael repeated.

"You must not think like a human in these matters."

"How can I not? I will be fortunate to live to twice the age I am now!"

"But we are hindered by our own dangers," said Penro. "Thou has disease. We have the sunlight. Thou has physical toil. We have heartbreak. Centuries of it. For us, if we allow it, agony such as that persists, until it consumes all things. And this is not the first time Her Majesty has known such agony. Leave any wound open for long enough, and it shall fester."

Raphael lowered his eyes. In a way, he could understand that. He had never begrudged anybody in his life, but all those around him had always glared at his family. Even Father Fortésa had made his dislike known. And for what?

"What happened to her?" Raphael asked.

Penro sighed. "'Tis not my place to say. But I am glad I came upon thee tonight, Raphael, because now I can ask thee for a boon."

Raphael backed away. "I don't wish to endebt myself. I cannot linger here."

"Thou seeks thy brother," Penro nodded. "I'm aware. We all are. And I assure you, he is alive. I saw him with my own eyes."

Raphael's heart leapt. "Really?"

"Aye. All will be well. I promise that," said Penro. "But with that knowledge, I beseech thee. Thy brother… His intentions may have been good, but he went about things very badly. You have come here in different circumstances. You have helped Her Majesty while he trapped her. You have spoken softly to her and shown kindness. Kindness which she has reciprocated, in her way. That she is even abiding thy company is something I never would have believed her capable of."

Raphael swallowed nervously. "What will you from me?"

Penro smiled. "I ask thee to remain for just a little longer. We cannot watch over her during the hours of daylight, but soon, she will finally be able to return home. On that night, the Rise, we shall all come to the surface, celebrate our ageing, and see her coronation."

"What makes you think she will tolerate me further?" Raphael asked. "I… am used to snide comments, but the look in *her* eyes when she beheld me…"

"I feel you may be able to break through where all others have failed," Penro said softly. "Thou art a gentle one. Show it to her. Prove her wrong."

"Why should I?" Raphael said. "I mean no disrespect, but I have my family…"

"Your brother will go to them," Penro assured. "And I dare say that, in doing this, your efforts will not be wasted for thy family, either. Merrin is among the most powerful of us. There is much she could do for you in return."

"Like what?"

"Again, *I* cannot tell you. The rest shall be up to her. 'Tis her burden, and she has forgotten what it was like to not carry it. I beseech thee, Raphael Atégo. A two-night. That is all it would be."

Raphael bit the inside of his cheek. The idea of remaining with Merrin set his nerves ablaze. But, he reasoned, had she not let him live?

His mind raced. He needed to go; find Silas, get back to his mother and siblings… But what then? The same thing, every day, until Raphael himself became ill? And then Silas? And poor Abraham would be long dead soon. In just a few short years, there would be nothing left of them. But if Penro was right; if Merrin had the power to help… Could she *lift* the curse?

"I didn't tell thee my name," Raphael said.

"Thou didn't need to," answered Penro. "Wilt thou stay?"

Raphael nodded once. "A two-night. That's all."

Penro smiled. "That's all."

The Asræ slipped a bag off his shoulder: similar to the one Raphael had seen Merrin carrying. Then he gave a silent nod, walked back into the centre of the lake, and disappeared into the depths.

Chapter XI
The First Shreds of Truth

WITH WHAT A DEEP DEVOTEDNESS OF WOE
I WEPT THY ABSENSE - O'ER AND O'ER AGAIN
THINKING OF THEE, STILL THEE, TILL THOUGHT GREW PAIN,
AND MEMORY, LIKE A DROP THAT, NIGHT AND DAY,
FALLS COLD AND CEASELESS, WORE MY HEART AWAY!

Thomas Moore

Merrin paced along the Lake, hoping the constant movement might shake the ire from her body. She kicked at the water and hit the air; she wanted to scream until her lungs burst. To endure all this at any time would be unwelcome, but now? On the cusp of becoming Queen; while she still held her father's face in her mind?

Tears stung her eyes. She blinked them away, but they came regardless. And with them, her energy swept out of her like a flood. She fell to her knees and curled in on herself, biting her finger so she wouldn't make a sound. She didn't want anyone to hear her. That human, least of all.

Raphael Atégo. Talking to him was like tearing off a scab. He had been kind – she admitted that. But why did he have to look so much like...

"Stop it," she hissed to herself. "Stop it... Stop..."

Time swallowed her. She felt arms around her middle, pulling her close; soft lips on the back of her neck. Such promises and pledges of love. Such lies...

She wanted to crawl out of her own skin. How long would it be, before she forgot the sound of his voice?

She paused. *Did* she want to? Dylana's words echoed in her memory. She had heard similar sentiments from her mother before, but never had they managed to touch her. Not until now, here, broken off from all she loved.

Merrin stared into the water beneath her. It was as black as pitch, the moonlight dancing silver upon the surface. Once again, she tried to push her hand through, but nothing happened.

That hand. She recalled the younger brother; holding him under, branding him with blindness. He had deserved it, the brazen fool. It was to be a lesson to all of them...

A lesson for what? To never cross the Wall? To continue calling her people *demons?* It might keep them away, but was that everything?

Merrin snarled at herself. She had thought about this enough. And these last few nights had hurt too much, without making it worse.

With a sigh, she got to her feet and walked back towards the bank. She stepped away from the Lake, and almost fell over an outstretched tree root. Then she paused. It wasn't a root. It was a pair of shoes.

She ground her teeth. "You're still here?"

Raphael emerged from the cave. "I'm still here."

"Why?"

"I wanted to check if you were alright. If I offended thee, I apologise."

Merrin scoffed, but she kept quiet. Apologising and ensuring her wellbeing? Those were two things his ancestor hadn't done.

"Thank you."

The words felt strange; her lips and tongue seemed separate from her. She took a step back and narrowed her eyes. But all the same, Raphael smiled warmly.

Merrin's heart flipped inside her chest, but she couldn't tell if it was from gratitude or impatience.

"Thou must have the utmost faith in thy brother, to not be running after him."

Raphael sighed: a sound filled with such pain and longing, Merrin's mouth turned dry. In a flash, she saw herself in the human before her.

"If you miss him, then you should go to him," she said. "I… appreciate what thou hast done, but I have no more need for you."

"You do," Raphael said. "You are alone here."

"I don't require your company to pass the time."

"I offer it anyway."

"And I refuse it. How many times must I tell thee to go away?"

Raphael looked straight at her. Then he reached back into the cave and withdrew a woven bag.

"Where did you get that?" Merrin asked.

"When you ran," said Raphael, "I met another of your kind. Penro. He gave it to me, for you."

"*Penro?*"

"Aye. He told me about the nature of the mantle thou must take up."

Merrin glanced down at the Bands. They were as strong as ever, but the one she had snagged on the branch was frayed. She would need to ask Penro to weave it back together properly.

A stone sank through her heart. She hadn't even worn them for a fortnight, and already, she had damaged them. Was there *anything* she could do without foil?

"What is't?" Raphael asked.

"Nothing," Merrin muttered, and took the bag without looking at him. But Raphael dipped his head to catch her eye.

"I'm sorry about thy father."

Merrin's breath caught in her throat.

"I… know how it feels," Raphael continued. "I don't suppose it will ever get easier. But at least we have our other loved ones to help us."

"Until they fall as well," Merrin said coolly.

"But until then, we have each other," Raphael insisted. He looked at her again, and smiled to himself. "Thou reminds me a little of my brother."

Merrin bristled. "I have never trespassed, or pulled anyone from their home."

"Nay… I don't mean like that. It's in your manner," said Raphael.

"How so?"

"You're both so driven, so passionate to lead. That is something I have always struggled with, even though I am the eldest son. Leadership is mine by birthright, but I don't have the heart to command my siblings like Si can."

Merrin's fin flickered. "That's called responsibility," she said. "And I will do well to hold to mine. I have a country to lead."

Raphael nodded. "Aye. And Silas, a family. To us – to him – that is just as important."

Merrin pursed her lips and turned away. She hated the weight in his eyes. They were so earnest, so open. No secrets. Unless, like all his kind, he was just very good at hiding them.

Raphael sighed again. "His only flaw is in his very nature," he carried on, more to himself than her. "In his responsibility, and his sense of it, he is blind to love. He knows not how to give it, nor how to receive it."

Merrin stared across the Lake so she wouldn't be tempted to fidget. *Love.* Such a simple word, filled with a thousand insidious connotations. Love had its place in the world. It was a brittle alliance. Allowing it to overstep its boundaries, one might as well hand over a blade.

"He's wise," Merrin muttered. But even as she spoke, doubt wrapped itself around her mind. She dug into the bag, grabbed a handful of watercress and thrust it into her mouth.

Raphael came closer. Merrin glared at him and shook her fin warningly, but he didn't heed her.

"Don't," she snapped.

"I won't touch thee," he assured. "Why do you hate humans so much? Penro doesn't."

Merrin refused to answer. Realising he had hit upon a dead end, Raphael dug into a pocket at his belt and revealed some small brown balls.

"Pignuts," he said.

"I know what they are."

"I dug them up whilst you were gone. You should have some."

"*Should* I?"

"Thou must eat. Watercress and half a trout will not

156

sustain thee for long."

Merrin exhaled harshly. "I don't like them."

"Beggars can't be choosers," said Raphael, and popped one into his mouth. "Please. There are enough for us both."

Merrin's arms tensed. For a moment, she was tempted to hit him. Insolent boy, trying to wear her down like water upon a stone! It was just like the last time.

But then she paused. It wasn't. Not really. A hundred years ago, she had been so easy to entice; so eager to fall in love. Easy meat, ripe for the taking, seduced by soft words and eyes as sweet as honey. Now, she was harder, colder, like a snake ready to strike. And even as she hissed, Raphael's persistence was more than his ancestor had ever shown.

Was there truly anything sly about this? Was she seeking things that were not there? *This one* had offered only courtesy and kindness. There was nothing hollow about it.

Merrin held out her hand. Raphael smiled, and dropped half the pignuts into it. She ate them quickly, so she wouldn't taste them, then cupped some Lakewater in her palm and washed out her mouth.

"Disgusting," she muttered.

"They're not that bad," Raphael said.

"Nay. Earth food in general. The taste of the soil. It turns my stomach."

"You don't eat of it?"

"Not if I can help it. I prefer the water. In all aspects."

"So you never come up here? Is that why you were so... out of sorts?"

Merrin crossed her arms angrily. "I have not been up here in over a century. And I wished for it to remain that way for many more. Until your brother came."

"Why did he?" Raphael asked. "I know he brought the net. It was missing from our house."

"I believe he wished to make a gift of it, or such like," Merrin spat. "Foolish creature."

"A *gift?*" Raphael frowned. "Why?"

"I don't care. It wasn't welcomed."

Merrin washed her hands, scraping around her nails until all traces of soil were gone. She hated the feel of it: hard and gritty, like sand, always working its way up her skin.

"Is anything welcome here?" Raphael asked.

Merrin pursed her lips. "Honesty. Sincerity. Everything your kind seems to lack."

Raphael sighed. "Well, I can't speak for all of us, but not everyone is dishonest or insincere."

"Like thee?" Merrin said sharply. But, once again, her tone seemed wrong. It scraped against her tongue like a dull blade, and she lowered her head.

"I'm... not used to doing this," she admitted. "Talking thus. I never thought I would again."

"And it's truly so terrible?" asked Raphael.

"It's difficult."

"Why?"

"That matters not."

"I disagree."

"Do not presume to make that decision for me, boy," Merrin snarled. "If I could, I would be away from thee right now. Back in my home. If only the Lake would allow me to return... I'd sacrifice my foot if it meant I could go now."

Raphael stepped closer, wincing with his blisters, and stood beside her. Merrin threw him a glance in her periphery. He was certainly handsome – she supposed girls would always be trying to catch his eye on the other side of the Wall. There was a mellowness to his expression which struck her, as though he were a curious child in a man's body. And when he looked at her, the fear was gone, leaving only respect. He was in the presence of a Queen, and he knew it.

"If the Lake would allow it?" he asked. "Thou speaks as if it were alive."

"Not it. *She*," Merrin said. "She is our Mother. All of this place belongs to Her, and exists because of Her. She is home to so many creatures, from trees to frogs. Birthplace and grave is Hers and of Her. We are all Her children. But I am Her voice. That is what it means to be the ruler of the Asræ. To speak for Her."

Raphael stared at her, then out over the water.

"What is it like down there?"

Merrin blinked. Why would he want to know about matters like that? What for? What could they possibly mean to him?

She breathed deeply; tried to remember what Dylana had said. Then she spoke.

"Bliss. Weightless, dark, cool… No harsh edges or cruel words. It's beautiful."

"Do you have houses?" asked Raphael.

Merrin nodded. "And a palace. It's been there for thousands of years."

"Extraordinary!" Raphael gasped. "Have any humans ever seen it?"

"Nay. It's impossible. Thy lungs are not like ours. That deep, the pressure would crush them."

"But humans *have* taken to the water here?"

Merrin breathed deeply. "Aye."

"What else is there?" Raphael asked.

Merrin's heart hammered. She forced herself to ignore it; to push through.

"Well… this forest is technically a part of our home. It's called Delamere: the forest of the Lake. And those flowers, the amarants? Those are the symbols of the royal family. Unassuming, but long-lived and hardy. They are the only real blossoms which grow here. Under the water, it's… You can't possibly imagine it."

Raphael smiled. "Let me try."

Merrin looked at him. "Bass and trout and shoals of minnow swim hither and thither. Pikes lurk in the shadows, and the weeds wave like hair. Everything is silver. And when one peers into the darkness in just the right way, there is the shine of magic."

Raphael's eyes widened. "*Magic?*"

Merrin couldn't hold back a grin.

"Are you all capable of it?" he asked. "Or only some?"

"Nay, all of us," Merrin explained. "But some more than others."

"By some, you mean yourself?"

"Aye. And my mother. She is the Mistress of Magic."

"Then… dost thee not have God?" Raphael asked.

"Not in the same way you do. But what does that matter? Are we not all for the same end?"

Merrin bit her tongue. She couldn't believe she had said that. She thought about the brother, Silas; how she had only been prevented from killing him by Penro's interference. And then there were all the other men in his family – Raphael's father among them. All dead by her hand. Her curse.

Could she bear to tell him?

"I… have not met a human like you for a long time," she

admitted.

Raphael glanced at her. "Is that a bad thing?"

Merrin fought the urge to squirm. But then she shook her head.

"Nay."

Raphael smiled again. It was more tentative than before, but the same warmth lingered in his eyes, like the late sunshine of a summer evening. And, to her surprise, Merrin returned it.

She inspected the sky. The stars had spun overhead, and hung at their midnight point. There would only be a few hours until dawn.

"Tomorrow evening, at dusk, I will go back into the north," she said. "That is where I will be crowned. There shall be only a short time before the moon waxes to full. Thou need not follow me."

Raphael peered over the shimmering Lake.

"Nay, I'll come," he said. "I need to journey north anyway, to return home. I may as well do so on this side of the Wall."

"It will be quicker for me without thee," said Merrin. "I can walk upon the Lake. You cannot."

"True," Raphael agreed. "But if the sunlight were not to touch thee, the journey could still be swift?"

"Thou know'st well I cannot travel during the day."

"So cover thyself. Wear my cloak, and walk under the trees. Would that protect you enough?"

Merrin hesitated. "If the light did not touch me directly."

"Then shall we attempt it?" asked Raphael.

"I suppose. Thank you."

"The pleasure is mine. I… enjoy the company I've found here."

Merrin eyed him. "Don't try to flatter me."

"I'm not. I'm merely being honest," Raphael replied. "When we get to the north, I shall scale the Wall and return to Fanchlow. Or continue searching for Silas, should he not be there. Thou shalt be ready for thy coronation by then, correct?"

"Aye," Merrin said. She heaved a sigh that filled her lungs, and let it out in one huge breath. "Well, thou cannot hope to keep pace with me. Not like that. Sit down thither."

She pointed at a raised root. Raphael did as she said, but still watched her with a nervous shadow lingering on his face.

"What is this?" he asked.

"Be quiet," Merrin said. She steeled herself, then laid her hands over his feet. White light seeped from her palms, as though she were holding a pair of stars. Raphael gasped and went to pull away, but Merrin held on.

"And still," she snapped.

She forced her power into his flesh, felt the blisters calming and the broken flesh closing. Raphael snatched at a nearby tree and screwed his eyes closed. Merrin didn't look at him. She just concentrated on her task, so she wouldn't have to think.

After a couple of minutes, she let go. Raphael's feet were still dirty and streaked with dried blood, but beneath that, his skin was as healthy as ever.

His mouth fell open. "How…?"

"Magic," Merrin said, hurrying to the Lake to wash her hands. "Don't expect me to do that again, boy. Now, clean thyself up. We have a long walk ahead."

Silas kicked out, but he couldn't move his legs. Water closed over his head. There was a hand in his hair, gripping him so tightly, he worried it might tear his scalp clean off. He didn't dare breathe in, else he would drown.

He looked down, into the darkness. An open grave lay below, a coffin within it. But the lid was missing, and his father was there, face pale and sunken. Drowned in air…

"Ai, awaken!"

Someone shook him. Silas's eyes shot open and he jumped up in alarm. As he moved, he smacked his head on the overhead beam, and the entire tent shook.

"Careful! Are yer alrigh'?" Irima asked.

Silas rubbed his temple with a snarl. "Aye."

Irima pushed a mug of ale towards him. "We really need to move that there bed."

"I won't be staying long enough for it to remain an issue," said Silas.

"I know. But I hate to see yer a'nightmarin'."

"I'm fine. What time is it?"

"Early. Not long until dawn. I had to wake yer. Else thou would have gotten the whole camp up."

"I'm sorry," Silas muttered as he sipped the ale.

The canvas was growing lighter; Irima didn't need to strike up the lamp in order for them to see. Silas glanced at his hand, and pulled off the glove to reveal the gleaming skin underneath. It was still red and angry, but had calmed in the days since he had escaped the demon. It would never go away.

How was he going to explain himself when he returned home? The mark would be easy enough – a simple burn on a pot – but the blindness? No matter what he said, he knew how his neighbours would react. And the Peregrini might have been nervous of him, but they didn't have generations' worth of warnings about crossing the Wall.

He thought about the demon. It had been difficult to get a good look at it in the darkness, but he remembered enough. Vaguely human, green hair like a briar, violet eyes burning with hatred. It had known who he was. But, Silas supposed, all those creatures would. They were the ones who had cursed the family in the first place.

"I don't know how I shall manage," he admitted in a tiny voice. "I suppose I could work at night. Continue the chores that way. The rest of the village would hate it, though."

"The noise?" Irima asked.

"Nay," said Silas. "Me. *Us.* They dislike us enough already. We've always been… different."

Irima smiled. "Comin' from thee, I'm not surprised!"

"I'm serious," Silas snapped. "Hopefully, my brother will be able to help with that. He has a kindly way about him. And he'll be the head of the household now. Perhaps he can convince them we're not to be feared. We will need it, now I'm… like this."

He shoved his hand back inside the glove.

"I can't remember the last time I spoke so much," he admitted.

"It's 'cause yer around a blabbermouth like me," Irima said jovially. But then an earnest expression swept over her face, and she inched closer to him.

Silas glanced at her. Her hair hung wildly around her face, and the pearls tinkled and shone like dewdrops. She had changed out of her stays and skirt, into an old one-piece dress which she slept in. It had slipped down a little, uncovering her shoulder. Silas's eyes strayed to the shadow of her collarbone.

"I'm sorry to hear about yer father," Irima said.

Silas stiffened. "I never mentioned anything about him."

"Yer did," Irima said. "Yer mentioned, just now, that yer brother be the head o' the house. So to yer Valley-folk, that means there's been a death."

Silas raised his eyebrows. "Thou art perceptive."

"Well, 'tis an improvement from bein' called rude," she smiled. "Look, I really am sorry. Yer've been through a lot, I know. But now I really see why yer must go back down there. What with not havin' yer father."

"Aye," Silas said. "But Raph will care for them until I return."

"Raph? That brother I saw with yer at the fayre? Do yer have others?"

"Another, younger. Uriel. He has a twin sister, too, Selena; and there's also the eldest daughter, Mekina. And our mother."

Irima whistled. "Big family."

"It's actually quite a modest size," said Silas.

"In the Elitland, perhaps. Not to us. One or two're enough."

"And none of them die? I know my parents lost one before Raph. Another two after me and Mekina."

Irima sighed. "Silas, it be work enough to wander without a babe in each arm. Thou has yer fields to always work; yer solid house to always go back to. We don't. So we care with all our strength to raise up our little-uns together. Everyone in the troupe helps."

Silas stared at her. "None would ever help us."

"Haven't *we?*" Irima replied softly. "Haven't *I?*"

"Of course. But…"

"But ye must go."

"Aye. I'll speak with thy uncle, see about him taking me

to Fanchlow."

Irima shook her head. "Stay one more night."

Silas frowned. "I have been away from my family too long already."

"I know," Irima said. "But we ourselves will be a'leavin' soon. And before we do, we'll celebrate Midsummer. I want yer to be there for it. Please."

"Why?" Silas asked warily. "Doth thou not wish me to go?"

Irima swallowed and began rolling one of the pearls between her fingers.

"There be none others 'ere who are my age," she said. "I know it's only been a couple o' days, but I'll miss yer. But I know why ye must leave. I won't stop yer. A promise is a promise."

She reached over and took his hand. Silas sucked in a breath through his teeth, but didn't pull away. He just focused on the pressure of her fingers through the glove; the way the soft light folded around her face.

And then, as slowly as ink dripping into water, his vision narrowed. He closed his eyes so he wouldn't see everything fade, and a tear dripped onto his cheek. Irima wiped it away with her thumb.

"'Tis dawn," she whispered.

Silas sighed. "Irima, stay here."

"I'm not goin' anywhere."

"Nay. Stay and listen. Thou asked for my trust. Thou hast earned it. I will tell the truth. I *did* cross the Wall. And whilst there, a demon attacked me. That is the reason why I am this way, and why I was fleeing."

Irima swallowed so hard, Silas heard it.

"Why?" she breathed. "You told me nobody crosses the

Wall."

"I had to," said Silas. "A long time ago, the demons hath cursed my family. I tried to appease them."

Irima's breathing became heavy and hard. Silas turned his head in her direction, wishing he could still see her.

"Please don't panic," he said. "I am no danger to thee."

"I know," she said shakily. "If yer were, darkness would 'ave come as soon as ye arrived. Tellin' me this now won't mean a thing."

"Thou isn't scared of me?"

"I'm scared *for* yer. Is that how yer father died?"

Silas nodded. "Aye. And it will be the same for myself and my brothers. I only tried to make things better. But this is the result." He buried his face in his hands. "I have disgraced them."

"Yer 'aven't," Irima insisted. "Yer tried to do right. An' this secret be safe with me."

Words tangled in Silas's throat. But before he could speak them, Irima grasped his wrists and gently pulled them down.

"I promise," she said.

Chapter XII
Midsummer

STELLA SPLENDENS IN MONTE UT SOLIS RADIUM
MIRACULIS SERRATO EXAUDI POPULUM.
CONCURRUNT UNIVERSI GAUDENTES POPULI
DIVITES ET EGENI GRANDES ET PARVULI
IPSUM INGREDIUNTUR UT CERNUNT OCULI
ET INDE REVERTUNTUR GRACIJIS REPLETI.

Author unknown

Raphael let Merrin lead the way, only walking in front of her when the undergrowth became too high, so he could flatten it with his feet. He marvelled at every step – it was as though the blisters had never existed.

"Do ye often use magic to heal?" he asked.

"Nay," Merrin replied, pulling his cloak tighter around herself. "Injuries are rare among my people."

"Really?"

"We have no weapons. Nothing which may harm us. The last time I helped with an injury was when a boy became trapped by a falling rock. That was five hundred years ago."

Raphael swallowed. He doubted he would ever grow used to the idea of how long-lived the Asræ were. Merrin herself only looked seventeen, but to think she was truly seventeen centuries old…

"I unnerve you," Merrin observed.

"Somewhat," Raphael admitted. "Thy age."

"Not my appearance?"

"Not now I've been in thy presence awhile."

"And not my manner?"

"Nay."

"Why?" Merrin asked suspiciously. "You afford me such courtesy. It's because thou knoweth who I am, isn't it?"

"I respect that, but I also respect how you've been honest with me," Raphael answered. "You told me about Silas. You explained your home and way of life. You allow me to walk with you. That speaks for itself."

"Does it?" Merrin said venomously.

"Aye," Raphael said, with such confidence, she was taken aback. "And *I* unnerve you, don't *I*?"

"Nay," Merrin snapped.

"Then why all this hostility?"

"Because I can't seem to get rid of you."

Raphael chuckled. "I'm sure you have the power to do that, if you really wanted."

"Do not test me, boy."

"*Raphael.*"

"I'll call thee what I like."

"And I shall correct thee every time."

Raphael pushed aside a clump of ferns, then swept his arm to Merrin. She glared at him as she passed. Under the hood, her eyes shone like embers.

He had never met anyone with such firm barriers around them. Even Silas, with his dour voice and sharp features, was nothing when compared to Merrin. Walking close to her, he almost felt her pushing him away; throwing up wall upon wall like a fortress.

The sun rose higher, towards its midday point. Merrin threw a nervous glance at the sky. The two of them had been careful to walk under the thickest trees, but Raphael knew this was the most dangerous time for her. If she was exposed now, there was nowhere to hide. Not even a hollow in the ground.

"Shall we stop awhile?" he suggested. "Once afternoon comes, we can continue unhindered."

Merrin nodded, and pointed ahead, to a cluster of oaks. A small stone ridge jutted out of the ground between them, amarants and roots trailing over the sides like overgrown fingers. It was hardly ideal, but it cast a small shadow, and that was enough.

Merrin settled upon the ground like a dancer. Then she wrapped the cloak around herself and drew up her knees, to make herself as small as possible. But even so, Raphael felt the presence of a giant rolling off her.

He could rip the hood away from her face and it would doom her. When was the last time she had allowed herself to be so vulnerable? He could tell, from her eyes alone, that it was long ago.

"May I wake a fire?" he asked.

Merrin blinked. "You seek permission?"

"This is your dominion," said Raphael. "I asked before I foraged. I'll do the same now."

Merrin stared at him for a moment, then nodded. "Just keep it away from me."

"It won't harm thee, will it?"

"No more than it would you."

Raphael gave her a smile, then gathered some twigs, hemmed them in with stones, and stuffed them with dry leaves. He took the flint pieces which Mekina had given him; struck them together until they sparked.

Merrin leaned forward to see better.

"It's... brighter than I remember," she said.

Raphael blew on the flame. "Does it hurt thy eyes? Being up here in the day, and now this?"

"It's a little uncomfortable, but not unbearable."

"Good."

Raphael fed the fire with larger pieces of wood, then pulled the last piece of bread out of his knapsack. He broke it in two, speared each half on a stick, and began toasting them.

Merrin tossed her bag towards him. Raphael looked up in alarm.

"Use that," she said.

He held both sticks in one hand, and opened the bag with the other. Inside lay half of her trout from the night before.

"Are you sure?" he asked.

Merrin rolled her eyes. "Nay, I just threw it at you to pass the time. Of course I'm sure."

Raphael smiled at her again. He laid the toast by the fire to keep warm, then took a knife from his belt, and sliced the trout on a flat stone. He laid the meat atop the bread and handed one to Merrin. They bit at the same time, each watching the other.

"Thank you," Raphael said.

Merrin returned his smile. "Likewise."

They ate in silence. Blackbirds and starlings flew overhead, filling the air with song. Spiders and beetles scurried through the undergrowth to escape the fire. Raphael picked up a leaf and nonchalantly held it out. The heat caught it and sent it flying upwards. It snagged on the amarant stalks above Merrin's head before fluttering back to earth.

Raphael glanced at the amarants. They were everywhere: scattered across the ground, trailing hither and thither in bursts of purple and red. He had never seen so much of it.

"Do any others grow here?" he asked. "Daisies? Gillyflowers?"

"I would not know," said Merrin. "I have never cared much for such things."

"Because they're not of the water?" said Raphael; more a statement than a question.

"Exactly."

"But don't you think this forest holds its own kind of beauty? The way the light cometh through the branches; the smell of the dew in the morning?"

Merrin's nose twitched. "I almost forgot the sense of smell. There's no need for it below the surface."

"Then is that not extraordinary?" Raphael pressed.

Merrin sighed. "In its way, I suppose. I'm surprised you care so much. Dost thou not spend thy days slaving away in some pitiful square of land, or shovelling animal waste? 'Tis a wonder you have time to notice anything."

"It's those small things which make it worthwhile," said Raphael. "Outside our house, we grow roses. It smells glorious at this time of year. It's the only thing we have which serves no use, except to sweeten the air."

Merrin cast her eyes down. "I haven't seen a rose for over a hundred years. They are overrated. Full of thorns, and they only last for a moment before they die."

"True," Raphael said, "but beautiful, all the same."

He took another leaf, tossed it above the fire, and watched as it danced up into the trees.

Silas walked around the camp slowly, tapping with his cane, one hand stretched out. He concentrated on the soft roll of the ground; the warm southern breeze as it moved his hair. The smell of smoke became closer as he drew near the central fire. And everywhere, he heard movement: wood being chopped, meat being sliced, conversations so light, he knew from sound alone that people were smiling.

He was stunned by how quickly he had managed to adapt to his blindness. There was no need for Irima to accompany him now.

"Silas."

He stopped still. "Garrett?"

"What're yer doin' out n' about? Ye shall get in the way."

"I know," said Silas. "I'm sorry. But I wanted to find thee."

Garrett sighed. "Alrigh'. I need to take the horses for a drink. Come hither an' we can talk."

He led Silas to where the animals were tethered, then pushed a couple of reins into his hands. Silas followed his footsteps towards the lake. He hoped Garrett had hold of the black stallion – the memory of its kick made him wince.

Scree crunched underfoot as they reached the water, and Silas slackened his hold so the horses could bend their heads.

"So, how be yer this morn?" Garrett asked.

"I'm well, thank you."

"Yer gettin' a lot better at findin' yer way around. I just didn't want to see yer get knocked over. Stay out o' the way, is my advice. There be much to do today. Tonight we'll celebrate Midsummer."

"I know. Irima told me," Silas said. "She wants me to stay for it."

Garrett chuckled. "Well, to be honest, it would be easier! Even if yer wanted to leave, today ain't the time for it. I have enough to get done afore the morrow."

Silas nodded, then set down his cane, removed his glove, and knelt to wash his hands. One of the horses nickered beside him.

"That's what I wanted to speak to thee about. I must return to my family. Tomorrow, wilst thou please take me to Fanchlow? If you leave me by the village lanterns, I can find my way back."

"I'll take yer straight to yer door," Garrett said. "I'm not leavin' yer scramblin' about. Yer won't be able to see. Or, what say ye to this: I take yer at sundown? Then yer will still have sight."

Silas bit his lip. It was a good idea. It would give him time to prepare himself for facing his mother and siblings. And it would mean they wouldn't be too horrified when they saw him again.

"Thou hast been so kind to me," he said. "I shan't forget it."

"Ai, 'tis fine," said Garrett.

"Nay, it's not," Silas insisted. "I haven't been fair to thee. I presumed so many wrongs…"

"Well, now yer know better. There ain't no harm done. An' now yer know the truth o' us, that we ain't wicked or thievin', ye can tell the others. Maybe our welcome will be a bit warmer at the next fayre!"

Silas sighed. "I will try. But they barely give us much warmth, either."

"So yer prove 'em wrong," Garret smiled.

"I don't think that will ever happen," Silas said sadly. "Sometimes, I wish I could be someone else. That we all could be. Not to disappear... Just to start anew. Some folk never change."

"True," Garrett agreed. "But that's not yer problem. Silas, ye have already proven this to me; to all o' us 'ere. Yer might be a strange one, but that heart be an honest one. An' it shows ye are better than them, with their small minds what might never open. Thou must remember that."

Silas swallowed. Silence fell upon him like a mist, but it wasn't the cold distance which he had clung to all his life. This was warmer, as though a mellow summer day had engulfed his heart.

He shook his hands dry and pulled his glove back on.

"Thou reads me so well," he muttered. "Only my brother has ever been able to do that."

"Well, I'm sure he'll be happy to see yer again," Garrett smiled. "Now, go an' rest. Yer eyes look mighty heavy. Did ye not sleep?"

"Not very well," Silas admitted.

"Get some now, then. It will be a long celebration tonigh'! Don't worry, I can take the horses back."

Silas nodded, picked up his cane, and walked away from the lake. He concentrated on the sun's warmth on his body, felt for a dip in the ground with his toe. Finding his bearings, he quickly reached the sick tent and crawled inside. Flint pieces and boxes rattled as he knocked them over. He snarled to himself, swept them into as good a pile as he could manage, and laid down on his mattress.

He didn't realise he had fallen asleep until his entire body jolted. He went to sit up, but remembered the beam overhead and stopped himself. When he opened his eyes, all was black. The sun mustn't have set yet. But outside, he heard the Peregrini, even louder than before. Music was playing softly, and Silas could tell, by the sound of the fire, that they had piled it high.

"Irima?" Silas said.

She didn't answer. Silas touched her mattress, but it was empty, so he fumbled for the ale bucket and dipped a cup into it. He drank slowly, breathing between each mouthful so he could smell the incense. Irima hadn't burned any the day before, but it had permeated every surface in the tent. Silas supposed that no amount of washing would get the scent out now.

He suddenly heard music outside, followed by footsteps coming closer, and a soft tinkling sound. Irima.

"Ai, yer be awake," she muttered. "I stuck me head in before, but yer were away like a babe."

"Thou could have roused me."

"I didn't want to. Ye shall need yer strength."

She knelt beside him. Silas held out his hand and she took hold of it.

"How long until sunset?" he asked.

"An hour or so," Irima replied. "But we'll be startin' soon. Shortest night, an' all. Can't wait too long, else it will be over too soon."

"The fire sounds large," Silas said. "We do that too, in the Valley. And at Midwinter. Balefires."

"Well, it will be one o' the last ones, before we move on," Irima said. "Might as well use up all the wood. We're not in the habit o' leavin' waste behind if we can help it."

"Where wilt thou go next?"

"I don't know. It will take a month to get out o' these mountains. There's only one safe route, y'see. After that, maybe back to the sea. Catch some fish, sell 'em on. Keep 'em for winter, or to trade for more spices."

"Are the sea-fish different to here?" Silas asked. "Are they all like the oysters?"

"Very different," Irima said wistfully. "There are some with teeth as big as knives. Could swallow yer whole. An' others, what look like stars."

Silas scoffed. "Thou's but telling fantasies."

"I'm not," Irima insisted. "I wish I could show yer."

"Well," Silas said, "perhaps, when your troupe returns here, thou can bring one of those teeth to show me."

"I'll do more than that," Irima said. "I'll bring a string o' pearls. But... until then, 'ere. Yer can have one o' mine."

She let go of him and slipped something over his head. Silas traced it with his fingertips: a leather thong, and threaded onto it, a small hard ball.

"Let me trade for it," he said.

"No. Yer 'ave nothin'. An' I don't want nothin'. 'Tis a gift."

Silas opened his mouth, then closed it again. What was he supposed to say? Nobody gave gifts in the Elitland without expecting something in return.

"Ai, don't get all emotional on me, now," Irima chuckled. She jostled his shoulder, then reached over to the corner and tossed a bundle of material into Silas's lap. "There. Yer can't be a'wearin' that old thing on a night such as this."

Silas recognised the feel of it at once. It was the garment which had been loaned to him while she dried and stitched his tunic. With a grateful smile, he stripped to his waist and pulled it on.

"Yer almost look like a Peregrini in that," Irima said. "Come hither. Let's go an' celebrate."

She swung the flap wide and guided Silas out of the tent. At once, the heat of the fire hit his face. Now he was outside, he also caught the smell of stew and roasted meat, and the spices made his head spin. His belly rumbled, and he went to walk towards it, but Irima held him back.

"Not yet!" she cried. "How will ye dance, if yer stomach be full?"

Silas blushed. "I don't dance."

"Well, yer do tonight!" Irima smiled.

Silas stumbled over his own feet as she pulled him. He smelled ale, then heard the merry laughter of people gathered around the keg. Irima filled two tankards and passed one to him.

"Merry Midsummer," she said.

"Merry Midsummer," Silas replied. He tapped his tankard against hers, and drank all the contents in one breath. The alcohol swam inside his head like sunlight. It was stronger than the stuff in the tent.

He breathed deeply. He hated hangovers at the best of times, but now more than ever, he needed to stay sharp. He had to concentrate, for seeing his family again…

He sighed. His family would be fine. By this time tomorrow, he would be ready to step across the Atégo threshold. And everything would go back to…

Normal. The word felt sour in his mind. Normal was snide whispered words and suspicious glances; back to living in the shadow of the Wall, and all the shame he would face. If anyone ever found out that he had crossed it…

Irima tapped his shoulder. "Yer alrigh'?"

Silas nodded. "Just lost in thought."

She leaned close. Silas swallowed when her hair brushed his cheek.

"Don't be a'thinkin' tonight. Just have some fun. All will be fine."

She took his tankard, tossed it aside, then dragged him closer to the fire. As they walked, the musicians struck up a tune. Silas listened, trying to pick out the instruments. Tambourine, drum, shawm, lute…

A woman began singing.

"Radiant star on the mountain,
Like a beautiful sunbeam,
Hear the divided people.
All joyous folk come together,
Rich and poor, young and all;
Climb the mountain, see with your own eyes;
And return filled with grace,
O radiant star…"

Suddenly, a tiny pinprick appeared in Silas's vision. He gripped Irima's hand. The light expanded, growing brighter, forming colours and shadows. Within moments, he saw everything: lines of dancers, shadows waving over the ground, the blazing fire spitting sparks into the sky. The sun had disappeared from view – all that was left was a golden cast at the edge of the clouds.

Silas looked at Irima, and gasped. She had woven a scarf into her hair, and others hung about her hips in a waterfall of colour. The flames reflected in her eyes like stars, and when she smiled, Silas's stomach flipped over.

"There yer are," she said softly. "Now, come on."

She tugged his arm, but Silas shook his head.

"I told thee–"

"An' *I* told *thee*," she snapped jovially. "Come on, yer ninny! Nobody will judge, even if yer fall over yer own feet!"

She pulled him off balance. Silas caught Garrett's eye, standing near the meat joint, and threw him a desperate glance, but Garrett just laughed and waved a hand in encouragement.

Silas groaned, but didn't speak again as they approached the dancers. Ida and Andreas immediately made room for them in the line, and linking their hands in a chain, they began to swirl around the fire in a giant circle. Everyone kicked their legs to the rhythm of the music, and Silas did his best to copy them. He had never heard this tune before. In the Valley, everything was always the same, repeated year after year...

The song swept him up like a wave. The fire filled his eyes with gold. Sweat broke out on his brow, but he didn't let go of Irima to wipe it away. His feet felt as though they were barely touching the ground, and even as he became breathless, he wanted to laugh.

He couldn't remember the last time he had felt so carefree. Everything that had happened was a distant memory. There was only the music, and the heat, and the stars whirling overhead like a million diamonds.

Chapter XIII
The True Enemy

THOU WAS NOT BORN FOR DEATH, IMMORTAL BIRD!
NO HUNGRY GENERATIONS TREAD THEE DOWN;
THE VOICE I HEAR THIS PASSING NIGHT WAS HEARD
IN ANCIENT DAYS BY EMPEROR AND CLOWN.

John Keats

The sun swung low, then disappeared behind the Western Ridge in a blaze of gold. Shadows stretched long and deep through the forest. As twilight fell, Merrin finally untied the cloak and pulled it from around her shoulders.

"Are you alright?" Raphael asked.

"Aye," Merrin replied. She stretched out her fin from where it had been pressed against her back, and handed the cloak to him. "You should have this. It will become cold soon."

Raphael took it with a smile, and draped it over his arm.

Darkness crept across the land. They came closer to the Lake, and Merrin stepped out from beneath the trees to walk on the surface. But she kept pace with Raphael, so he wouldn't be left behind, and trailed her toes over the water.

"How does it hold thee?" Raphael inquired.

"'Tis part of our magic," Merrin replied. She didn't take her eyes off her feet.

"I hear thy longing," said Raphael. "Only one more day, and you can return?"

"Aye."

"And will you never come up here again?"

Merrin hesitated. "I don't know. Perhaps I will. It's... proven to not be as terrible as I remember."

Neither spoke again as the night swept in. Luckily, the moon was now so bright that Raphael could still pick his way through the undergrowth, and after another hour, the little island came into view.

Merrin threw it an anxious glance. That was where, in just one day's time, she would be formally recognised as Queen.

Then she spotted the boats. Just the sight of them turned her blood to ice. She quickly steered Raphael away and over a hillock, to where the cave lay. Raphael took the hint immediately, and settled down inside. His eyes went to the scuffed earth near the back.

"Thou hast sheltered here before," he noted. "Recently."

Merrin nodded. "This is near where thy brother netted me. When he did so, dawn was imminent. This was the only place I could shelter."

"He took one of those boats?"

"Aye. They have been thither for decades. I don't know how they haven't fallen apart."

"They're from before the Wall?"

"I have a mind to smash them to pieces. But... not tonight."

Merrin sat opposite Raphael, with her back against the wall. Raphael watched her for a moment, then started combing his hair with his fingers. His skin was dusted with dirt from their hike through the forest, but his locks were as red as ever.

"How are your feet?" Merrin asked.

Raphael paused. "You really want to know?"

"Just answer me," Merrin snapped. But for as sharp as her voice was, there was no venom in it. She swallowed, held a hand to her throat as though it might come apart.

Raphael frowned. "What's the matter?"

"Nothing," Merrin muttered.

Raphael pulled off one of his shoes.

"They're fine," he said, with a hint of surprise. "Aching, but that's to be expected. No blisters. Thank you."

Merrin nodded once, not looking at him.

"So," Raphael said, "we are not far from Fanchlow here?"

"I wouldn't know. I have never been to your human villages. But this is closer to my home, at any rate. Didst thou see the island down yonder? With the willow tree?"

"Aye."

"I shall be crowned there." Merrin twisted her dress between her fingers. "You… You may attend it, if you wish."

Raphael dropped his shoe and stared at her. "Beg pardon?"

"Thou heard me," Merrin replied. "I admit I owe thee my life. Twofold. And… I admit that you have done more than that. I never believed I could abide your kind again, much less hold a conversation or walk alongside you."

Raphael swallowed. "So… Do you trust me?"

"I suppose I do."

"Have… any other humans ever witnessed such a thing?"

"Not a coronation," said Merrin. "Rises, yes, but hundreds

of years ago. I remember when thy kind first came hither, centuries before the Wall, and all the banks were lined with humans while we danced."

"Are you sure about this?" Raphael asked anxiously. "I'm most grateful, but–"

"'Tis your choice," Merrin said. "I have nothing I may give in thanks for thy service. So I offer this. But you may leave now, if you want. Find your brother. I won't stop you."

"Stop me?" Raphael chuckled. "This morn, thou wanted nothing more than to be rid of me!"

Merrin raised her eyebrows, then lowered them. "Your company has proven tolerable, after all."

"So, if I were to ever come back, wouldst thee attack me again?"

"Nay."

"What about others? My brother?"

Merrin's throat turned dry. "Can you tell me for certain that if it was so, there would be no nets or lies? Nobody would come to hurt us in any way?"

Raphael opened his mouth, then shut it again, and shook his head.

"I can't promise anything. But neither does thee know everything."

"I know enough. I have seen much more than you."

"But have you felt as much?"

Merrin leaned forward. "Be careful, boy."

"*Raphael*," he said. "I know not what I can do. I don't think I have ever seen any creature so afraid."

"*Afraid?*" Merrin repeated incredulously.

"Aye," he said. "Not just of my kind. Afraid of what you must do; what you must become. Afraid to let go of whatever you believe."

Merrin felt as though he had slapped her. She screwed her eyes shut so no tears could escape. It was almost like having Dylana in front of her, speaking the same words Merrin had heard for decades.

Somewhere far away, a nyhtegale whistled. Raphael began humming under his breath.

Merrin stiffened. "What are you doing?"

"What's wrong?"

"Don't. Not *that* song."

"Why? Thou hast heard it before?"

"Please, just stop."

Realisation fleeted across Raphael's face like lightning.

"It's about *thee*, isn't it?" he gasped. "*Thou* is the lost love it speaks of."

Merrin glared at him, hoping her eyes might chill him into silence. But for as hard as she tried, she couldn't pull her vitriol to the surface. It felt thin and diluted, like moonlight on the wane. She could hurt him; she could do so much... and yet, she didn't want to.

"Who wrote it?" Raphael pressed. "What is't thou not telling me? It weighs thee down. I can see it – you carry it like a boulder. Someone hurt you, didn't they?"

"All in this world are hurt at some time," Merrin muttered.

"But not all who, for as long as they live in this world, none other will they seek," Raphael quoted.

Merrin sucked in a breath. She looked past him, through the trees, to the Lake, and let out such a huge sigh, her entire body moved. Her face was betraying all her feelings, and she knew it.

"Seek, for the wrong reasons," she said softly. "'Twas a foolish first love. I imagine everyone has them."

"Perhaps," Raphael agreed, "but to the extent of holding onto it for so long? *How* long ago was it?"

"A while," Merrin said. "What of thee? Thou must have many… admirers."

"Not really. And even if I did, I wouldn't care for it."

"Why?"

"Because most people don't wish to get close to my family. We have garnered a rather unfortunate reputation in our village. And further afield, as I've recently learned."

Merrin watched him carefully. "How so?"

"They claim we are cursed," said Raphael. "I've heard that it's because one of my forefathers came here, before the Wall, and his dealings with thy people turned sour. Is that true?"

Merrin pursed her lips. "Sour is one way to describe it."

Raphael's eyes widened. "Thou knew him? So is it real? The curse?"

Merrin's heart pressed against her chest as though it might burst. She opened her gills in a frantic attempt to breathe better, but they just flapped uselessly in the empty air. There was no skirting around it now. She owed it to him. The truth, at long last.

But how could she tell him? His face was calm and jovial, but even she couldn't deny the cloud of sadness which shadowed it. He had already lost his father, at *her* hand. He would hate her. Perhaps even harder than *she* had ever hated…

"Aye," she whispered. "It is real."

"And… which one of you did it?"

"I did."

Merrin didn't dare blink. She felt as though she had just turned her chest inside out. Just a week ago, she would have admitted it easily, perhaps with pride: the topmost stone in her own mighty wall.

But now, the bricks cracked. The words turned sharp on her tongue and her skin grew as cold as winter. The moment hung still with horror.

Raphael stared at her, and his eyes took on a flat shine.

"*Thee?*" he said shakily. "I… had my suspicions all this had something to do with you, but I wanted them to be wrong. *You* did this to my family? All my forefathers? My father? He died because of *you?*"

"You don't understand," Merrin said. She steeled herself; gripped the hem of her dress as if bracing for a blow. "I know you have heard of… Adrian Atégo. It was all because of what he did."

"His *dealings?*" Raphael snapped. "He was in love with you. Wasn't he?"

Merrin shook her head. Invisible pain crept outwards from her chest, turning her veins to ice. Love. The lie. The waiting blade…

"Nay. He just knew how much *I* was in love with *him*. From Averyl until Septymbre, he came to me, riding upon his white mare, speaking all his promises and adorations. He was humble, kind; everything I wished for. 'Twas a summer of light. And then… Oh, you have called my kind demons, and perhaps *I* am deserving of that. But you only know whatever *he* said. His tale, twisted, as it always was. Have you any idea what he did?"

"Was it terrible enough to lay a curse upon us all?" Raphael hissed.

"He almost killed me," Merrin said. "It would have been the end of our monarchy."

Raphael got to his feet and stormed out of the cave. Merrin ran after him.

"Wait! I beg thee," she called. "I will tell you. You should know."

"Hast thee not told me enough?" Raphael retorted, not looking at her. A sob strangled him; he barely sounded the same.

Merrin grabbed his hand. His flesh was so warm against her own; calloused and dry from long hours of toil under an unforgiving sun. But she didn't let go. The scab was ripped off; the heart exposed, ready to be struck. It needed to be struck. Dylana had been right all along.

"Please," Merrin said. "He already had a wife, and still he came to seduce me, knowing exactly what he wanted. To take me away and hold me captive. I trusted him blindly, and then he went to tear me asunder. I was furious. He hurt me!"

"So you hurt him back? You drove him insane with your own blindness, then killed him? Killed *all* of us?"

Merrin's shoulders sagged as though Raphael had thrown a mountain onto them.

"I did nothing to him that he would not have done to me," she said. "I branded him; made him blind during the hours of daylight. I wanted to make an example of him. I wanted vengeance, but it didn't satisfy. It wasn't long enough. So after he built the Wall, I struck him with a sickness. One which would make him die in my grasp, as I would have died in his. But his name… That would outlive him, every single time there was a son. I let it continue. I was content to let it be so, until whichever would end first: thy line, or my life."

Raphael stared at her. Merrin saw the shine of tears in his eyes, and she clung so tightly to his hand that her fingers hurt.

"I'm sorry!" she cried. "Despise me for this; 'tis no more than I deserve! But I beg thee to know that I am sorry!"

Raphael pulled away from her. His lip quivered, then he stumbled down to the Lake. Merrin followed him.

"*Please*," she said pitifully. "I don't ask thee to forgive me. I understand thou never could."

"Why are you telling me this now?" Raphael asked tightly. "That's why you hated me so much, isn't it? 'Twas bad enough that a *human* came to your aid when you were trapped upon the tree. But I saw thy expression when you noticed my face. It's not my name alone. Do I look like him?"

Merrin tried to swallow, but she couldn't. Her throat felt as though a rope had been wrapped around it.

"Face me," she choked out.

Raphael's jaw tensed as he gritted his teeth. Then he turned, slowly, and locked eyes with her.

The force of them almost made Merrin stagger. Standing like that, with the moonlight striking his hair, he was the spitting image of Adrian. But even through his anger, there was a kindness which his forefather had never possessed. Something genuine, working into her, as softly as breathing in pollen on a summer breeze. A million conversations with her mother had never equalled all he had made clear in two nights.

"You are not him," Merrin said. "Neither is your brother; nor any others who came before you. I held onto the image of him for all of you. I... wish I could bring back thy father. But I can prevent thee from meeting the same fate."

Raphael blinked in surprise. "What?"

"Thee, thy brothers, thy sons," Merrin said. "I swear to you, I will lift it."

"Why? After thou was so desperate to see me gone? Why didn't you kill me as soon as you had the chance?"

"I have spent longer in your company than I have any human, since Adrian."

"A two-day! 'Tis nothing! *That* is enough to change thy mind? Thee, who hath lived for centuries? Hogwash!"

"You doubt me?"

"Entirely!" Raphael snapped. "Penro claims that you detest liars. So what wouldst thou call this?"

Merrin bristled. She had a mind to grab him in anger, but held herself back.

"This is me being honest for the first time in a hundred years," she answered. "This is me promising to save you, because I owe you more than simply protecting me from the sun."

"The sun," Raphael repeated. "Penro asked me to remain here to ensure you would not come to harm. And he mentioned thee might help me – I hoped, perhaps, in lifting the curse."

"And I shall!" Merrin insisted. "I promise thee, I shall! Just stay until the Rise. That is the height of our magic. I cast the illness upon Adrian during the last Rise. This time, I will rid thee of it. But please stay. Please, Raphael!"

He blinked, slowly, as though she had stabbed him.

"Say that again," he muttered.

Merrin looked straight into his eyes. "Raphael."

She reached out, carefully, as though he might strike her. But he didn't move. When she took his hand, he didn't wrench away.

Tears spilled down his face, and they cracked her wall even more. Every single one was a life lost because of her.

Murder, Dylana had called it. Merrin hadn't wanted to believe it. But it was true.

When she spoke, her voice was so small, she barely recognised it as her own.

"I have done wrong by all of you. I have… done worse than him. And I am so sorry."

Raphael's eyes burned into her, worse than the sun, worse than anything. Then he wiped his cheeks on his sleeve; stared out

190

across the Lake, towards the island.

"Thou is in earnest?" he said. "The curse will be lifted?"

"I promise," Merrin replied. "But please wait until tomorrow night. The Rise. Mark me: no more harm will be dealt before then."

Raphael drew a shaky breath.

"Very well."

Merrin's tongue stuck to the roof of her mouth. "Really?"

"I know you told me you don't have God as I do, but we are taught to exercise forgiveness," said Raphael. "*The same soul that sinneth, shall die: the son shall not bear the iniquity of the father, neither shall the father bear the iniquity of the son.* I shall hold thee to that."

Merrin was speechless. She wanted to run, to stay; to do anything to shatter the moment which had fallen over them. How could he, who knew so little of life, so swiftly let go of something she had clung to for a century?

"Is this... easy for you?" she asked.

Raphael stiffened. "Far from it. You are responsible for everything my family has suffered. Dost thou realise that?"

"I do."

"But I endeavour to understand. To see it from where thee stands. So to that end, I will remain. But I ask thee to leave me be. I can't... I need to be away from you awhile."

Without another word, or glance back, Raphael slipped his hand out of Merrin's, and headed into the forest. He placed each foot clumsily, woodenly, as though he were sleepwalking. It was completely different to the steadiness he had shown before.

Merrin felt like her entire body had been hollowed out. She stood rooted to the spot, her fin shaking, her breath coming in short gasps. A hole had opened beneath her, all around her, waiting for her to fall. But she didn't. She remained, as she had for so long – and this time, she had no wall to protect her.

She decided to not tell him about his brother. She had hurt him enough already. At the Rise, she would be crowned, then lift the curse, including the brand she had placed onto Silas.

After over a hundred years, one more night wouldn't hurt.

Chapter XIV
Fires in the Night

I HAD A DREAM, WHICH WAS NOT ALL A DREAM.
THE BRIGHT SUN WAS EXTINGUISH'D, AND THE STARS
DID WANDER DARKLING IN THE ETERNAL SPACE,
RAYLESS, AND PATHLESS, AND THE ICY EARTH
SWUNG BLIND AND BLACKENING IN THE MOONLESS AIR;
MORN CAME AND WENT - AND CAME, AND BROUGHT NO DAY.

Lord Byron

The celebrations continued long into the night. The Peregrini drank the ale kegs dry and danced until their legs folded underneath them. The musicians played constantly, the tunes becoming slower as time drew on, until they eventually abandoned their instruments and helped themselves to food. And all the while, Silas's head spun, barely keeping up with his feet.

Irima refused to let him rest. Even without drinking much of the alcohol, his blood felt as though it were filled with air. He couldn't remember the last time he had moved so fluidly, so freely. There were no fields to till, no siblings to watch, no father to mourn. Only joy, and peace.

The stars spun through the sky. The fire crumbled in a burst of sparks. One by one, everybody retreated to their tents, staggering against each other in bursts of drunken laughter. A hiccupping Irima held the flap open for Silas, but he shook his head.

"Nay, I'm not tired," he said.

Irima chuckled. "After all that? Lord above!"

"I'll come anon. I want to take some fresh air first."

"That ain't goin' to do anythin' for yer tomorrow! Even yer hair will be a'hurtin'!"

"It won't," Silas insisted. "I know my limits."

Irima puffed out her cheeks and dragged her hands down her face. "Suit yerself. I need to sleep!"

She flashed him a smile, then disappeared inside the tent. Silas stood still, watching as she lit the lamp. The kindling flared, and her silhouette appeared on the tarp like a ghost. Even the pearls in her hair were still visible, hanging down in their long strings.

Silas touched the one around his neck. It was large, with a faint yellowish tinge, like a drop of sunlight. How could it be that something so simple, so beautiful, could be coughed up by a sea snail? And to be given it as a *gift*, without any expectation of trade…

He wandered past the fire, to the lip of the corrie, and gazed into the dark gash of the Valley. The moon beat down from above, bathing the entire place in a frost of soft silver light. Behind him, over the Eastern Ridge, the sky held the faint pink of dawn, but there was still time before the sun truly rose. His sight would last for a little while longer.

High up, level with the pastures, he could see for miles.

He even spotted the line of the Wall. But Silas ignored it all, and instead looked north. There, nestled among the mountains, the pass snaked into the distance like a ribbon. He had never paid much attention to it before. But now it called to him in a whole new way, as he thought of all the things Irima had told him about; all the wonders which lay outside the Elitland.

How could the world be so huge? How could it be filled with water that took days to sail across, or buildings the size of a whole village? Silas pondered those words he had never heard before: castles, oceans. They didn't seem real. They couldn't be.

But they were. She was proof of it. What a life she had led, in her simple, rootless fifteen years.

Silas ran his hand over his tunic. He would need to return it tomorrow, and change back into his own: the simple brown woollen one. The one which he had lived in for the past year, which looked just like everyone else's in the Valley. But even that plain little uniform had never been enough. Not with hair like his. Not with a name like his.

He glanced at his hand. It was hidden beneath the glove, but he still felt the flesh tingling, as though he had slapped it against a rock. What would everyone say? What would his mother and Raphael think?

The wind changed, blowing from the south. Silas caught a whiff of smoke.

He glanced over his shoulder, at the remains of the balefire. It was almost dead – too far gone to smell that strong. And it was thicker, with more than just logs. There was peat, fibre, the sharp sting of grass.

No, not grass. Thatch. And then, carried on the breeze, came something else. Voices, raised in anger. Somebody screamed.

Silas ran to the other side of the campsite. At once, the smell became stronger. His heart leapt into his mouth.

Down there, he spotted Fanchlow, bordered by its village lanterns. But those were not all which were burning. An entire building was in flames. They licked up the wattle and daub walls; consumed the roof in a blaze of orange. Smoke churned into the sky like a monster. And surrounding it: the glow of torches stabbing the air.

Horror pierced Silas's body like lightning. That was *his* house.

Adrenaline shot through his veins. He spun around, suffocating on his own panic. He should wake Garrett, wake everybody... No, they would all be passed out from drinking, and even if he did manage to rouse them, the stupor would render them useless. He was alone.

His eyes fell upon the horses. He didn't pause to think; he just bolted towards them. The black stallion saw him coming and leapt to its feet. Silas faltered, remembering how it had kicked him, but desperation snapped through his fear. He had to get to the village, before dawn. If he tried to make it on foot, he would be too late.

He pulled his knife from his belt and cut the stallion's rope. Then he snatched its mane and swung up onto its back.

The horse gave an alarmed snort and tried to buck him off, but Silas clung on and dug his heels into its ribs. At once, it sprang into a gallop.

He pulled on the stallion's mane, and it tore over the corrie lip, barrelling through the pastures like a thunderbolt. The steep fields transformed into copses of trees, and the wind screeched in Silas's ears like a demon, but he didn't dare let go. If he fell now, he would break his neck as soon as he hit the ground. He gripped the stallion's sides with his knees, ignoring every uncomfortable jolt when its hooves hit the earth. He could bemoan the pain later.

The flames grew nearer. They were more vicious now; out of control. The acrid smell burned Silas's nose. He heard the screams again, and recognised them. Mekina.

His sister's face flashed in his mind. Then his mother; Selena, Uriel, Raph...

The ground finally flattened out. The stallion leapt over the hedgerows surrounding Fanchlow – almost throwing Silas, but he wrapped his arms around its neck to keep his balance.

It rounded the rear of the house, swerving to avoid the fire. Silas raised a hand to shield his eyes. A mob was standing there: all his neighbours, headed by Father Fortésa. They all cursed and spat on the floor, brandishing torches and pitchforks like spears. Before them, cowering wretchedly on the ground, were Araena, Uriel and Selena. Mekina was standing, her hands raised, but one of the men slapped her so hard, she fell to her knees.

Rage burst through Silas like scalding water. He pulled the stallion to a halt, slid off its back, and leapt in front of his family. The crowd staggered away, their shouts dimming to shocked mutterings.

"Si! Thank God!" Araena cried.

Silas didn't reply. He was too incensed, too focused. The heat stung his back like a whip. His mother and siblings were alive and unhurt. That was the most important thing.

"What's the meaning of this?" he shouted.

Father Fortésa raised a gnarled finger at him. "*You!* What are you doing here!"

"This is my home!" Silas cried. "Speak up! *Now!*"

"Thou should never have come back!" one of the villagers snarled. "Thy cursed family! Dost thou think us blind? Every one of your men drowned in air, and then the two eldest sons disappear without trace? 'Tis evil work!"

"Nonsense!" Silas snapped. He looked at Mekina. "Are you alright? Where's Raph?"

She only whimpered in response. Silas's heart thundered in his head, and he looked straight at Father Fortésa.

"Where is my brother?" he demanded. "If thou hast harmed him, I swear–"

"I know not where he is!" the priest hissed. "And thee! Vanishing not one day after we spoke at thy father's grave! Where did you go? What did you do?"

"He's in league with *them!*" a woman shrieked. "They all are! Hell-kissed demon folk! Thy family has no place hither!"

"Silence!" Silas shouted. "We are Valley-folk as much as any of you!"

"Cursed!" cried Father Fortésa. "I tell thee, we have had enough of it!"

"So you burn a poor widow out of her home?" Silas raged. "How can such actions come from a man of God, Father?"

The crowd's gasps turned to outraged snarls. Silas raised his arms to keep his family behind him. Sweat ran into his eyes like rain.

"Wicked boy!" Father Fortésa yelled. "If thou is truly so innocent, then where did thee go? Sneaking off in the night like a serpent – and thy brother next! Slithering with those creatures of darkness!"

"Aye!" someone else shouted. "Look at the garments he wears! They are not of the Valley!"

"They were loaned to me by the Peregrini!" Silas snapped.

Uproar welled at the unfamiliar word.

"*Peregrini!* You see, he confirms it! He has been with the

demons!"

"Nay, the... the Cart-folk! The Wanderers!" Silas cried.

"The Raptors!" a man said. "Do you all remember when they stole my sheep? Disgusting creatures!"

"They are not!" Silas insisted. "Thou trades with them! I'm not the only one here who travelled to the fayre!"

"Listen to him not!" Father Fortésa barked, slashing his hand through the air like a blade. "He lies, I tell thee! Look! Look at the glove upon his hand! A single glove! Take it off, boy! Let us see what thou conceals underneath!"

"Aye, off with it!"

"What have ye to hide?"

"Demon family! Folks of darkness! Thou art not welcome here!"

Two men suddenly sprang forwards. Before Silas could fight, they snatched him.

Selena burst into tears. Mekina staggered upright and tried to pull Silas free, but one of the men shoved her away. The other got his fingers underneath the glove, and wrenched it off.

A horrified gasp spread like a wave. All the onlookers fell back. The men released Silas as though he might burn them.

"Dear God..." a woman breathed. "Look at his palm..."

"You see?" Father Fortésa cried triumphantly. "I told you! The touch of demons! I always knew he was too strange to not be under their influence! How came you by that, boy? What wickedness hast thou done?"

Dread settled over Silas like freezing rain. The torches seared his vision; the pitchforks cut the air. There were too many of them. And the sky was growing lighter by the moment. If these people saw what would happen to his eyes...

He threw Father Fortésa a ferocious glare, then whirled

around. He bundled Uriel under his arm. Mekina grabbed Selena; both of them pulled Araena to her feet, and they ran.

Outraged, the mob began to follow, but Silas led the way past the burning house, and their own numbers hindered them. Araena shrieked as the cruck beams crashed through the walls, shooting a fireball into the air.

"Where's Raph?" Silas demanded.

"He went looking for thee!" Mekina replied, her voice ragged with fear. "Where were you?"

Silas didn't waste time replying. He spotted the stallion, hurried towards it and seized its mane before it could bolt.

"Get astride!" he ordered, practically throwing his mother onto its back. Then he placed Uriel in front of her, Selena behind. Mekina held the mane on the other side, and they ran up the hill, away from the smoke, into the darkness.

Silas didn't halt the horse until they reached the trees. It pawed the ground and raised a leg to kick him, but he sidestepped it. The animal didn't scare him anymore.

They stood in terrified silence. Silas peered out from behind the trees. The fire was still raging, but the torches hadn't come any closer. The villagers must have realised they wouldn't be able to catch up. Either that, or they had done what they wanted. The family was driven away.

"Are they following?" Selena whispered.

"Nay," said Silas. He turned around, grasped Mekina by the shoulders and peered at her cheek. Even in the gloom, he saw a bruise beginning to form.

"It's fine," Mekina muttered, but Silas felt her shaking. He looked at her face: freckled and framed by her wild, flaming hair – a face that he had known all her life – and *saw* her for the first time in so long.

"What happened?" he asked. "Is anyone else hurt?"

"Nay, we're alright, thank God," Araena said.

"They were throwing stones at first," Uriel said in a tiny voice. "Then they threw fire. They took the donkey…"

"We've lost everything," Mekina whimpered. "Oh, God… we've lost *everything!*"

"Calm thee. Thou art safe. That's the important thing," Silas insisted. "Now, where's Raph? He went looking for me? When?"

"He set off days ago!" Selena said.

Silas's heart skipped a beat. "Where did he go?"

"He went south, towards the lake at Ullswick," said Mekina. Tears welled in her eyes and she hit out at him. "Si, for God's sake! Why didst thou leave us? You just disappeared! What were we to think? Where were you?"

"That doesn't matter."

"It does! What happened to thy hand?"

"I burned it on a pot. I've been with the P… the Cart-folk. Up yonder."

Mekina stared at him. "You've been *there* all this time? Why did you mix with *them?* Why didst thou not come home?"

Silas hesitated. "I…was injured. I went to the river to fish, but I fell and hit my head. They found me and tended to me at their camp."

He forced himself to not sound wooden. Lying was like a stone in his heart, but he couldn't bear to tell them what had really happened. Not after everything which had befallen them.

And Raph… How could *he* have left? The eldest; the one with the most power by birthright? The neighbours had hated the Atégos for long enough, but with both sons gone, of course they had smelled meat. There would have been no better time to turn the family away.

Silas felt as hollow as an old tree. Guilt beat at him; swirled with anger at what he had just seen; relief that his family were unhurt. Then it overwhelmed him, and he threw his arms around Mekina.

She froze. "What are you doing?"

Silas didn't reply. He couldn't remember the last time he had embraced her. She smelled of smoke and stale sweat; she was thinner than he had been expecting, but he didn't care.

He glanced over her shoulder, through the trees. Dawn was creeping closer by the moment. In just a few minutes' time, the sun would rise.

"I love thee," he said, and he meant it. "I haven't told any of you often enough. And I'm so sorry. I had no intention of being gone for this long. But... I can't leave Raph out there. Not with them."

"You're leaving us again?" Araena cried. "Nay, Si!"

"I must," Silas insisted.

"Be not a fool!" Mekina argued. "What if they catch thee? What if they do more than throw stones?"

Silas's mouth turned dry. He thought faster than he ever had in his life.

"Thou must get to shelter," he said. He pulled the pearl from around his neck and pressed it into Mekina's hand. "Take this. Ride up to the corrie, to the Peregrini, and show that to Garrett and Irima. Tell them that you are my family. They'll help you."

"Up there? With *them?*"

"They are good people, Mekina. The kindest I've ever met. Trust me."

"But what of thee? You can't stay here!"

"I won't," said Silas. "I'm going to find Raph. Worry not for me, I'll stay clear of Fanchlow."

"And go where?" Araena asked. "We don't even know where Raph is! Even if thee had been at the other end of the Valley, he should have come back by now!"

Silas's stomach turned to ice. If they had thought he had gone to the lake at Ullswick, and Raphael hadn't found him there, then perhaps his brother had gone to search somewhere else. Not the other end of the Valley, but the other *side*.

He turned around. Through the trees, the Wall waited like a creeping monster. This high, Silas could even see over it: the dense forest, the distant shimmer of water.

His palm tingled as though in anticipation of a blow. Surely, Raphael hadn't been that stupid...

But in his heart, Silas knew. Dread seized him like iron; he beat it down. There was no time.

"I'll be as swift as I can," he said shakily. "Just get to the corrie and stay there."

"Don't go, Si!" Uriel cried. "Please! Come with us!"

Silas caressed his little brother's cheek. "I'll return to thee, I promise. And when I do, I'll never leave thee again."

Mekina shook her head. "Si, please–"

"Enough," Silas said firmly. "Hark, Mekina: keep high on the slopes, else they'll see ye. Go, now!"

He pushed her towards the horse, and as soon as she was holding its mane, he slapped the animal on the rump. At once, it moved off, Mekina clinging on. She threw him a glance over her shoulder, then the trees swallowed her, and the entire family vanished into the shadows.

Silas waited until they were gone from sight, then hurried in the opposite direction. There was hardly any trace of night left.

His heart pounded – he had no chance of crossing the Wall before sunrise. But if he could get close enough to it: around the village and over the river, before his vision was lost, then he would manage.

Fear weighed upon his tongue like a sheet of heavy cold metal. To be going back *there*, into the land of the demons…

He tried to draw upon the same strength he had found when he first climbed the Wall. He had done it before. He could do it again. He knew what awaited this time, and hopefully the monsters would be weaker in daylight.

But he would be weaker, too. In that place, blind, defenceless…

"Ai! Silas!"

He spun around. He heard hooves pounding the ground – had Mekina turned back for him? No, that voice was too nasal to be her…

Irima appeared out of the trees. She rode bareback upon a dapple grey horse, skirts hitched up around her knees.

"What are yer doin'?" she demanded, waving a hand in the direction of the fire. "We saw that, noticed yer were missin'… I ran into yer family on the way down!"

"You saw them?" Silas gasped. "Are they safe? I gave them thy pearl!"

"I saw," Irima said. "Don't worry, I sent 'em onward. Me uncle will take care o' 'em. What happened?"

Silas held a hand to his chest in relief. "Thank you… Bless ye, Irima! The villagers have turned against us!"

Irima's eyes widened. She glanced towards the blazing house, her face painted with horror.

"Then it ain't safe for thee 'ere," she muttered. "Why didn't ye flee with yer siblings? Come hither, jump up!"

Silas shook his head. "My eldest brother is missing. I must find him too."

"What? In yonder flames? Yer mad!"

"Nay, he wasn't there. He's... I think he crossed the Wall. Looking for me."

Irima's cheeks turned pale. "Yer can't be plannin' what I think yer are."

"I'm going back," Silas said resolutely.

Irima looked at him for a long moment. Then she slid off the horse's back and clicked her tongue loudly. At once, it turned and cantered back towards the camp.

"What are you doing?" Silas gasped.

"Comin' with yer," Irima said. "Worry not for the horse. He knows the way home."

"Nay, you mustn't!" Silas cried. "'Tis too dangerous for thee!"

Irima scoffed. "I told yer, don't be tryin' to boss me about. The sun's about to rise! How do yer hope to manage without me, eh? They'll find yer in a heartbeat, staggerin' around blind. An' what will they do to thee? I suspect it won't be a kindness! So, I'm a'comin'."

Silas gritted his teeth. "I don't want thee with me."

"Tough," Irima said. "Yer want to bring thy brother back? Well, I'm bringin' *thee* back."

The final wall of the house collapsed. Fire shot into the sky. And at that moment, the sun finally broke over the Eastern Ridge. Silas's vision shrank down to nothing.

At once, he put out his hands to keep his balance. He didn't even have his cane...

Irima grasped his wrists and held him until he was steady. Then she turned him around and gently pulled him onward.

Chapter XV
Across the Wall

SUETE LEMMON, Y PREYE THEE,
OF LOVE ONE SPECHE;
WHIL Y LYVE IN WORLD SO WYDE
OTHER NULLE Y SECHE.
WITH THY LOVE, MY SUETE LEOF,
MY BLIS THOU MITES ECHE;
A SUETE COS OF THY MOUTH
MIHTE BE MY LECHE.

Harley MS.

The two of them scaled the Wall as swiftly and silently as they could. Irima climbed first, then sat astride the top and pulled Silas after her. As soon as his feet touched the soil, a shiver coursed through his bones. He drew the cross over his chest and muttered a prayer.

He heard the crunch of a footfall as Irima landed beside him. Then she pushed a branch into his hands.

"'Ere," she said. "Use that to help yer."

Silas's breathing shook. Even the wind whispering through the trees sounded wrong, like a million voices.

"They know I'm here," he muttered. "God, help me!"

"Ai, don't be scared," Irima said, but Silas heard the nerves in her voice. She felt it, too.

Fear. The whole place was filled with it: a breeding ground for shadows and darkness. Silas remembered the way the whole forest had seemed to swarm around him like a wild, freezing trap. Now it lay open again, waiting to ensnare them both.

What if the demons already had Raphael? What if they had killed him? Silas thought of the green-haired creature which had forced him under the water...

Come, unwelcome fool, the trees seemed to be saying in his head. *Come, to the doom thee set down upon thyself, foolish human who dares to return...*

Irima grasped his hand and began leading him. He swung the branch back and forth to feel the way. Every time he struck a tree, an eerie hollow sound bounced back. Low branches whipped over his face like fingers.

"Where are we? What do you see?" he asked.

Irima's pearls tinkled as she cast her head around.

"Just trees," she whispered. "Hundreds o' trees."

Silas hesitated. Were they even going in the right direction? How were they supposed to find Raphael in this labyrinth? This forbidden land stretched the length of the entire Valley...

"Head south-west," he said. "We won't miss it if we go that way."

"Miss what?"

"The lake."

"Is that... where the demon attacked yer?"

Silas swallowed. "Aye. Dost thou see any of them? They look human, but they aren't."

"Nothin' like that," said Irima. "Would they be a'walkin' about in daylight?"

"I don't know. I hope not. The one which I saw seemed distressed at dawn being so close."

"Then let's hope they're all hidin' away. Try callin' for yer brother."

Silas's heart slammed against his ribs. The idea of raising his voice to normal volume was terrible enough, let alone yelling. But if he didn't, they could be searching the forest for weeks.

He shouted Raphael's name. The cry echoed off the mountains like the wail of a ghost. Silas heard alarmed birds flapping into the air. A crow cawed nearby. He heard its anger. He wasn't welcome here…

His shoe caught a tree root and he crashed onto his face. Demon laughter rippled through his mind.

"Are yer alrigh'?" Irima asked as she helped him up.

"I'm fine," Silas said. "Please tell me thou can see the lake."

"Not yet. Ai, yer've cut yer lip!"

Silas held a hand to his mouth. He tasted blood and spat it out. Hopefully that wouldn't draw the monsters closer. They were things of the water, but for all he knew, they might descend on him like rabid dogs.

"*Raph!*" he shouted, so loudly, his throat burned.

Suddenly, he heard something: twigs snapping, the rustle of clothing. Footsteps. Running.

Irima spun him behind her and bent to snatch a branch of her own. Her breath came thick and fast. Silas strained to listen, forcing himself not to panic.

The footsteps came closer, then stopped.

"*Si?*"

Silas's heart melted with relief.

"Raph!" he cried. He tore past Irima and bolted towards the voice, but tripped again, and this time, he tumbled down a slope. Stones and twigs pierced his skin. He threw out his arms, but found nothing to grab, and eventually, he slammed into a tree. Pain exploded through his wrist.

He heard Raphael and Irima coming after him, and then hands appeared on his shoulder. He recognised them: large, strong, calloused. Raphael carefully turned him over and supported his head, but Silas kept his eyes closed. That was better than opening them and not being able to see his brother's face.

"Si?" Raphael said shakily.

"Is he hurt?" Irima asked.

"I don't know. Who are you?"

"I'm his friend. We came a'lookin' for yer. Let me see him."

Raphael stiffened. "To do what?"

"To check him," Irima snapped. "Come on, what am I goin' to do, eh? Move over!"

Silas heard her kneel beside him. She ran her fingers over his arm, lighter than feathers. When she reached his wrist, he sucked in a breath.

"Ai, it's broken, yer daft fool," Irima muttered. There was a fumbling of fabric, then she held a thick twig along the back of his hand and bound it in place. "Try not to move that, alrigh'?"

Silas groaned and tried to nod, but his head hurt too much.

"Raph?" he said softly.

"Aye, I'm here," Raphael assured him. "What was thou thinking? How could you disappear?"

"No time," Silas mumbled. "I'm sorry… We need to get out of here!"

"You can't move like this," Raphael said. "Don't worry. We're safe."

"We're not. The demons…"

"It's alright. Don't be afraid. There are no demons."

Silas froze. "There are! I saw them!"

"Nay, nay, listen," said Raphael. "There *are* beings here, but they aren't demons. Everything we have been told is… well, not completely wrong, but… I met them. They are not what you think – what anybody thinks."

"What?" Silas cried. "Raph, they're evil! What have they done to thee?"

"Nothing."

"We can't stay hither! We must go! Now!"

"Calm thee!" Raphael insisted. "Look at me. Open thy eyes."

Silas tensed. "Nay. My… my head hurts."

Raphael stayed quiet. Silas bit the inside of his cheek. He never admitted when he was in pain. Even when he had caught a cold and could barely heft a sickle, he had carried on without complaint. His brother would see right through this.

"Silas," Raphael said firmly. "Open thy eyes."

"Do it," Irima whispered. "Show him. Let him behold what they did."

Silas drew a deep breath, bracing himself, then did as she said. He looked out into darkness, and raised his hand, so Raphael could see the mark.

Raphael's muscles became as solid as stone.

"What is this?" he cried.

"I came hither, to try and appease the demons," Silas

210

explained. "But the one I met struck me down thus. Raph, for God's sake, do you understand? We must go, before they hurt you, too!"

Raphael's breathing grew hard. Silas stilled in alarm. He had never heard his brother sound so angry.

Raphael slid his arms under Silas and lifted him. Silas sighed in relief. He had seen sense; they would return to the Wall, escape this place…

"Where are yer goin'?" Irima suddenly shrieked. "That's the wrong way!"

"It's not," Raphael growled. He stormed through the forest, down the slope. Dread chilled Silas's blood. If they were heading *downhill*, then that could only lead to the lake.

"What are you doing?" he cried.

"Hush," said Raphael. Then he raised his voice and bellowed, "*Merrin!*"

Silas flinched. Raphael never shouted. Ever.

The ground levelled out. Silas smelled dampness; heard the soft whisper of waving rushes and lapping water. Then the sun's heat vanished completely, and Raphael's footsteps took on a peculiar echo. They had entered a cave.

"Where art thou taking me?" Silas demanded. "Raph, what are you doing?"

Raphael ignored him. "Show your face! What is the meaning of this? Didst thee do this? Hath thee blinded my brother?"

Something shivered. It sounded like some kind of membrane. Then came more footsteps, inhumanly light.

"I hoped thou would not see this."

Panic set Silas's body alight. He knew that voice.

"*Nay!*" he screamed. He kicked and scrambled, trying to

get free, but Raphael didn't let go of him. "Get back! Raph, keep away from it!"

"Lie still," Raphael hissed. "I won't let her harm you."

"'Tis too late for that!" Irima cried. "What is that thing? Oh, sweet Lord in Heaven…"

"Peace," the demon said softly. "Raphael speaks truth. I mean no harm. Not to any of you."

Silas whimpered in terror. The creature was definitely the same one which he had ensnared that night. There was no malice in its voice now, but he would never forget that lyrical tone, undercut with darkness.

"Answer me," Raphael snapped. "Is this thy doing?"

The demon sighed. "Aye."

"And you didn't think to inform me?"

"I didn't think there would be a need to."

"Raph, why are you talking to it?" Silas whispered frantically. "We must go!"

"We're not going anywhere until this is done!" Raphael said. "Why didn't you tell me? Did you think I would leave? Just like what you wanted all along?"

"I kept secret to spare thee," the demon said. "One more night. And then, as I promised I would lift one affliction, I would have done so for the other."

"But you did this to him when he came hither?" Raphael demanded. "Is this what you would have done to all of us? Just like how you drove Adrian Atégo to insanity?"

"Please listen," the demon cried. "I'm sorry! I tell thee, once again, and I mean it! I know I have done wrong, so many times, and thou knoweth it too. But thou also knows how I have pledged to end it. This time tomorrow, it shall be over. Raphael, of all the conviction thou hath placed in me these past nights, I beg of you, grant me that one final shred of trust, even if you never do so again."

Raphael didn't reply. More blood welled in Silas's mouth. Frightened of drawing more attention, he swallowed it rather than spitting it out. It tasted awful; dried his throat like sand. What was happening?

"What would you do?" Raphael asked shakily.

The demon walked closer. "What I did to thee. I shall heal him."

"Don't listen!" Silas hissed. "It tried to murder me!"

"And for that, I apologise, Silas Atégo," the demon said gently. "Thou can thank thy brother for this. Give me your wrist."

Silas cradled it against his chest.

"I won't hurt you."

"Nay! Lies!"

"It's alright, Si," Raphael whispered. "Do you think I would still be here if it were not?"

"Don't!" Silas protested. "Oh, God, Raph, please! It's evil magic! What payment will be asked in return?"

"I ask for nothing, save you remaining here until nightfall," said the demon. "And magic is neither good nor evil; only its intention. Now, don't move."

Cold fingers suddenly appeared on Silas's mouth. He recoiled with a yelp, but Raphael held him firm. His lip tingled as though he had rubbed it with nettles. Then the swelling lessened; the cut grew smaller. Within moments, the leftover blood was the only trace there had been a wound at all.

"What is this?" Irima gasped.

But the demon didn't reply. The fingers moved down, to Silas's wrist, and the same sensation swept through his skin. He whimpered in pain, but the creature didn't release him. He felt his bones moving of their own accord, slotting back together like a puzzle.

"Almost there," the demon muttered.

The bone clicked. Silas jolted in alarm, then the demon untied the scrap of material and let the branch fall to the ground.

"'Tis done."

"Thank you," said Raphael. "Now heal his eyes."

"I cannot. Not yet. Thou must wait until tonight."

"Raph, I can live with this!" Silas protested. "I don't trust that thing!"

"She's not a thing, Si. She is no demon," Raphael said. "Trust me, if not her."

"And thou might live, but it will drive thee mad in the end," said the creature. "Listen to me. It will take time yet for me to be completely comfortable around thy family, but you committed only an innocent mistake. My own mistake was different, and I shall undo it. And... I ask thy forgiveness. Your brother has granted it to me, but I beg it of you, too."

Silas couldn't believe what he was hearing. *Forgiveness?*

"I pardon thee for coming here," it continued. "And for pulling me from the Lake. Wilt *thou* pardon *me?*"

Silas swallowed nervously. The words caught in his throat like a half-eaten morsel. This was hardly what he had expected to find upon crossing the Wall again. But the more the creature spoke, the less bitter fury he heard in its voice. In fact, he heard something which sounded almost human. It wasn't like the Valley-folk, but, he supposed, neither were the Peregrini. And had they not overturned all notions of what he had believed?

This being might have attacked him, but he still had his life. It might have blinded him, but only during the day. Matters could have been so much worse.

"Aye," Silas said quietly. He wasn't sure if he believed it wholeheartedly, but he would trust in Raphael. His brother had never let him down.

"Thank you," the creature said.

"Thou should remain in here, shaded," Raphael said tightly. "I must speak with my brother. He deserves to know everything."

He clutched Silas tighter, as though he were no older than a babe, and carried him away into the forest, with Irima hurrying along behind.

Silas felt the sun on his face. A soft breeze whistled through the trees, and he tried not to shiver. Raphael wouldn't be so calm if there was anything to fear.

"I can walk," he insisted.

"No need," Raphael said, setting him down. "Sit here. We can be still awhile."

Silas swept his hands over the ground. He felt grass, dry leaves, tiny stones. The air smelled cool and damp. Nearby, the waves of the lake swept back and forth in a chorus of tiny whispers. A frog croaked and leapt into the water with a plop.

"Are you alright?" Raphael asked.

"Aye," Silas said shakily. "Irima, are you here?"

"Right behind yer," she replied.

"A Cart-girl," Raphael said in surprise. "How came you by her?"

"She cared for me," Silas explained. "But *thee!* That demon tried to kill me!"

"She didn't take kindly to me, either," Raphael admitted. "But she's no demon, Si. The demons don't exist."

"Nonsense!"

"It's true. Her name is Merrin. She's a Queen. That's one

of the reasons she was so angry with thee. That and... well, something else. I'll tell thee. But they are just another race of people. Like thy friend here."

"*I* don't have green hair," Irima snapped. "Those are what yer speak of? Why yer built that there Wall?"

Silas fell silent. The creature was a Queen? Such a thing existed among them?

He moved his hand out, feeling for Raphael. His brother took hold of it and squeezed his fingers.

"She'll lift thy affliction, Si," Raphael said. "The family curse, too."

"She knows about that?"

"Aye. In many ways."

Silas turned his head, then bared his teeth and drove his free hand into the ground.

"How I wish I could see thee!" he cried.

"A few hours yet, and yer shall be able," Irima said gently, but her words brought little comfort to Silas. All at once, the events of the past few days slammed upon him like rain in winter.

"Raph, I'm so sorry I left," he said. "I didn't mean to be gone for so long. I never meant for any of this to happen! I just... Father Fortésa told me... Oh, there's so much to say! I don't know where to start!"

"At the beginning," Raphael said gently. "Tell me, and then I'll tell thee."

Silas drew a deep breath that filled his lungs, and began to speak. He relayed his journey across the Wall, taking the boat out and catching the creature, what it had done to him, and how he had been rescued by Irima's people. Raphael listened quietly, only asking the occasional question. And when Silas was done, it was his turn to speak.

Silas's mouth fell open at what he heard. By the time all was said, the sun had climbed higher and the heat beat down upon his shoulders like a whip. It almost didn't feel like the same sun he had lived under all his life. How could anything be the same now? How could anything be *normal?*

"*She* was the one who cursed us?" he whispered.

"She had her reasons," Raphael said. "I don't agree with all of them. Not in the slightest. But I've already spoken with her about it. She is contrite, and it is all in the past now. We must remain just a few hours longer, and then we shall be safe."

"But we won't," Silas argued. "We have naught hither. The house is destroyed. Ma and the others escaped with only the clothes on their backs. We... we cannot return to Fanchlow. We *can't.*"

Raphael's grip grew tighter. "It's truly so terrible?"

"Aye. Father Fortésa hath turned all the neighbours against us. I don't know what they might have done, had I not arrived when I did. It's not only the house. The donkey is gone, too. If they haven't taken our chickens and crops yet, then they shall."

"Perhaps we could go to our kin in Ullswick."

Silas shook his head. A horrid realisation drew itself over him like ice.

"It's not enough," he said. "We'll never be accepted. We'll never be safe. Not with our name. And when they drive us from Ullswick, where then shall we go?"

Irima suddenly leaned forward and took Silas's other hand.

"Come with us," she said.

"Back to thy campsite?" Silas frowned.

"And yonder," Irima said. "When we leave, join us. We'll

217

take care o' yer. We'll take yer to a kinder place than 'ere, where thy name means nothin'. Or yer can stay with us, if yer want. Silas, yer know we be gracious hosts."

"Leave the Valley?" Raphael said in a small voice. "That's… We can't…"

"Yer can," Irima insisted. "If the two o' yer can come 'ere, break all your rules an' still be standin', then yer can put one foot in front o' the other, an' walk through those mountains."

"That's not the same," Raphael said. "We know this place. It's our home."

"It ain't," Irima said firmly. "Yer family is yer home."

Silas nodded. "She's right."

Raphael grasped his shoulder. "Don't be hasty."

"I'm not. I'm being realistic. There's nothing for us here, Raph. But I hath seen the kindness of the Peregrini. It exceeds all Valley-folk I've ever known. Thou asked me to trust that creature in the cave; that it will restore my sight and lift the curse? Then I ask thee to trust the Wanderers."

"But what of Abraham and Nalina? Couldst thou leave them behind in good conscience?"

"I can sort that," Irima said. "Once we're back, I'll ask me uncle to send a convoy down south. We'll collect yer kin an' ask them to join us. All thy family will be welcome. I promise."

Silas licked his lips nervously. It was a massive decision – one which he never would have imagined making, least of all now, after everything that had happened. But the more he thought about it, the stronger his conviction became. There wasn't really a choice anymore. Perhaps their family had ceased belonging to the Elitland a hundred years ago, when their forefather had made his terrible mistake. And now, at last, it was time to own what everybody else had always known.

"Raph, thou art the head of the family now," Silas said. "'Tis your decision."

Raphael didn't speak. He let go of Silas's hand and groaned loudly, as though the weight of the entire world had been thrown upon his shoulders.

"I might be the eldest, but you are my equal. We shall decide together. Dost thou believe this is the best course of action?"

"I do. The Valley is just that: a valley. A place. *We* are what is important."

Raphael let out a huge sigh. "Then I am in agreement."

"Really?"

"Aye. We shall stay until tonight, so Merrin can do her work. And then..."

Raphael broke off. Silas frowned.

"What's wrong?" he asked.

"Nothing," Raphael said quickly. "I just..."

"I know," Irima cut in. "'Tis not only the thought o' leavin' which troubles ye, is it?"

Raphael chuckled. "Nay, it's not. It's... *her*. Merrin. She hath hated us so deeply, but I don't know if I have the heart to do the same in return. Not even after all she has done."

"Thou hast never had the heart to hate anybody."

"But can others say the same? If we leave, we are the only ones who know the truth. It shall all continue. The Wall shall always stand. There will always be *this*."

Silas reached out, found his brother's shoulder, and squeezed it.

"That cannot be our responsibility anymore," he said softly. "If she is truly as long-lived as thou claims, then perhaps she can take up that mantle. If she is willing. Has all this not proven how much things can change?"

"There yer go," Irima said, and Silas heard the smile in her voice. "*That's* the only thing that never changes."

She slipped her hand into Silas's. He nodded to himself, then turned his face towards the lake, listening to the waves and the frogs. A cloud passed overhead and the air grew heavier, cooler.

One more day. Then it would all end. But he dared to hope, deep in his heart, that wouldn't be a terrible thing.

Chapter XVI
The Rise

AND THE EARTH WAS WRAPPED IN A STARRY NIGHT,
AND THE ONLY LIGHTS THAT THE EYES MIGHT MARK
WERE THE COLD STILL SPHERES OF A MOON SNOW-WHITE;
EV'N THEN, OF THE DEW AND THE CRYSTAL AIR,
AND THE MOONRAY MILD, WERE THE ASRAI MADE;
AND THEY WALKED AND MUSED IN THE MIDNIGHT AIR.

Robert Williams Buchanan

The day passed in silence. Merrin sat surrounded by it, her dress spread to cover herself from any wandering sunbeams. Guilt beat against her like a whip. She had hoped to spare Raphael the pain of knowing what she had done to his brother. But, she supposed, it was no less than she deserved, to be faced with the result of her own deed. A sharp stab of anger still flared when she thought of Silas, but it was smaller than before; tampered with shame and pity.

Never mind his hair. Never mind his name. He was just a frightened, misguided child. Just like all of them.

Just like her.

She heaved a sigh, and slowly waved her fin back and forth, matching it to the speed of her fingers as she drummed them over her leg. She half-hoped Raphael might come back, but she knew he wouldn't. She had done too much.

She rested her head against a pillow of moss growing on the cave wall. Better to sleep than to think.

Dreams swelled around her, and she floated above them, snapping in and out of consciousness. She was in the cave, but no longer alone. Arms were around her waist, holding her close, pressing her against a warm chest. Then those same arms were moving through the water beside her. She swam with him, dived with his hand in hers. In the wonderful, weightless dark, she kissed those lying lips.

Merrin, wilt thou be mine?

She didn't wake up. She held onto the moment, and looked straight into Adrian's eyes. Even now, her heart leapt as she beheld him. So much time had passed, but she could never forget it: the angles of his cheekbones, the mole beside his nose, the luscious timbre of his voice. So sweet, so seductive. So false.

And it was *only* him. No Raphael. No Silas. Nothing of any who had come after him. Just him, and her, alone.

Nay, she said. *Never, ever again.*

Each time she thought it, something broke inside her. Stone split. Ice cracked. One by one, bricks fell from the wall she had built around herself.

And love has to my heart gone
With a spear so keen,
Night and day my blood doth drain
And my heart, to death it aches.

Merrin opened her eyes. A reddened land greeted her

beyond the cave mouth. Dusk was sweeping in, and between the scarlet sky and the deep purple amarants on the ground, it was as though all of Delamere was ablaze.

She crawled closer, careful to keep back so the dying rays wouldn't touch her. Through the trees, she glimpsed the Lake, glowing like a bronze mirror. Every leaf was edged with gold; every blade of grass waved perfectly in the soft breeze. Deep in the forest, nyhtegales began their song.

A tear rolled down Merrin's cheek. In all her times above the surface, she had never seen it so beautiful.

She watched until the Western Ridge swallowed the sun, and then finally stepped outside. Each time she brought her foot down, she thought she might fall straight through the earth. Never had she felt so heavy, as though her entire body had turned to stone.

She walked in the direction Raphael had taken, and after several minutes, she came across him. Where the ground swept into a small dell, he was sleeping; Silas beside him, the black-haired girl nearby. Merrin supposed Silas had fallen asleep first, because Raphael's cloak was spread over him.

She smiled to herself. They looked so serene, lying there like little mice. So vulnerable. So innocent.

"Merrin."

She turned around, and spotted Dylana, water streaming off her hair. Penro came behind her, a smile etched onto his face.

Merrin's heart swelled. She hurried to the Lake and threw her arms around her mother.

"You did it," Dylana whispered.

"Thank you," Merrin said, her voice breaking. "And Penro... Both of you, I owe you so much!"

"Thou owes nothing, Your Majesty," Penro replied

respectfully, but his eyes still flashed with knowledge.

Dylana released Merrin, then surveyed the slumbering humans.

"Two more?" she noted.

Merrin nodded. "His brother, and a friend."

Dylana gave her a pointed look. "The brother who pulled thee up here?"

"The same," said Merrin tightly.

"And thou hast not harmed him?"

"Nay."

Dylana smiled. "I'm proud of you."

"Thou doesn't sound surprised," said Merrin. "You knew, didn't you?"

"That the other boy would return?" said Dylana. "Nay. But I hoped you would refrain from causing harm regardless, and you have proven me correct. My sweet girl… My wonderful girl. Thy father is so glad."

Merrin gasped. "Thou spoke to him? In the Tomb Garden?"

"Indeed," said Dylana, as she caressed her daughter's face. "And he shall be with you tonight, as shall I. All of us. Are you ready?"

Merrin turned her eyes skyward. The moon had risen, full and bright, and it lit up the night in liquid silver. Already, she could feel its power soaking into her.

"Aye," she said. "Is everyone else?"

"Indeed, Your Majesty," said Penro. "Upon thy word, we shall call the Rise."

Merrin nodded, then glanced over her shoulder at the humans.

"I have one request first," she said. "I wish for them to be present. When the coronation is concluded, there is something I must do."

Dylana raised her eyebrows. She knew exactly what Merrin was talking about.

"Very well," she smiled. "Penro and I shall await thee on the island. But first… Thou hast lived in that dress for days. 'Tis no garment for such a night as this."

She raised her hands towards the moon, until they glowed white under its light. Then she swept them across her daughter's head. Merrin closed her eyes as the magic flowed over her. A crystal circlet threaded itself through her hair. Her gown lengthened; the gossamer fabric bloomed into a full skirt and huge bell sleeves. Finally, Penro approached and handed her a belt of braided rushes, which she fastened around her hips.

"You look radiant, Merrin," he whispered.

Merrin smiled at him. She touched his cheek with the tips of her fingers.

"Thank you both," she said. "I couldn't have done this without you."

"You could," Penro replied softly. "Because you have. But I dare say you could not have done it without him."

He stepped away from Merrin and followed Dylana. Merrin watched until they reached the water, then turned around and regarded Raphael. The moment had come at last. Not just to take up her mantle, but to cast off the weight of the old one.

She gently shook Raphael awake. He rolled over and stared at her as though she had struck him.

"My God!" he gasped. "You look…"

"'Tis time," Merrin said. "Wilt thou still be my guest? I extend the offer to all of you."

Raphael swallowed. "Aye. Your Majesty."

"Then rouse thy companions. I bid thee all to come hither."

Raphael quickly tapped Silas's shoulder. Merrin watched as he opened his eyes. Sure enough, they were no longer the milky white which she had first seen, but the same warm walnut brown as his brother's.

When Silas saw her, he shuffled away in fright, bumping into the girl as he moved. She sat bolt upright in alarm.

"It's alright," Raphael said to them both. "We're in no danger. Oh, Si, thy eyes! Can you see?"

Silas nodded. "Aye. It's gone."

"And ye shall not be blind for any day longer," Merrin promised.

She beckoned them to follow. As she walked, her skirt trailed over the ground, as thin and light as spiderwebs. The humans kept their distance, to avoid treading on it – but Merrin suspected it was for more than that. Silas and the girl were still frightened of her. Perhaps, deep down, Raphael was, too.

She might have revelled in that once, but now, it just felt hollow. She looked over her shoulder. At once, all three of them stopped.

"Don't," Merrin said. "Please don't be afraid."

Silas fixed his eyes on her. Never had she seen a stare which burned like that. He was sharp and firm in all the places Raphael was soft and welcoming.

"I don't think I shall ever *not* be afraid of thee," Silas said.

"And I shall bear that burden," said Merrin. "But no harm shall come to you."

Silas pursed his lips. Beside him, the girl slipped her hand into his.

"Come on," Raphael whispered. "We'll be alright."

Merrin managed a small smile. He spoke to his brother the same way he had spoken to her: full of respect, but laced with kindness. And sure enough, Silas relented. Raphael nodded towards Merrin, and she led them onwards, to the bank.

Raphael gasped in wonder. The surface of the Lake was shimmering, and with each moment, Asræ stepped through: a crowd of green bodies, all dressed in immaculate white clothes. There were men, women, children of every age, rising up one after another. They looked at her, some calling out her name and sighing with relief. Dylana and Penro would have told them that she was safe, but to see her again with their own eyes brought smiles unlike any Merrin had seen.

They began to dance. Each movement was perfect – they spun across the water in a flurry of skirts and green hair, slipping under each other's arms and leaping into the air. Even Merrin had almost forgotten how beautiful the sight could be. In her cold fury, she had carried herself with the same icy magnificence as a harsh winter's frost, but now, she realised just how different she had been from the rest of her people. There was such warmth, such authenticity. It radiated like a sweet summer breeze, and she felt it soaking into her, just as it had with Raphael.

Love. This was what it was. Not an empty promise, not a hidden blade waiting to strike the heart, but this.

The old boats caught Merrin's eye. She swept a hand towards the nearest one.

"Get inside and come with me."

Silas stiffened. "I don't think that's–"

"It's fine, Si," Raphael whispered. "Come, climb in."

He waited until his brother and the girl were seated, then shoved the boat down to the water. The Lake took the weight into Her gentle embrace; Silas didn't even need to counterbalance it as

Raphael leapt over the side. The two of them each took up an oar and began to row.

Merrin stepped onto the surface and walked alongside them. When the Asræ saw her coming, they parted like a curtain, all smiling and bowing their heads. Merrin straightened her spine, waved her fin gently back and forth. Every single person here knew what she had done, but even so, they had never ceased believing in her – her ability to rule, her ability to survive.

Perhaps even her ability to let go.

She turned towards the island. Lachlan and the guards flanked it, while Dylana and Penro stood beneath the willow tree. Merrin's heart fluttered when she saw them. The Lake opened before her in a sweeping silver carpet. This was the moment. *Her* moment.

"Wait here," she said to Raphael. She ran her hands over the Royal Bands, swallowed her nerves, then glanced at Lachlan and nodded once.

"Asræ!" he shouted. "I bid thee greet thy Queen!"

At once, her people moved aside, forming a shimmering moonlit path for Merrin to walk. They all bowed as one; so synchronised, so perfect, it seemed like the movement of a single giant creature. Merrin glanced at them as she passed, at every face she knew, every pair of eyes she had looked into as she grew into womanhood.

She stepped off the surface. The island's amarants swallowed her feet up to the ankles. She tensed, acutely aware of the great crowd behind her. She could feel them watching, and their silence seemed a thousand times worse than if they had shouted. That silence held all the words and knowledge of the world. Of all the hurt she had dealt, all the mistakes she had made to trap herself up here. She was the fool who had fallen for the false love, and almost doomed herself…

"Don't think of them," Penro whispered. "Forget everything else, and just focus on me."

Merrin sucked in a breath through her teeth, and nodded.

"Asræ," Dylana said loudly, "here I present unto thee Her Majesty Merrin, daughter of King Zandor. Do you accept her as your reigning Queen, the Voice of the Lake, from this night until the end of her nights?"

The Asræ replied, in one voice, "This I do."

Merrin breathed a sigh of relief, then sank onto her knees, and spread her arms wide, so everyone around her could see the Royal Bands. Dylana towered above her. She no longer looked like Merrin's mother, but the powerful magic-weaver she was; the one who, millenia ago, had seen their people through the mountains to the Elitland.

"Dost thou come here of thy own free will, to stand in the place of thy father, King Zandor?"

Merrin swallowed. "This I do."

Her voice shook, but she held firm. Dylana shot her the quickest of winks.

"Dost thou solemnly swear to take thy title, thy residence in the Queen's Room, and to wear the Royal Bands around thy wrists until thy dying moment?"

"This I do."

"And dost thou solemnly swear to rule justly and fairly, without discrimination or unfounded judgment, and to grant care to all who stand present here tonight?"

Merrin bit the inside of her cheek. Every part of her wanted to turn and look at Raphael. But she didn't. She just kept her eyes straight ahead, holding onto the dream; the moment when she had finally denied Adrian's hold over her.

"This I do," she said.

Penro beamed. Then he reached behind him and withdrew a circlet, woven from amarants and reeds.

"Turn around," he whispered.

Merrin did so. She gazed straight down the centre of the gathering, to the little boat. Raphael, Silas and the girl were all staring at her, their mouths agape.

Pride swelled in Merrin's chest. She had extended the invitation tightly, as the closest thing to a peace offering she could think of. But now she saw the Atégos sitting there, she knew it had been the right thing.

Penro placed the circlet onto her head. It was only a symbolic crown – the true mark of the Monarch were the Bands she already wore – but Merrin carried the weight of its meaning as though it were made of gold. This headdress, made of the royal flowers, showed how she was now the true Voice of the Lake.

She stood as still as she could; forced herself to project all she was becoming. She could almost feel her eyes taking on a new shine. This was a pocket in time, which would now always be hers. She had done it.

When Dylana spoke, her voice brimmed with joy.

"Asræ, under the moon above, atop the great Lake below, and with honour to all our forefathers, I present unto thee Her Majesty, Queen Merrin."

"Hail, Queen Merrin!" Lachlan shouted. "Long may she reign!"

A chorus of cheers rose into the air, and like a spreading ripple, the Asræ bowed. Penro and Dylana did the same. And then, so did Raphael. Silas and Irima threw him an uncertain glance, but followed suit.

"Thank you," Merrin said. "I shall do everything in my

power to be the best Queen I can. But... I know this is the time when we would celebrate. But first, I ask you to bear witness."

Raphael looked up. Merrin kept her eyes on him as she spoke.

"It's no secret that the humans' Wall is a result of my actions. It is also no secret as to why. I... would like to tell you all that I will allow misdeeds to pass. As proof of this, tonight, the descendants of Adrian Atégo are among thee. They are innocent, and I shall make them so again. I shall lift the curse I laid down upon their line a century past."

The Asræ muttered among themselves. Merrin heard it as though from a distance. But she didn't pay any mind. She just walked off the island, across the water, towards the boat.

"Hold out thy hand," she said to Silas.

Silas's cheeks turned pale, but he did as he was told. Merrin turned it over so she could see his palm. The flesh glistened where she had touched it. In a heartbeat, she remembered how firmly she had grabbed him, how ferociously she had forced her anger into him...

She pressed her own hands around it, and drew the moon's power into herself. It was more than simple light. It was the star beyond stars: the most splendid one of all, which pulled at water and breathed life into the night.

She pushed. Silas gasped and went to pull away, but Merrin didn't let go. She gritted her teeth until her entire jaw ached. She hadn't focused so intensely in so long. But the time above the Lake had dragged itself through her bones... Would she even have the strength to undo both curses?

Then she felt more power entwining with hers, and looked around. Her heart swelled. All the Asræ's hands were aglow. Even Dylana and Penro had joined in. Dylana met Merrin's eyes, and she smiled.

The Rise was the height of their magic. They had all seen her intent. And now they would help her realise it.

The light flowed into the water, until the entire Lake shone silver. Then it shot towards the boat, and into Raphael and Silas. Merrin heard them both cry out. The girl said something frantic, but Merrin didn't listen. She just kept her attention on Silas's hand, forcing the curses away like a dark mud stain; harder, *harder*…

And then, in a heartbeat, she felt it break.

Silas yelped. Raphael snatched hold of him, panting, and the two of them fell backwards into the bottom of the boat.

"What did yer do?" the girl shrieked. She tapped Silas on the shoulder. He stared at her, then at his palm.

Merrin smiled. Just as she had intended, the brand had vanished. His flesh looked no different to how it did before he crossed the Wall.

Raphael sat up. He grasped Silas's hand and stared at it.

"'Tis gone!" he gasped. "Are you alright?"

Silas nodded woodenly. "I think so."

Raphael turned to Merrin. "It's done? Thou healed his eyes?"

"Not just his eyes," she replied. "Thy curses are lifted."

"From both of us?"

"From *all* of you. And all your sons to come. Just as I promised."

A huge smile broke across Raphael's face. Then he scrambled forward and threw his arms around Merrin.

There was a subdued gasp from the crowd, and a few light-hearted chuckles, but nothing in malevolence. Merrin froze. She had a mind to push him off, to snarl at him, to slap him… But instead, she breathed deeply, and allowed him to hug her.

"Thank you so much," Raphael choked out.

"You are welcome," Merrin said woodenly. "Enough, now."

Raphael swiftly let go. "I'm sorry. Your Majesty."

Merrin shook her head. "Don't call me that. Thou art my guests." She reached out and took Raphael's hands. "However… I'm afraid thou cannot linger. The ageing of my people is something sacred, which I dare not break the tradition of by having you witness it. And it would do thee well to move now, whilst the moon is high and the night is young. Otherwise, you shall be seen crossing the Wall."

Raphael's grip tightened. His eyes darted back and forth over her face.

"We shan't see thee again," he said.

Merrin swallowed. "Nay."

"But…"

"Thou cannot tell me you are suddenly against leaving now."

"It's not that," said Raphael. "I… I'm afraid. Everything is gone."

A sob stole up his throat and choked him. At once, Silas reached out and grasped his shoulder in comfort.

Merrin shook her head slowly. "Thy life is not gone. Surely you realise that you shall meet no foe worse than I."

She released him with one hand so she could take Silas's as well.

"I'm sorry our dealings were so harsh," she said, "but I must thank you equally in part for them. Thy curses have been broken tonight, and you made that happen, just as much as my people. Do not fret, and do not fear. You shall be safe."

Tears of relief and gratitude rolled down Raphael's cheeks. At the sight of them, the final lumps of ice within Merrin's heart melted away. Such respect, this boy had managed to earn, in just a few short days!

She plucked an amarant from her circlet and slipped it into the front of Raphael's tunic. Then she leaned in, pushed his hair aside, and kissed his forehead.

"*A sweet kiss of thy mouth may be my cure,*" she whispered. "Now, go. All of you. Take with you the lessons you have learned, and plant a new seed, as I will."

Raphael smiled. The depth of it ripped Merrin's breath away. In that moment, he could not have looked more different to Adrian. That grin was so deep, so sincere, it could have brought spring after the harshest winter.

"God bless thee and thy people," Raphael whispered.

"Bless you," Silas agreed. "I shall be grateful to you for as long as I live."

Merrin nodded. "Likewise."

No more words were spoken. Merrin kept her eyes on Raphael as he bowed one final time, then grasped the oar and began to row towards the bank. She stood still, watching. The brothers hauled the boat out of the water; Silas took the girl's hand in his and waited for Raphael.

The eldest Atégo stared across the Lake, at the moon, at the island, at all the Asræ. Then he vanished among the dark trees of Delamere.

Merrin's knees knocked together. It was done. The wound would always be there, but this was a cleaner sting, and she would learn to live with it.

Chapter XVII
Homecoming

AFOOT AND LIGHT-HEARTED I TAKE TO THE OPEN ROAD,
HEALTHY, FREE, THE WORLD BEFORE ME.
THE LONG BROWN PATH BEFORE ME
LEADING WHEREVER I CHOOSE.
HENCEFORTH I WHIMPER NO MORE,
POSTPONE NO MORE, NEED NOTHING.

Walt Whitman

Raphael, Silas and Irima walked through the forest hand in hand. Raphael didn't dare look back, not even for a moment. Every single step across the amarant-laden ground was a step further into an unknown abyss. He wasn't just leaving the forbidden west. Even after they reached the eastern side, he would be leaving the only home that he had ever known.

The Wall appeared. Raphael climbed it first, then reached down to help Silas and Irima. They sat astride it for a moment, catching their breath.

"Are you both alrigh'?" Irima whispered.

"Aye," Silas muttered. He looked at his hand again. "I

can't believe it's gone."

"It shall be strange, not seein' yer walkin' around with a stick!" Irima said. She spoke jovially, trying to lighten their spirits, but Raphael still felt the weight upon his shoulders. Nothing would be the same now. Nothing, ever.

He squinted towards Fanchlow. Where their house had been was now just a pile of smouldering timbers. The flames had burned out, but if Raphael looked closely, he could see the redness of embers.

"No sign of anybody waiting for us," said Silas.

Raphael nodded in agreement. "We should go there. Salvage anything we can find."

"I don't think there will be much left," Silas said. "But… I want to go somewhere, too. On the way. I want to visit Pap."

Raphael gave him a small smile and squeezed his hand. "Then we shall."

They clambered down the other side of the Wall and crept across the meadow. The village lanterns beckoned in the distance, but Raphael and Silas didn't need them – the moon made the entire Valley as bright as day.

They came to the river, and walked down its course until they reached a narrow spot near the mill. The brothers leapt across first; held out their hands to catch Irima. Then they headed around the side of Fanchlow. All the houses were dark – there weren't even signs of rushlights burning inside. But Raphael still placed each foot with care, terrified that the slightest noise would raise the alarm. Based on what Silas had told him, he wasn't about to take any chances.

To his relief, nobody appeared. So he led the way towards the church, and crept through the gate. Irima hung back as Raphael and Silas approached the freshest grave. A wooden crucifix was stuck into the earth to mark the spot, but even in the darkness, Raphael could tell it had been moved. Somebody must have kicked it down before it was set upright again.

His heart wrenched. Even as an innocent, and even in death, their father hadn't been safe from hatred.

"I don't want to leave him," Raphael whispered.

"Nor do I," said Silas, "but what choice do we have?"

Raphael shook his head. The grave blurred as tears filled his eyes.

"'Tis not just him, though. It's all who came before him. Our grandfather. His father. Even the one Merrin knew. Our blood is of this land, just like everyone else."

"Aye," Silas said softly, "but did the first Atégo not need to travel here, once? There's a first time for everything."

"I know. I just never thought that would fall upon *us*."

"But what future did we have here, truly? There is more than jeering and throwing stones. Pap once admitted to me how difficult it was for him to find Ma. After all we've done, who would marry thee, Raph? Or me? We could never have lasted hither. Never."

Raphael bit his lip. He knew Silas was right. But that didn't make it any easier.

He laid his hand over the grave. The soil was still loose.

"I'm sorry, Pap," he whispered. "I tried. We both did. I wish thou were still here with us! God, Si, if only he had held on for one more week…"

"I know," Silas said sadly. "I know."

Sorrow consumed Raphael like a wave. How could it have only been a week? He had been so focused on caring for the family, searching for Silas, accompanying Merrin; there had been hardly any room for his own grief. But now, it struck him in the heart and refused to recede. A cloud settled over his shoulders, and he lowered his head and cried.

Silas didn't speak. He didn't need to. He just stood close, not letting go of his brother. Raphael pulled him into an embrace and wept against his shoulder.

Irima approached. The decorations in her hair tinkled with each step.

"Are you alrigh'?" she asked quietly.

Raphael sniffed his tears away. "Nay. But I will be."

He turned back to the grave and made the sign of the cross over his chest. Silas did the same. Then, fighting against a weight which threatened to crush him, Raphael got to his feet, and the three of them walked away.

They crept through the streets, towards the house. Some of the timbers still held the basic shape, but the wattle and daub walls were completely gone. Everything inside had been swallowed by the flames. Raphael spotted the charred frame of a cot; warped cauldrons and cooking utensils. Nails protruded from the ash like thorns. The stones of the hearth had turned black with soot. The only thing which had escaped the blaze was the rose bush.

"And I suggested cutting that back," Silas muttered, running his fingers over one of the flowers. "Do you see anything we can save?"

"Nay," said Raphael. His voice sounded small and empty, like a raindrop falling into a cave.

"Well, yer have the most important thing," Irima said gently. "Up at the corrie. We should go, afore anyone spots us hangin' around 'ere."

Silas nodded. "She's right. Come on, Raph."

Raphael's heart leapt into his mouth. He breathed deeply,

trying to keep himself under control, as he looked at the house one last time. This was where they had all been born, had all grown, for generation after generation.

He turned his back, steeled himself, and followed Silas and Irima towards the campsite. The ground rose into a slope, steeper and steeper, until his calves burned from the effort of scaling it. He didn't take his hand away from the front of his tunic. He hated the idea of the amarant slipping out and being lost among the shadows.

Tents appeared, glowing in the darkness, lit from the inside by flickering lamps. Raphael spotted horses too, and tents and carts. Irima and Silas immediately quickened their pace, all but dragging him onwards. They paused only to snatch a quick drink at the lake in the bottom of the corrie.

"Irima!" a man called.

Irima looked up, then ran to him. "Uncle! I didn't realise yer might be awake!"

"*Awake?*" the man repeated incredulously. "Thy mindless girl! I haven't slept! Yer gave me such fright! Don't yer ever run off like that without tellin' me! Dost hear, eh?"

Irima shied back. "I'm sorry. I just... I needed to help. Did yer see the fire?"

"Oh, I saw it. An' I saw to the folks who ran up 'ere to escape it. On *my* horse." The man pointedly turned his eyes on Silas. "But they were in need. I've put 'em in the sick-un's tent."

"Garrett, are they safe?" Silas asked frantically. "I'm sorry I took thy horse. I had to reach them swiftly."

"Ai, 'tis no worry," Garrett replied. "They're a little shaken, but fine. Stay 'ere."

He crossed to a tent further from the others, drew back the flap, and leaned inside.

"Ai, wake up. Yer sons are back."

There was an urgent scramble, then Araena stumbled out, followed by Mekina, Uriel and Selena. Raphael's heart melted when he saw them. They all looked exhausted, with their hair sticking in all directions and clothes smeared with ash, but they were alive.

He and Silas ran forward. The entire family threw their arms around each other, almost falling over with the force of it. Raphael planted kisses all over his mother's face. Never, in his whole life, had he been more grateful to see them.

"Thank you, Lord!" he whispered. "Ma, are you alright? Are you hurt? Mekina, thy face!"

"'Tis nothing," Mekina assured him, but she still touched the bruise on her face with a grimace. "Oh, God, Raph, I was so frightened! I thought thou wouldn't come back!"

Raphael shook his head. "I'll always come back," he assured, then glanced at Silas. "Both of us."

Araena burst into tears. She fell against him, trembling with shock. Raphael held her as tightly as he dared, worried that too much pressure might snap her like a twig. She had endured so much; they all had… But they were together now. Everybody was safe. Silas had been right. That was all that mattered.

More of the Cart-folk appeared from the other tents. They walked barefoot upon the grass, and were dressed in nightclothes: old shifts which had worn too thin to serve daytime use. They whispered among themselves, some pointing at Silas, but they all hung back, as though an invisible line had been drawn between them and the family.

Silas looked up at Garrett and Irima.

"Thank you," he said. "How can we ever repay thee?"

Garrett's face softened. "Well, yer all must stay in that

tent, like yer did. A few days, until yer be clean. That will be all."

"Uncle," said Irima, "May I suggest a repayment?"

"Go on."

"They've lost everythin'. I saw the house. There's nowt left, an' I fear for their safety, should they stay 'ere. Could they a'come wanderin' with us awhile? Even if it's only until we get out o' the mountains? An' they can repay with their labour along the way."

Garrett fell silent. Raphael watched carefully as his eyes moved over the family, one by one. Then they settled on Silas.

"Really proved a little troublemaker, ain't ye?" he muttered. "Very well. Yer can come along. If that's what yer want."

Raphael's heart swelled. Silas leapt to his feet and approached the Peregrini leader.

"Thou cometh from God in Heaven. I can't thank thee enough."

"Just promise no more o' this insanity, yer fool. Alrigh'?"

"There is one thing more," Irima said. "They have kin in the south. Can we fetch 'em and bring 'em along, too?"

Raphael eased his mother away and walked to Silas's side.

"Please, sir," he said. "They are but a man and his daughter, trapped among unforgiving neighbours. They may not wish to come. But my soul would be heavy to abandon them thus. They are good people."

Garrett sighed. "'Tis our way to believe that all people be good, unless they prove otherwise. How far south are we talkin'?"

"Ullswick. A two-day's walk, there and back."

Garrett sucked in a breath. "Ai, that's too long. It will be swifter on horses."

"I shall come too," Raphael said at once. "I know the way.

They'll listen to me. Oh, sir, thank you for all thou hast done!"

Garrett smiled at him. "I ain't no sir, lad. I just know a strugglin' soul when I see one. Same as ye, I think. Yer 'ave that look in yer eyes."

He clapped his hands and addressed the Peregrini.

"Everyone, 'tis all fine. Go back to sleep. Ai, Andreas, can I speak to yer? I've somethin' needin' to be done upon the morn."

He walked towards one of the men and gestured to the horses. Irima shot Silas a wink, then headed to one of the carts and began rummaging under the tarp.

Silas looked at Raphael, beaming.

"I told thee," he whispered. "You convinced me to put trust in that... Queen. Now you can put your trust in these folk. Who in Fanchlow ever treated us like this?"

Raphael nodded in agreement. "They are kind. This won't be easy for me, but I will be strong for thee."

"We'll be strong *together*," Silas insisted. "Thee, me, all of us. Wouldst thee wish me to come tomorrow?"

"Nay, stay here and mind the family," said Raphael. "They have been alone from both of us for too long. At least this means only one shall disappear."

"You're going away again?" Uriel whimpered. He ran to Raphael and grabbed him around the waist. "Nay, Raph! Please don't! I'm frightened!"

"So am I!" Selena said. "What if they come back for us?"

"They won't," Raphael promised. "Si and I walked by the house on the way here. Everybody is abed."

"They didn't come seeking us today, Selena," said Mekina quietly. "Our hosts have been... more generous than I expected."

She withdrew something from her pocket and passed it to Silas: a shimmering white ball on a leather thong, just like the beads Irima wore in her hair. He took it as though it was as precious as gold, and tied it around his neck.

Irima returned, with several slices of dried meat in her hands.

"'Tis not much, but it should fill a hole in yer bellies," she said, passing it between the family. The smell overwhelmed Raphael before he even bit into it: heavy with salt and the spices which he and Silas traded for.

No. Which they *had* traded for. That would never happen again. They would never visit the fayre, nor walk the donkey to the field, nor pick berries in the woods.

He chewed the meat without concentrating, and wandered to the lip of the corrie. The Elitland rolled beneath him like a huge black carpet, spotted with the lights of distant village lanterns. The ribbon of the river twisted into darkness. The shadow of an owl flew below him, as silent as a ghost.

He turned his eyes westward. The Wall looked so tiny up here, as though it had been drawn with a stick of charcoal. And beyond, in the black mass of Delamere, was the Lake.

The Asræ would still be there. Raphael couldn't see them, but he fancied he could hear them, as the wind whispered through the trees.

Feet became still. Hands lifted into the air. Merrin stood in the centre of her people as they fanned out around her like petals on the breeze. She was breathless from dancing, barely able to stand from the amount of magic she had wrought. But now, midnight had arrived. The moon sat at its highest point in the sky, directly overhead, like a giant silver sun. It was time.

The Asræ all fell silent, waiting. And then, slowly, the Lake itself began to shine. Everything became white, spreading up Merrin's legs, over her hips and through her chest. She let her head roll back as it consumed her. It was like floating in the water, but even more weightless than that, as though her entire body were coming apart from the inside out.

Her spine stretched by an inch. Her hair lengthened. Her fin spines protruded further from her spine. She silently counted off all the years as they became one with her. One thousand, seven hundred. Seventeen centuries into her age-old life. And, for the first time in so long, she felt truly alive.

Merrin held to it for as long as she could. But slowly, the moon's magic flowed out of her. She sank onto her knees with a gasp.

Her eyes snapped open. She stared at her hand where it landed. It had slipped under the water.

She hardly dared to breathe. She pushed down, felt the tiniest resistance, but then the surface gave under her palm like thin ice.

She cried out with joy. Tears stung her eyes and rolled unhindered over her cheeks.

Somebody knelt beside her. Merrin knew it was Penro before she even looked up at him, but when she did, her heart leapt. He had aged, too: his cheekbones were a little sharper, his hair a little thicker. It was subtle, but when a hundred years came all at once, she noticed the differences straightaway.

"It is finished," he smiled. "Thy mother was right. You can come home at last."

He offered his hand. Merrin took it and allowed him to help her to her feet. Children giggled to see themselves a little taller. Friends ran to each other and embraced. All around, she heard gasps of joy.

Dylana walked towards her. Merrin's heart skipped a beat when she saw her mother. She looked as though she had grown much older than anyone else. Lines had eaten into her face, and there was more grey in her hair than there had been before.

She cupped Merrin's face in her hands and kissed her cheeks.

"That was… my first Rise without thy father," she muttered.

Merrin took her mother's shoulders, then pulled her into an embrace.

"I'm proud of you," she said. "I miss him too. So much."

Dylana bit back a sob. "I know, my girl. But he is proud of thee. As am I. I told thee you would be wonderful. You are truly ready to be a Queen."

Merrin nodded. For so long, like a frightened child, she had shrunk at the thought of this night. But now it had arrived, it felt as natural as waking up after a deep sleep. The Bands around her wrists were not a burden. They were an honour. And it was no longer one which she had inherited, but one which she had earned.

Epilogue
Rose and Amarant

A ROSE, IN YOUTH AND BEAUTY'S PRIDE,
GREW BY A MODEST AMARANTH'S SIDE.
SO FAIR A FORM, AND TINTS SO BRIGHT,
ALL STOPT TO GAZE AT WITH DELIGHT,
AND STOOD ENCHANTED TO ENHALE
THE FRAGRANCE OF THE PASSING GALE.
"NEIGHBOUR," SHE BLUSHING SAID, "YOU SEE,
NONE GO WITHOUT OBSERVING ME;
WHILE I PERCEIVE THAT VERY FEW
SEEM ANY NOTE TO TAKE OF YOU."
"SWEET ROSE," THE AMARANTH REPLIES,
"NO FLOWER WITH THEE IN BEAUTY VIES.
NOT OBVIOUS TO THE VULGAR EYE,
MY HUMBLE MERITS DEEPER LIE;
LESS EXQUISITE, THEY LONGER LAST;
UNCHANG'D, ALAS, WHEN THINE ARE PAST."
LOVE IS THE ROSE-BUD OF AN HOUR;
FRIENDSHIP THE EVERLASTING FLOWER.

Brook Boothby; from Aesop

Suns rose and set over the Valley. Dew turned the grass into fields of diamonds. The mill wheels turned, the moon began to wane, and the final beams of the Atégo house collapsed into a mound of ashes.

Silas tried not to think too hard about it. Another week had passed, and each day, he had put on a brave face, for Raphael's sake, as much as for his siblings and mother. But this was difficult for him, too. No matter the hostility they had always faced, and despite all its shadows, the Elitland was branded upon his heart. This landscape had fed him and clothed him and sheltered him. His forefathers had worked the same land and looked upon the same mountains, for hundreds of years. Deep down, like Raphael, he couldn't imagine existing anywhere else, or in any other way.

But he trusted Irima. There was more out there. A bigger world. One which, hopefully, would accept them.

He looked around at his family. They were all inside the sick tent, sleeping top and tail, covered with as many blankets as could be spared. The smell of the incense wormed up Silas's nose. After realising that Uriel was restless, Irima had burned more of it, and Silas has never known his brother sleep so soundly.

He heard soft snoring from the neighbouring tent: Abraham and Nalina. As they had promised, Raphael and Andreas had set out for Ullswick, and after a few days, returned with the other two Atégos. They came with barely an argument, with only as much as they could carry. They were nervous of the Peregrini at first, but Silas quickly helped to break the ice, and now the two of them would be joining the convoy out of the Elitland.

Silas sighed. There wasn't long to go now. And no point in trying to get back to sleep. He pulled on his shoes, then stepped over Mekina, and and emerged into the night air.

The sun hadn't risen, but the dark didn't sway him. Now,

he knew his way around well enough. Even though he could see, he still moved his feet carefully, feeling for the familiar bumps in the earth which told him exactly where he was.

The campsite itself was almost stripped. Everything unnecessary for one more night had been packed atop the carts. The last of the firewood was burned. The cooking utensils were cleaned and tied down with rope. Even the horses were prepared, with their tack lying in wait nearby. As soon as dawn came, they would move out.

Silas went to the lake, washed his hands and drank until his stomach could take no more. Then he looked at his left palm. The mark hadn't come back, and every day since the Queen had healed him, his sight had remained. But in a way, it felt strange. There might be nothing to see, but he would carry it forever: an invisible penance for everything that had happened.

He heard footsteps. He didn't even need to turn around to know it was Raphael.

"Are you alright?" he whispered. "I've been awake for ages. It stinks in there."

Silas smiled. "I thought the same when I first came hither."

The two of them walked away from the tents and past the horses. Silas toyed with the pearl around his neck.

"Will Abraham be able to walk up the pass?" he asked. "I thought thee said he was ill."

"He was," Raphael replied. "But that proves to me that Merrin really has lifted the curse. He looked just like Pap did. And now... well, he's still coughing, but not like he was. He will not die. Not like the others."

Silas heard the smile in his brother's voice, but it was tempered with a deep dart of sadness.

"I know what thee is thinking," he said. "We cannot

flagellate ourselves with what happened, Raph. I wish as much as thee that Pap was still here. But if he was, neither of us might have ever discovered the truth, or rectified it. I have faith that the Lord is caring for him. And he shall always be with us. Thou knows that."

Raphael sighed. "I do. But it makes it no easier."

Silas took his hand and squeezed it. "I hope things will become easier – as much as they can – when we depart. Then, at least, we will have some distraction."

"How long will it take to get out of the mountains?"

"Irima told me several weeks. It's good to go now, though, before the snows. Apparently, in some places, the summits are covered in Auguste."

Raphael shook his head. "I don't believe it."

"Nor do I. But I suppose we'll see it soon enough."

"Part of me thinks we have seen enough already."

"Enough of *this place*. I have faith, Raph. We're doing the right thing."

"I hope so," Raphael groaned.

He reached into his pocket and pulled out the amarant blossom. It had withered a little, but still held its vibrant colour, like woven blood upon a stem.

Silas glanced at it, then at his brother.

"You came to care for her, didn't you?"

"Aye."

"Even after all she did?"

"I've told thee. It's not as clear-cut as Father Fortésa would claim. Demons… pah! Nay, there were never demons. Just pain. Pain which fermented into hate. And are we humans not also guilty of that?"

Silas nibbled his lip. "Didst thou love her?"

Raphael shook his head. "I respected her. I endeavoured to understand her."

"And nothing else?"

"Nay," Raphael said. "There was no need to be anything else. What we did share was enough."

He replaced the amarant, then turned to Silas.

"I want thee to promise me something. And I shall ask the same of everyone, Atégos and Peregrini alike."

Silas frowned. "What?"

"When we are gone from this place," Raphael said firmly, "I want no word about Merrin and her people."

"But thou was insisting that we would be the only ones who know the truth. You don't want others to know there are no demons?"

"Merrin told me that Adrian Atégo tried to abduct her. If we spoke of the Asræ to strangers, would it not entice people to the Valley for all the wrong reasons? Si, the Wall may yet come down. I hope to God that it will, one day. But what happens here must remain here. I will not burden my conscience with the idea that we helped her, only to doom her. Dost understand?"

"I didn't think of it like that," Silas said. "Aye. I promise."

Raphael hugged him with one arm. "Thank you, Silent Si. Though, I must say, thou art hardly silent anymore!"

Silas smirked. "Is that a bad thing?"

"On the contrary," Raphael replied. "It makes for a pleasant change!"

The two of them stood side by side, looking over the Elitland, as the sky transformed into the blue and pink of dawn. The sun rose, but Silas didn't turn away. He kept his eyes open, watching as the light bled its way over the ground. It was so beautiful. He would never take it for granted again.

One by one, the Peregrini emerged. As soon as they exited the tents, they pulled the tarp off the poles, and folded it as small as it could go. The floor mats were rolled up; nightclothes were tossed into bags. Busy chatter filled the air, but nobody got in the way of each other. Silas had the impression that they could have struck the entire camp with their eyes closed.

Irima stepped into view, still lacing the front of her stays with a large bone needle.

"Ai, there yer are!" she exclaimed. "Come on, give us a hand! We'll have some breakfast once we're through the pass."

Raphael and Silas sprang into action. They loaded the tents onto the already-bulging carts and oiled the wheels in preparation for the journey. Mekina and Nalina brought a final bucket of water to the horses, then Silas and Irima led the animals to the carts.

"Hold that there harness," she instructed, and began arranging all manner of ropes and leathers over the black stallion. Silas watched in awe. Compared to the simple way he had always hitched up the donkey, this was like another language.

Irima noticed his expression.

"It's got to be sturdy," she said, "else those trails will shake everythin' off. Loads o' loose rocks an' stuff up there. How are yer feelin'?"

Silas swallowed. "Nervous, now the time has come."

Irima peered over the horse's withers and gave him a gentle smile. "It won't be as bad as yer a'fearin'. I promise."

"How can ye?" Silas said. "This life is all thou hast ever known."

"True," Irima agreed. "But there still be places I ain't seen, and I always feel like that when I go to 'em for the first time. Now, do yer think yer shall stay with us after we're free o' the mountains?"

Silas hesitated. "Perhaps."

"Would yer want to?"

"*I* would. But whether Raph would say the same is another matter."

"What's another matter?" Raphael called. He finished tying some tent poles atop a neighbouring cart and wandered over. "I heard thee say my name. What is it?"

"Whether we remain with our hosts," said Silas anxiously. "Or would ye prefer to settle again? Farm the land, like we have done?"

Raphael's eyes moved between him and Irima. A thousand thoughts chased themselves across his face.

"Well, anything is possible," he said. "If the land is poor in the new places, then what are we to do? We have nothing with which to buy a new farm. So for now, I think the sensible thing is to stay with thee, Irima."

Irima's face lit up. "Yer will always be welcome. I'll have to sort out some clothes for yer, mind! Time to break out me embroidery hoop again!"

Silas chuckled, but didn't speak again; just helped her raise the horse poles into position and secure them with a length of rope.

Soon, everything was ready. The women and children climbed onto the carts, balancing on the heaps of tarp. Then Garrett took the black stallion by the bridle and raised his hand.

"Move out!" he shouted. "Let us go a'wanderin'!"

"A'wanderin' we shall go!" Irima replied loudly.

The horses began to move. Silas and Raphael walked beside the last cart, which held the rest of their family. Everyone was seated backwards, so they could look down on the Valley one last time. Mekina and Araena clung to each other for mutual support, while Nalina and Abraham wiped tears from their eyes.

The world was changing with every breath, every passing moment. Normal was a distant memory. Nothing would ever be the same.

"Si?" Uriel asked in a tiny voice.

Silas glanced at him warmly. "Aye?"

"Where are we going?"

Silas reached up and touched his cheek. "We're going together."

errin knelt in the Tomb Garden and gazed at her father's grave. Every night since she returned to the Lake, she had come to be with him, making up for all the time she had lost. A pale orb hovered before her face; she moved her hands through the water, almost close enough to touch it. She could feel him there, as certainly as if he had been beside her, alive.

I miss you, she said in her mind. *I'm so sorry for everything I did. I hope thou can forgive me.*

I do, my daughter, the reply whispered.

It feels wrong to have led a Rise without thee. That I am...

Do not fight thy title, Merrin. 'Twas always meant to be thine. I was with you. I always am. And don't ever doubt the pride I hold for you.

Merrin closed her eyes. She wanted to cry, but the water pulled her tears away. So instead, she just focused on the feeling of her hair floating above her head; the weightlessness and coolness; the way her gills opened and closed on her neck.

Home. She had been so grateful for it after escaping Adrian, but that time was coloured by fury and fright. Now, she drank it into herself; felt it taking her shape like a perfect garment. There was no anger, no darkness. Only freedom.

"Your Majesty?"

She looked over her shoulder, and spotted Penro floating in the water at the outskirts of the Tomb Garden. She blew her father a kiss, then swam away.

"What is't?" she asked.

"I thought I'd find thee here," said Penro. His fin flickered anxiously. "I wanted to ask if thou might come to the surface with me."

"Why?"

"Why not?"

Merrin smiled. "Well, I have nothing else to do. Come."

The two of them moved upwards. Slowly, the rippling skin of the water drew closer, and Merrin closed her eyes as she broke through it. Her gills closed; she opened her mouth and filled her lungs with air.

Penro surfaced beside her. He pushed himself up, until he was standing, then stooped down to help her. The night opened overhead: a huge black sky filled with thousands of stars. The moon hung lazily over the trees, half-faced, on the wane. In the distance, two swans glided across the Lake, and somewhere deep in the forest, a nyhtegale sang.

Merrin glanced at the bank. The boats were still there.

"I didn't think I would be back here so soon," she muttered. "What did you fetch me for? Is something amiss?"

"Nothing to be concerned about," Penro replied softly. "I was just up here, thinking, and I passed by the island where thee was crowned. And I saw something there. I wanted to ask if thou would wish me to remove it."

Merrin's brows lowered. "What is it? Show me."

"Art thou sure?"

"Aye. Let me see it."

Penro nodded, but Merrin still noticed the nerves dancing in his violet eyes. She followed him across the surface, trailing her toes in the water with each step. They passed the spot where Silas had netted her; the place where he and Raphael had watched the coronation.

Merrin's heart thundered. Where were they now? Had they returned to their home, just the other side of the Wall? Or had they left the Elitland forever? She would never know.

She and Penro reached the island. He parted the branches of the willow tree, and Merrin stopped dead in her tracks.

She hadn't noticed it during the ceremony, but growing there, above the amarants, was a small bush, covered with dark green leaves. And protruding from it, still in bud, were heads of snow white roses.

The most beautiful flower in the Valley, the wicked voice whispered in her mind.

But she didn't listen, and pushed the memory away. She didn't see him in those flowers anymore. Instead, she recalled a conversation she had shared with Raphael, when they had sat around a fire, watching leaves fly on the updrafts.

It's those small things which make it worthwhile.

"I'm sorry," Penro said hurriedly. "I'll have it removed. I shouldn't have brought thee here."

"You should," Merrin said. She approached the bush and ran her fingers over the roses, trying to convince herself they were real. So soft, like silk; so delicate.

"Are you alright?" Penro asked. "I'm sorry."

"There's no need to apologise," Merrin insisted. "This does not hurt me. I'm glad thou showed me."

"Really?"

"It will take more than a simple flower to pierce my heart now, Penro. Even if it does have thorns."

"I'm glad to hear that, Your Majesty."

"Call me by name," Merrin said. She turned around so she was looking straight at him.

Penro gave her a small smile. "As you wish. Merrin."

She grinned. "Will you say it again?"

Penro didn't blink. "Merrin."

He stepped closer to her, close enough to touch. Merrin forced herself to stand still. Penro's fin shuddered again; when she glanced down at his hands, she noticed they were shaking.

"I have a confession to make," he said. "Thou may very well deny it, and I will take no offence. But I… I know Adrian hurt you. I know you have guarded yourself and sought to cast away your frivolity. I don't blame you for that. But *I* want *you* to know that I have always admired your strength. That I have admired *you*."

Merrin's tongue stuck to the roof of her mouth. He had always been so kind to her. Far from simply being an advisor, she had been drawn to him for decades; denied herself the possibility of ever letting it seem real. Love was the hidden blade and nothing more.

But the hidden blade, itself, was nothing now. Raphael had proved that to her.

"And I have admired you," Merrin said. She reached out, across the abyss between them, and touched Penro's face. "I am not healed yet. I don't know how long it shall take."

Penro's eyes almost melted her with their warmth. It was so different to how Adrian had looked at her, even when he had been pretending. This was real. This was true.

"Then I shall wait for thee," Penro said. "Even if it takes centuries."

Merrin shook her head. Before she could convince herself it was a bad idea, she stepped closer, and kissed him on the lips.

It was quick, chaste, as though the touch might burn her like the sun. But it didn't. And when she drew back, warm relief spread through her entire body. The final stone in her wall crumbled to dust.

"It won't be centuries," she smiled.

Penro stroked her hair away from her face. And they stood there in silence, gazing at each other in the shade of the willow tree, as the swans glided across the water.

origins

Once upon a time, long before the Peregrini people began their wanderings, a tiny Kingdom lay nestled within the peaks of the Ironbelt Range. With homes built into the mountains themselves, it lived its own existence, separate from the rest of the world. Rocky paths followed the rugged shape of the land, through the carpets of purple heather and hardy pine trees. A mosaic of tiny lakes lay captured in the bottoms of the corries, each so still, the water caught the reflection of every star above. It was after this striking nature the Kingdom was named: Delamere – the Forest of the Lakes.

Dylana sat on her yard wall and gazed at the faraway summits. The dusk had turned the sky pink, streaked here and there with golden-edged cloud. The air smelled crisp, and far below in the distant valleys, clouds of mist were settling for the night. In the soft twilight, there was no boundary between earth and sky, and if she squinted, she could almost imagine herself flying, or perhaps swimming in a bottomless pool; a sanctuary with no need to breathe or speak.

Sunset was her favourite time of day. No matter the season, she always made sure to be out of bed early enough to watch. Darkness was the time when the Asrians lived; the light was too bright for their sensitive eyes and the heat prickled their pale skin. So they existed with the moon, not the sun. They would close their windows against the day, and when the stars emerged, so did they.

As Dylana sat there, Delamere slowly became alive. Doors opened and their occupants flooded out, ready to begin the night's work. A group of women came walking along the path, wooden tubs clutched in their arms to be filled at the lakeshore. They would ask permission from the water to take some of its bounty, then haul the tubs back up to the slopes, so they could launder at a respectable distance.

One of the women, an elderly lady named Fenella, noticed Dylana, and nodded in greeting.

"Good eve to ye, dear," she said. "Wilt thou come today?"

Dylana smiled, but shook her head. "Nay, I have no need."

"Thou is always welcome, know that," said Fenella. She withdrew a bag from her belt and handed it over. "I kept it back from yesternight. I shall bring more later."

"Thank you," said Dylana.

"Fare thee well, sweet girl."

The women took their leave. Dylana watched them in silence. They knew she never went to the lake. She had never stepped foot in the water in her entire life. But, driven by politeness and custom, they never stopped inviting her along. She might have grown irksome about the whole thing, if the lakes were not such an integral part of being Asrian.

Her people were even named Asrians after the largest lake in the region. Dylana could see it from her door: a near-perfect circle of water which had turned almost black in the growing darkness. It looked like a massive hole which no light could penetrate, and she couldn't even imagine how far it might stretch into the earth. Nobody knew that; nobody dared swim deep enough. Not for fear of drowning, but of what lived there.

There, in the darkest part just before the corrie lip, was the magic of the Wise Ones. Everyone knew it and revered it to the utmost. The Wise Ones were not human, but of an entirely different race; part of a family which cared for all aspects of nature. They had the power of the water in their veins and lived for millennia. It was said that for every century that passed, they only aged the equivalent of one year. It was they the Asrians appealed to on a daily basis, for everything from fish to wishes. It was to them the songs were sung at Midsummer; in their water, newborn babes were washed to be granted their blessing.

Dylana had often asked her father if their lake was the entrance to another world. Every time, he would simply smile and say, "Who knows?"

She watched the women until they were little more than spots in the distance; then she headed inside to cook her breakfast. Her home was tiny: only one room, but cosy, and it was all she needed. She combed her thick silvery blonde hair, tied it back with a strip of fabric, and perched by the fire pit in the centre of the floor. She opened Fenella's bag and pulled out the trout within, speared it on a spit and set about roasting it over the flames.

Since Dylana didn't go near the water, Fenella always made sure she was well-stocked with food. In the three years since her father's death, she had looked after herself. The neighbours kept a watchful eye on her and helped when they could, but for the most part, she remained on her own. And that was exactly how she liked it.

As she turned the spit, her mind wandered to the empty corner where her father's bed had lain. It was gone now, but she could still remember the shape of it. Fifteen Midsummers ago, she had been born in that bed; her mother's last breath drawn at the same time as Dylana cried out her first. Her father had buried the bones in the Tomb Garden and raised Dylana alone. But he was old and sickly too, only managing to make it until her twelfth birthnight.

And just before he died, he had grasped her arm and urgently begged her to never go near the lakes.

"I am no longer able to protect thee... Use caution, my daughter!" he had cried as his lungs failed. "Keep to thyself... that is all you may do now. Heed me and stay away from the water as thou hast done all thy life!"

"Protect me? From what?"

"Swear to me!" he cried. "Keep away from the Asria, Dylana!"

She had quickly agreed, and word of her vow passed around the Kingdom as her father was laid to rest. But nobody had actually believed she would keep it so seriously. They had told her she was free now, and didn't need to keep the strange tradition which had been once forced upon her. To never go down to the lake was like the girl had cut off a hand.

And yet she stayed in the summits, taking her water from the little stream behind her house. Not once did she relent.

She was an outsider because of it. She knew that well. It was difficult enough being the only one in Delamere with purple eyes. Everyone else's were blue or grey. But she had been born at odds from the start; her irises shone violet from the moment they opened. She had taken them as a gift from the mother she had never known. But she had her own suspicions why her father had made her promise.

She could see things – things which should have been impossible to comprehend or identify. She would sense massive storms weeks before they struck; how many fish would be caught, right down to the single number. Sometimes, she knew instinctively when somebody was going to die. And she hadn't cried at her father's passing, because she could still speak with him.

She wondered what her neighbours would call her if they found out. She had no proof, but was sure she would be the quiet solitary orphan no longer. Instead she would be a demon; a necromancer. How else could it be labelled? How could she predict how they would react?

It was better not to risk it. Better to be a little strange than completely outcast.

She took the trout off the flames and ate half of it, wrapping the rest in the bag to save for supper. Then she hung it off the floor, smoothed her skirt and walked outside.

It was true night now. The final blue glow had disappeared into the west, but she saw as clearly as the owl and bat. The moon was climbing high in the star-spangled sky; the waters of Asria caught its light and threw it in all directions. Close to its shore sat the King's home: not large or grand enough to be called a palace, but still unique enough from the houses on the slopes to leave no denial as to who lived there.

Between there and her own home was the Tomb Garden. The Asrians did not bury their dead – the rocky ground was far too hard to dig, so instead, they gave their loved ones a sky burial: allowed the birds to pick the bodies clean. A stone engraved with their name was erected in the shadow of the King's home, so they would know they were never forgotten, and then their bones laid to rest at its base.

Dylana followed the warren of paths until she reached the Tomb Garden. The faint whispers of the deceased drifted around her as she moved. They could sense her; knew she could hear them. She listened as she passed their stones. None were shocked or appalled by her. She was their only link to the world now. They would often ask her to pass words to their relatives, but she never did. It was too risky. If only the living were as accepting as the dead.

She rounded the corner where her father lay, and sat in front of his stone. A little orb of light hovered above it. Many of the stones had them: the bones within the earth cast memories of themselves into the air. Everyone was aware they were there; it

263

was how they could recall their loved ones so clearly when they came to the Tomb Garden. But only she could see them.

The one before her pulsed faintly, and Dylana heard her father's voice inside her mind.

Good eve, my dear.

Father, she thought back. *How does ye?*

I am most content. And thy mother too… She speaks of thee often.

Dylana smiled. Once, as a child, her father had brought her here, to show her where her mother lay. She had tried to play with the memories like balls, and when her hands slipped through them, she quizzed her father about what they were. It was then he had realised the extent of her powers.

"Why canst thou not see them?" she had asked.

"Because I am not special like thee."

"Could Mother see them?"

"Aye, as clear as day. She was like thee in many ways, but also held her tongue. It does not do to take such a gift and hold it aloft, Dylana. The eye will see what it wants to see, remember that."

Then he had swept her onto his shoulders and carried her home.

Now, in the present, ignoring the voices and memories was like an attempt to shut out the moonlight. Dylana could try, but it went against her very nature. She could no easier do that than fly.

She went to speak again, but then a sound cut through her thoughts. It was hard, guttural. Someone else was in the Tomb Garden, and they were sobbing.

"What is't?" she muttered. *Father, pardon me.*

Without another word, she crept through the undergrowth

in the direction of the sound. Soon enough, she spotted a figure, crouched over and looking intently at one of the stones.

It was a young man; she could see that much. His face was turned away from her, but there was no mistaking the two Royal Bands around his wrists. Only one person wore those.

It was the King.

Dylana drew in a gasp before she could stop herself. The young man spun around. She was so shocked that she almost fell backwards over a stone.

Forgive me, she silently muttered to the bones resting there, then turned to the King.

"I'm so sorry, Your Majesty. I did not realise."

"There's no need for apology," he replied, but kept his eyes downcast. "I have not seen thee for some time, Dylana."

"There has been no reason for me to trouble anyone," she said. "They have their own lives to live."

"And so you live yours *here*," said the King with a glance at her.

Dylana shrugged. Like many Asrians, she was on friendly terms with their ruler. Even though he was the leader, he was still one of them. And like many, she felt sorry for him. He had only become King two months ago, at the age of just fifteen, barely out of his boyhood. The Bands – the sign of the monarch – had been woven off the dying Queen's wrists and onto his own, passing the mantle to him. Before that, he was like any other youngster: playing with his peers and running along the lakeshores. But now he was sullen and withdrawn, still mourning his mother's death. Now, he was a prince no more, but King Zandor.

He wiped a tear from his cheek.

"Thou cometh here more often than others. I have seen it," he remarked. "Why? It's been several years since thy father's death."

"And yet he remains family," answered Dylana.

The memories shone in every direction, invisible to Zandor, but brighter than the stars to her. She motioned to the stone in front of him.

"I know you miss her."

Zandor managed a thin smile. "More than any words may say."

He knelt down again and ran a hand across the name engraved into the smooth surface.

"I wish I could speak to her again," he said. "I didn't have an opportunity to say farewell. She was not awake when the end came. I had to stand at her side and simply... wait. It was the worst thing. No parting words, no final kisses."

Dylana sighed. "I'm terribly sorry."

Zandor was looking away, so she nodded her head respectfully to the old Queen's stone.

The dead woman's words echoed in her head.

Pass my love to him... pass my love.

I cannot, Your Majesty, Dylana replied. *I dare not.*

Pass my love to him... It pains me to see him suffer so.

I beg thee, do not ask this of me. I cannot let him know what I do, lest the others discover it.

The Queen's voice grew fierce.

Pass my love to him!

The harshness was so sudden that Dylana cried out in shock. Zandor stood up again.

"What is't?" he asked, voice laced with concern.

Dylana turned away so he wouldn't see the alarm on her face. When her own father died, it had been a peaceful thing. Dylana never worried for a moment about never seeing him again, because she knew he was still there. She knew it better than anyone. But for others, when it was less peaceful, and when there was none of that comforting knowledge, what was there to do?

Zandor and his mother had been torn from each other so slowly. Nobody could prevent the end from coming, but to have no chance to accept it either… It would leave a puckering wound on anyone's heart. Dylana could sense it in the air: invisible throbbing waves of depression and loneliness – and frustration that the other was so close and yet just out of reach.

The Queen's words echoed in her mind, pitting themselves against those of her father. Could she? Should she?

She hesitated – she had never promised anything about her powers, only about going to the lakeshores. She wouldn't be breaking any vows.

"I… think I may be able to grant thee a favour," she muttered uneasily.

Zandor's concerned expression changed to one of confusion.

"What dost thou mean?"

Dylana chewed her lip. "If I tell thee, wilt thou promise to keep my secret?"

"What secret?"

"Please, Your Majesty. I would not ask this if it were not important to me. Please, swear thy silence."

Zandor looked at her for a long moment. "I swear it."

"Thank you," said Dylana, then took a deep breath and watched him closely.

"I can see her. Thy mother."

The King's eyes widened, but Dylana didn't wait for an answer. The longer she hesitated, the more likely her resolve would flee.

She lowered herself to the ground and cupped her hands together over the memory. She had never done this before; she had no idea if it would even work, but it felt as though it was the right thing.

After a few moments, the air between her palms grow thicker, as though it were half water, pressing against her flesh. Zandor gasped behind her. She opened her eyes a crack and found white light shining through her fingers. She slowly drew her hands apart, and sure enough, an orb was hanging there, exactly like the ones she saw. But this time, it was denser; less ghostly-looking.

"Do you see it?" she asked quietly.

He nodded, mouth hanging slack. Inside the memory, the old Queen's face peered through a film of mist. Her eyes settled on her son and shone with love; pearly tears of happiness flowing down her cheeks.

Dylana smiled to herself. It had worked. She had made the memory real.

Zandor appeared beside her on his knees. He reached towards the orb, fingers trembling, but he stopped before he could touch it. His lips didn't move, and neither did his mother's, but Dylana could still hear their exchange as loudly as if it had been spoken aloud.

She regarded him. Already, his face was brightening; the sadness seeped away like rain into a river. This was what both of them had needed, and she had given it to them.

She drew back, so as not to eavesdrop, and glanced at her hands. She hadn't realised her power ran so deep. It was one thing to see the memories; hear the words of the dead. It was another completely to bring them forth for others.

She wondered if her mother had also been able to do this.

Then she looked up, and her stomach flipped. Straight

ahead, beyond the low border wall, were Fenella and the other women. They had seen everything.

Dylana struggled to breathe. She hid her hands behind her back as though they were stained.

"What hast thou done?" Fenella choked out.

"Is it true?"

"She shows herself!"

Dylana thought she might faint with horror. She went to run, but Zandor's fingers closed on her wrist.

"Be still," he said in an undertone. He put his other hand on her shoulder, silently urging her to calm down.

Dylana's knees knocked together. She wanted the ground to swallow her; the sun to rise and put an end to the night... Anything to take her away from this moment. It dragged out around her and pulled at her bones; every breath hurt as panic swelled in her chest. But she managed to keep herself under control, and when Zandor was sure she wouldn't flee, he spoke.

"What she has done is nothing short of a miracle," he announced. "She has allowed me to say goodbye to the Queen. She has a gift. Whatever it is, I'm grateful for it. Ye need not be afraid."

Dylana threw an anxious glance between him and their audience. The secret was out. Fenella was the greatest gossip in Delamere; soon all the Asrians would know about this.

Would they drive her away? If they did, where would she go? To the next valley with its giant ribbon lake, which was still half-full of ice from the melting glaciers? Nobody lived there; it was too cold and dangerous. She would be alone forever, with only the trees for company, without even a single dead soul to listen to...

"Please!" she cried before she was even aware of her

mouth opening. "Have mercy on me! I meant no ill!"

Zandor turned to her.

"Do not fret, Dylana. No harm will come to thee. You know we are a people above that. What you have done is something to be applauded, not feared."

"But it's unlike any other, Your Majesty," Fenella insisted. "I know her well; she's a harmless one. But she's strange, have no doubt of it, and her father had his secrets. Now it be out, we should seek guidance from the Wise Ones."

Dylana's stomach twisted into a knot.

"I cannot," she protested. "All of you, feel free to go to Asria, but leave me be, up here."

By this point, several others had arrived, all gazing in wonder at the hovering orb. Fenella was quick to fill in any newcomers on what she had seen, and soon the Tomb Garden was filled with hushed voices. It even drowned out the whispers of the dead, and Dylana had to fight the urge to cover her ears. There was so much noise; too much noise…

"Thou must come," Fenella said. "Ye may have the power to grant all of us one of those… visions. So we may all remember our loved ones forever, with our own eyes. The Wise Ones will know! They know more than any of us!"

Her words acted as a rally to the gathered people. Before Dylana could draw a breath, they had entered the Tomb Garden and rushed towards her.

As though sensing the King may be trampled, several guards appeared seemingly from nowhere and formed a barricade. They tried to push Dylana back to the throng, but Zandor kept hold of her.

"She is to stay with me," he said firmly.

The guards didn't reply, but none of them moved for

Dylana again. Her father's words cut through the wall of sound and stabbed in her ears like needles.

Keep to thyself... Listen to them not and remain up high... Thou swore an oath...

She clutched at Zandor's wrists.

"Please, Your Majesty, I beg thee! Don't take me to the lake!"

Zandor frowned. "Why not? All Asrians are welcome there."

"It's not a case of welcome. My father bade me to never go to Asria. I have kept it so and vowed on his deathbed to uphold it. I dare not enter there."

Zandor hesitated. A strange determination had set in his eyes.

"The Wise Ones will understand in these circumstances, I'm sure. And dost thou not wish to discover why thee possesses such a gift? May they not have given it to thee themselves?"

The crowd shuffled and whispered.

"Do you not want answers, Dylana?" Zandor pressed.

"Of course I would like to know," she insisted, "but I promised. I must not go. It would be dangerous for me."

"Dangerous? How so?"

"I know not, but I believed my father."

Zandor looked at her earnestly.

"The Wise Ones are only dangerous if they're offended. You know that. What if these powers have been given to thee for a purpose, to help others in their times of need? Who else can tell thee these things except those among us who are also powerful? Thou hast the eyes of someone otherworldly."

Dylana's lip trembled. She threw a glance in the direction of her father's stone.

Forgive me, she said. *They will not leave me be until I consent.*

Do not go, daughter!

I have no choice.

Twisting her hands together anxiously, she nodded.

"This one time only."

Zandor smiled. "This one time only," he promised. Then he raised his hands and motioned for everyone to follow.

The walk to the lake was the longest Dylana had ever taken. Her heart pounded with a raging cocktail of emotions: pride at helping the King, guilt over breaking her promise, relief and worry that her powers had been revealed. More and more people swarmed to join the crowd, many craning their necks to get a glimpse of her. She hunched her shoulders in discomfort.

They reached the rocky banks of Asria. The surface was still and glassy; the moon's reflection hung fat and bright over its centre. Dylana couldn't see the bottom, only boulders and scree at the edge which gradually melted away into the depths.

A sudden heaviness overcame her, as though the entire weight of the water had crashed down on her body. She fell to her knees and gasped for air.

"What's the matter?" Zandor asked under his breath.

Dylana looked up at him urgently. "There's something wrong… I cannot be here! I feel it!"

To her dismay, the King only shook his head.

"You are merely nervous. There's nothing to fear."

"Not from *thee,*" she replied. "But here… I must leave! Let me go!"

She staggered upright. The Asrians had pressed together like a wall in their excitement. There was no way out. Dylana's panic surged, and like a frightened rabbit, she ran into the water, trying to cut around the side of them.

She had barely taken three strides before she fell. Something was grasping her ankles and rooting her to the spot. When she tried to get free, she realised the restraints were part of *the water itself*, somehow made dense and firm enough to hold her still.

The lake suddenly rippled. Silence fell over the muttering crowd. Out of the depths rose a sinuous figure, long hair flowing down to its heels. It stood on the surface as though it were as solid as ground. Every single inch of its flesh was transparent and sparkling, made entirely of water. Two fierce eyes fixed themselves on Dylana.

She trembled. Those eyes were the same colour as her own.

Everyone on the shore sank into a bow. Never before had they seen such a creature. But the Lady ignored them.

"You have brought her here," she said, in a voice older than the mountains. "She with the eyes of the Arncæ."

Dylana frowned. What were the Arncæ?

"She has granted me a gift, O Wise One," Zandor said shakily.

"If that is how you choose to view it," the Lady responded. With every syllable, her tone became colder. "But it is a gift which she should never have possessed. We know of thee, Dylana. We have been waiting for this moment for a long time, ever since thou was born."

Dylana swallowed. "Why? What dost thou want of me?"

The Lady regarded her as though deciding whether she would make a tasty meal.

"Thy mother was my sister."

Dylana was so shocked, she almost fell over again.

The crowd started muttering, but their voices seemed a thousand miles away. There was only her, the Lady, and the water between them. That short distance was terrifying; the same lake touched both of them, held her in place, forced her to look into those chilling eyes, so like her own, but empty of everything…

"You are a crossbreed of the humans and the Arncæ – the beings of the water," the Lady continued. "Why else would you have our violet gaze, or be able to deal our powers with no ill effect? To do what you did; to even experience life as you do every day, hearing the dead, speaking to them… If thou were simply human, then it would kill you instantly. Thy father knew this. Why else would he always come with thee to the lakes, if not to keep thee safe? Why else would he make you promise to stay away when he passed on?"

Dylana's mouth fell open. A *crossbreed?* That couldn't be… Her mother had been a common girl; that was what she had always been told…

As though reading her thoughts, the Lady carried on.

"They all knew about thy mother," she said, and swept her arm towards the crowd.

Dylana stared at them. Sure enough, many of her neighbours' faces were cast down, like guilty children who had been caught out.

"Thou knew?" she cried. "Thou knew all along and never told me?"

"Oh, they did not know about thy powers, or even hers," said the Lady. "But they were aware of thy origins. Of how thy father used to come to the tarns in the middle of the day when thy people do not walk in the sun. All to entice my sister. And then, how he awoke one evening to find a babe left on his doorstep. Why else would they find thee odd, thou foolish girl? They always knew you were not one of them."

Dylana whimpered in shock. None of the Asrians dared meet her eyes. The only person still looking at her was Zandor. He was the same age as her; he would never have been aware of this secret his Kingdom had covered up.

Dylana gritted her teeth. She was still shaking, but the Lady's words cut deep, and her fear slowly drained into anger.

The Lady smirked.

"How I behold thee! Such fury; such human rashness! What wilt thou do? Punish them? Will you summon the dead to scream in their ears forever, just as you have always heard?"

"Would my power stretch that far?" Dylana growled.

"Perhaps. If only thou had been born a true Arncæ. You descend from the strongest of our line. But my sister was foolish, as you are."

"How am I foolish? Why has thou waited for me?"

"Your resistance of the water is all that has protected you. But now you are here, defenceless, and having revealed your stolen powers to those who should never receive them. Such a display – and such an existence – goes against all that must be. Thy heart and lungs and life represent a mixture which should not be. I refuse to allow it to continue."

"I had no choice in being born, or to whom," Dylana argued. "No babe knows such luxury. I meant no harm and I will stand by my vow forevermore. Never again shall I use the power. Dost thou accept this?"

"A promise to a dead man means little to we who live for millennia," said the Lady. "Thou shalt die this night, Dylana the Asræ. And as for your people, by taking one of ours into their midst, having the nerve to bring thee back here... My punishment extends to them. All of you will die."

The low whispers turned into a scream. The crowd tried to hurry back towards the path, but the bottleneck was too narrow to take them all.

The Lady raised her arms. Her entire body glowed white, until it hurt to look at her. She focused on the Asrians, ready to bring the curse upon them.

Dylana's panic reached its peak. She wrenched herself free of the watery grip.

"Nay!" she shrieked. "Leave them be!"

The guards quickly surrounded Zandor, but Dylana knew it wouldn't be enough to protect him. She sprinted towards him, just as the Great Lady brought her arms down.

The light shot from her like a knife – and Dylana leapt in front of it.

For a horrid moment, she lost all feeling in her body. Was she dead? She was floating somewhere above herself, with no breath in her lungs nor heartbeat in her ears. But then she sensed a growing heat in her hands; the air growing denser, as it had when she pulled the memory into sight. Before she could even think about what she was doing, she drew it closer, opened her eyes, and threw it back at the Lady.

The Lady pushed harder, trying to force her out of the way. Dylana stood like a shield. No matter what happened, she couldn't move. If she did, the light would strike Zandor, her neighbours, all her people, and the entire Kingdom of Delamere would be lost forever.

And all because of *her*...

No. She had to stop this. She *could* stop this.

She resisted with all her might, until she felt the curse absorbing into her, filling her with its influence. Like water held within a bucket, it did not breach her defences. Instead, it fuelled her in a way she hadn't thought possible. It strained against her body, bursting to get out. She couldn't hold it much longer.

Then a sudden thought came to her. She hadn't created the memory orb for Zandor, only changed it into a new form so he could see it. She knew, instinctively, that she couldn't destroy or stop the Lady's power. But she could *change* it.

She grasped the Lady's magic in an iron grip. The strength of it caught the Arncæ off guard; Dylana felt her hold slacken. Then she wrenched it towards herself, and let go.

The light erupted from her, fracturing as though it had hit a mirror, and struck every single Asrian in the heart. But Dylana was in control now. She sought every single person, as she had sought the dead in the past, ensuring not a single one was left. When the light had reached everybody, she switched to her own power, and sent a little of it to all she had reached.

We will survive! she thought. *Come water, sun, the ravages of time... we will survive together!*

The words echoed as though she had shouted them. The last of the magic finally flooded out of her, and she fell onto all fours.

She exclaimed in shock.

She was not kneeling in the water, but on top of it. Her hands were pale green, with webbed flesh running between her knuckles. The green was all over her body; her feet were webbed too, and her hair had transformed into a deep emerald. She tried to stand, but the movement made her wince, as though she were carrying a bundle on her back. Reaching over her shoulder, she found a large fin protruding from her spine. It had torn straight through her clothes and ran from the base of her neck to her hips.

She turned to the Asrians. Like her, they were transformed; every man, woman and child. And every single one of their eyes were purple.

"Very clever," the Lady said.

Dylana spun around again. She wasn't sure she could fend off another attack.

But despite the Arncæ's frustration, it was clear she would not strike again. She was shaking her head in disbelief.

"I underestimated thee," she said. "Thou took my magic, combined it with thy own, and altered its intent. And look what thou hast done with it!"

"I know what I have done," Dylana replied. "All of my people now have a piece of me within them. A piece of *thee*. Thou said thyself, this very night, that I was strong enough. I knew my power would stretch that far. And it protected us."

To her surprise, the Great Lady sniggered.

"You believe you have saved them? You have struck them with a double-edged sword, fool! Yes, you have now forced them all to share in Arncæ power – you will age as we do, one year for every hundred that pass. You may breathe under the water and walk upon its surface. These are blessings, but only if you had been strong enough to repel all of my malice! I sensed what thou was doing, and so I also altered my power! If you so much as step one foot into the sunlight, it will not merely harm you, but melt you like ice in the spring thaw. All those who see your twisted bodies will look upon you in fear and revile you as monsters. Is that truly what thou wanted, Dylana the Asræ?"

The Lady shook her head slowly.

"Thou art Asrians no longer. Thy Kingdom will return to the rocks and the lakes, and become dust so small, none shall remember you. And you have brought it all upon yourselves."

She cast one final glare at Dylana, then receded back into the depths, leaving not even a ripple to mark her presence.

The rest of the night passed in a haze. Dylana fled to her home and slammed the door shut. She snatched a chair and wedged it under the handle so nobody could come in. People shouted for her, pounded on her wall, but she flung herself on her bed and did her best to ignore them.

What had she done?

She thought about Zandor. What were they going to do now? How could they survive without the lakes? No crops could grow up this high. No fish swam in the streams.

She screwed her eyes closed so she wouldn't have to look at herself. The fin on her back waved of its own accord; the webbing between her fingers snagged on the sheets. It felt terribly delicate, as though it was spun from spider silk.

Soon, the sky began to lighten, and silence fell across the Kingdom as everyone hurried home. Dylana eased the door open. As soon as she stepped outside, she let out a hiss of pain. Her skin stung as though it had passed through flame. She drew back in alarm and nursed her hand.

Tears rolled down her cheeks. Everybody else would feel the same now. Before, the sun's touch had merely hurt. Now it could kill them. She had doomed them all.

But she couldn't stay in her house, either. With every moment, the walls seemed to press in around her. She had to get out. So she snatched her thick winter cloak, wrapped it around herself until she was completely covered, and fled toward the Tomb Garden.

The paths were empty. Faint cries carried on the wind as others realised the light couldn't touch them. Dylana did her best to ignore them, and hid herself behind the wall. She crept to her father's memory and laid upon his stone.

I'm sorry! she wept. *I'm so sorry! Thou always told me not to go there! One time I waver in my resolve, and look at what has been done!*

I wish thou hast heeded me, came the reply, but it was laced with a tenderness which Dylana hadn't been expecting.

Are you not angry?

I was for a moment, but there's no need for such emotions among the dead, my dear. I am the one who should be sorry. I concealed the truth from thee. I bade all others to do the same. I should have been honest about thy mother, thy origins... It was my failing.

Nay, I am the one who has failed us, Dylana insisted. *I have mutilated us, destroyed all we are. Father, I don't wish to live! I cannot hold this burden upon my shoulders forevermore!*

Before the memory could reply, she reared onto her knees and pulled her hood off her face. The sun struck her and pain seared across her cheeks. She gritted her teeth and waited.

"What are you doing?"

Hands closed around her middle and dragged her away. She kicked out as hard as she could.

"Leave me be!"

"And let thee come to harm? Nay!"

She was thrown through a door and into a large room. She spun around to face the figure. It was Zandor, flanked by two guards.

Dylana forced herself to not cry out at the sight of him. He was still young and handsome, but her stomach flipped to see his pale skin and silvery hair turned green.

"What was thy intention?" he asked. "To die? To give up?"

"It's no more than I deserve, Your Majesty!" Dylana protested. "I have destroyed everything!"

"*We* are not destroyed," Zandor said. "I still stand, as does thee, and all our people. We should all be dead, yet we were saved."

"*Saved?*" Dylana repeated incredulously. She threw off the cloak and motioned at herself. "Thou dost think *this* is saved? What I did to thee, to everyone?"

"We are saved," Zandor insisted. "Changed much, aye, but saved, living. We shall not die."

"Not for thousands of years! And again because of me!"

"You are not listening! Dost thou think I have been sitting idle all night, not pondering our future, of how we may continue?"

Zandor took hold of her hands.

"Dylana, our people are not fragile. The light may always have hurt us, but if we were so dainty and easily-broken, why would we have lived as we have, up here, far from anyone else? Thou may have been different from us once, but no longer, and even before, not so much as might be thought! Thou cometh from the Wise Ones! Thou *is* a Wise One, who has given us life; a new existence. We are indebted to thee. And we will survive."

Dylana's eyes stung with tears.

"Then what wouldst thou have us do?" she choked out. "No lakes? No light? No Wise Ones? We will surely perish. It will be as she said."

A tiny smile curled Zandor's lips. Dylana had never seen such an expression: hope and sadness in equal measure.

"We will perish *here*," he said slowly. "But not elsewhere."

"What dost thou mean?"

"We leave. We cannot remain in Delamere. The land is too

dry; the air too thin. So we shall move on and create a new future. We can choose it: a chosen land above all others."

He gripped her tighter.

"And I would bid thee to help me rebuild. I shall be King, and thee the Mistress of Magic. Instruct us in how we may adapt to this, teach us the power thou hast given to each of us. We shall be as Asrians no more, but a new people, under a new home and new name. All is not lost. So, Mistress Dylana, wilt thou do this with me?"

Dylana's heart thundered. Leave everything behind? Was it possible?

"There's no other way, is there?" she said quietly.

"Not which I can see," replied Zandor. "Any way is better than none. Thyself is proof of that. Is it not preferable to live in an altered form than to join all our loved ones in death?"

Dylana pressed her lips together and looked away. She would have been happy to do that. She imagined herself lying over her father's grave, letting her bones become entwined with his; never again having to deal with the tangles and shallowness of the living.

It was a tempting offer. Blessed silence and stillness, floating in an abyss without beginning or end, sound or speech, breath or blood. Just nothingness, forever.

Zandor seemed to realise her thoughts, because he dipped his head to catch her eye again.

"Dylana, thou canst be of the dead anytime," he said, "but what's the hurry?"

When the summer receded and the longer nights swept in, all of Delamere gathered. They abandoned their homes and took no belongings. The only things collected were the bones from the Tomb Garden, carefully stored, so no two would accidentally mix. Dylana carried those of her father under one arm and her mother under the other, and kept her eyes straight ahead. There was nothing behind, not anymore.

The people made their way out of the pine forests. They walked through the peaks by the light of the moon, hiding in caves to avoid the sun. In the next valley, they would find a new home, Zandor had said. A new Forest of the Lakes would spring up and protect them, as the mountains had done before. And Dylana made a new vow to her people: that once they were there, she would place a protective spell around the entire place, so the Wise Ones would never find them again.

She had passed the power of the Arncæ to her people. And as a result, they were not Asrian any longer.

Like her, they were Asræ.

❧ Author's Note ❧

In 1998, the Asrai came into my life. First, through the poetry of Robert Williams Buchanen, and then as a legend. It told of a selfish man who caught a beautiful water nymph in his net, and refused to let her go, even when she grabbed his hand and pleaded for her life. In the folktale, she didn't survive, but the concept lingered in my mind. What if she had escaped? What if she was angry? What would she do?

The first draft of *Blindsighted Wanderer* was written in February 2007, when I was fifteen years old. Although not the first novel I had created by that point, it was the first which I endeavoured to complete within one month. I succeeded, even though I had to write it entirely by hand, due to limited computer access. In the corner of my school library and in the loft of a Victorian cottage, I scribbled until my fingers were sore. The story came alive like a beautiful painting. It was simple, but that simplicity was its power. It struck me deeper than I was expecting, and as I wrote, it transformed from a folktale retelling into a celebration of acceptance and kindness.

The inspirations behind the story were Victorian, but I deliberately avoided using that period for the setting. I wanted the tale to feel like it was truly somewhere long ago and far away— yet with a universal texture, which could happen in any place or time. In a way, like a folktale within itself. Even though the Elitland has no connection to actual historical events or real locations, I settled on the 13th century, as a nod to the tail end of the Dark Ages. But because I decided to play a little loose with the threads of accuracy, there are certain details which are either

285

equally loose, or altered for the sake of modern sensibilities. Namely, *When the Nightingale Sings* is a real medieval poem, and *Stella Splendens* (sung at the Midsummer balefire) is a real song with music. Both, however, are from the 14th century: 90-180 years after the time of the novel. And while the language of the 1200s would have been either Latin or Middle English, I used a simplified interpretation of Early Modern English. This isn't just to make the dialogue easier to understand for a 21st century reader. It's also closer to the kind of language used in the 17th century: a time which is infamous for widespread panic, accusation and misunderstanding, in the form of the European and American witch hunts.

At midsummer of 2012, a magic moment came. After years of tireless work, I received an offer from Staccato and Darkest Night Publishing. Several months later, *Blindsighted Wanderer* became my debut novel. I remember feeling as though I had reached the summit of a huge mountain; struggled my way to the top, been greeted by a breath-taking view, and now stood with one foot over the abyss. What would come next? Should I recoil or should I fly?

Ten years have passed. A part of me can't believe it's been that long, while another part looks back in pride and wonder at all I've accomplished. Nine more novels published, a stage script, multiple illustration and cover art commissions… If I had foretold all this to 2012 Emma, she would have been at a loss for words.

Over the past decade, I have moved into being completely independent. It's been a steep learning curve, on a very long and rocky road, and there are times when the difficulty of being a one-woman army overwhelms me. Imposter syndrome can rear its ugly head, and I feel like that wide-eyed twenty-one year old who somehow got lucky. But more than anything, I love how my creativity is not only unhindered, but celebrated and welcomed by so many. From the moment I began this journey, I have been supported by incredible people, and whether you've walked with me for ten days or ten years, I want to thank you from the bottom of my heart.

Thank you to my amazing parents, who have always stood by me and encouraged me in every way. Also to my grandparents Edna Baker and Eric Hibbs, both of whom passed before they could see me hold my first book in my hands. I love you all.

Thank you to all the friends who hold my hands and raise me up: Courts, Holly, Fletch, Carter, Emma, Iona, Kim, Tara, Emma, Nasha and Roger, Josh and Sally, Leanne, Maiken, Meeri, and Hannah. Extra special love to the original uni crew who were there from the very beginning: Rhian, Scott, Emily and Matt. And also to my late best friend Katie, who was with me on the day the offer arrived, as well as through thick and thin, hand in hand. I miss you and love you forever.

Thank you to all the phenomenal readers in the Batty Brigade, who remind me every day that I should never give up. Your support astounds me, and my love and appreciation for you is unparalleled. To know that my stories touch your hearts is a gift which never fails to lift me. Thank you for your kind words and reviews, for coming to see me at signings, for choosing to stick around and share this dream, all because of a book or two. I owe you everything.

Special thanks to my Patreon Batties for all you do to help me continue creating. You allow me to spread my wings in ways which would otherwise be impossible. Special mentions to Mariletty Blackrose and Heather Clawson. You are amazing.

Thank you to the Staccato gang for helping me take my first steps into the publishing world: Heather Savage, Donna

Milward, Jacinta Maree, David Fingerman, C. S. Yelle and Joshua Mims. Thank you also to all the book bloggers who propelled *Blindsighted Wanderer* into the light, especially Jaime Radalyac, Tammy Middleton, Becky Johnson and Derinda Love. I want to also give a shout-out to all the authors I have since connected and worked with, who have supported and championed my work, especially Anthony Galvin-Healy, Rose Titus, Serene Conneeley, Selina Fenech, Rachel Lilliman, Gretel Hallett, Cat Treadwell, Rhian Waller, and Catherine Smyth.

Thank you to my friends at the Australian Fairy Tale Society for your support and wonderful conversations; Tink Bell for your kind words and brilliant events; Willow, Karen, Steve, Christopher and all the others at CoP; my co-workers of past and present who always cheer me on; my friends across the world; and the Lapland and Tenerife families. Further thanks to Suzie K and everyone at The Secret Garden for your unwavering belief in me, and for hosting my launch parties.

I looked over the abyss, I leapt, and I flew. All the stories I have written since 2012; all those I am yet to discover and share with you… Their road will forever be paved with bricks laid down by *Blindsighted Wanderer*. Here's to the next decade, and many more to come!

E. C. Hibbs
Chester, England; June 2022

DID YOU ENJOY BLINDSIGHTED WANDERER?

PLEASE CONSIDER LEAVING A REVIEW!

Reviews allow you to share your thoughts, and also allow the book to reach others who might enjoy it.

Visit Blindsighted Wanderer's webpage to leave a review and discover extra content, including playlists and behind-the-scenes trivia!

To stay up to date with the latest news, releases and signing events, don't forget to subscribe to the official E. C. Hibbs newsletter!

Printed in Poland
by Amazon Fulfillment
Poland Sp. z o.o., Wrocław
14 July 2023